WINGS FOR PEACE

Books by Marian Talmadge and Iris Gilmore

PONY EXPRESS BOY

COLORADO HI-WAYS AND BY-WAYS

WINGS OF TOMORROW

WINGS FOR PEACE

WINGS FOR PEACE

A Story of Cadet Frank Barton of the Air Force Academy

BY *Marian Talmadge* AND *Iris Gilmore*

WITH A FOREWORD BY *James E. Briggs,* MAJOR GENERAL, USAF

SUPERINTENDENT, U. S. AIR FORCE ACADEMY

DODD, MEAD & COMPANY, NEW YORK, 1959

Library of Congress Catalog Card Number: 59-9619
Printed in the United States of America
by The Cornwall Press, Inc., Cornwall, N.Y.

*To the Class of '59
Vanguards of the Space Age*

Foreword

Wings for Peace is the second in a series of fictional books about the life of cadets at the United States Air Force Academy. In their first book, *Wings of Tomorrow,* the authors took their cadet characters through the strenuous first year at the Academy. This story carries their busy and eventful lives into the final year of studies preparing them for careers as Air Force officers in the Aerospace Age.

The four-year program of instruction at the Academy is designed to provide cadets with a balanced education and a firm foundation for further development in any of the numerous fields open to Air Force officers during a lifetime of service to their country. We strive to instill in our graduates the qualities of leadership and readiness for responsibility of future air commanders. I hope that this book, in addition to being entertaining, will give the reader a good understanding of the Air Force Academy and its objectives.

JAMES E. BRIGGS
Major General, USAF
Superintendent
U. S. Air Force Academy

Acknowledgments

It was natural for the authors of *Wings of Tomorrow* to write a follow-up book about the cadets in the first book and their further experiences at the United States Air Force Academy. An intimate study of the Academy's first years has been an exciting privilege. The authors have unbounded respect for the conduct of the Academy, the dedication of the officers on the staff, the cadets and their "way of life." Close association with the daily life and training of the cadets reveals two of the most important contributions of the Academy: the carrying out of the Honor Code by the cadets, and a basic emphasis that these future leaders of our country are training to be builders of peace.

Wings for Peace is really a co-operative project among the authors, the officers and the cadets of the Academy. This has involved hundreds of hours of conferences, class attendance and correspondence. Most generous sharing on the part of many persons has resulted in this book.

We wish to thank Major General James E. Briggs, Superintendent of the Air Force Academy; Brigadier General

Henry R. Sullivan, Commandant of Cadets; and Colonel Robert F. McDermott, Dean of Faculty, whose permission, co-operation and courtesy made this book possible.

Our grateful thanks to Colonel Max Boyd, Office of Information Services, and his staff; also to Major H. E. Swinney, Captain John M. Connolly, Jr., and Sergeant Richard Anderson. In addition, our thanks to Major Harold Basham and Captain H. L. Emanuel.

Our deepest appreciation to Colonel John L. Frisbee, Colonel Jerry Kutger, Colonel Gabriel D. Ofiesh, Major William Fuchs, Captain John M. Connolly, Jr., and Sergeant Richard Anderson for the many hours they spent reading and correcting the manuscript.

Our thanks to these officers and men at the Civil Air Patrol Headquarters in Washington, D.C., who supplied us with material about cadet training for the CAP: General Walter Agee, Major James W. Hickman, Captain James Ves'sells and Mr. Frank Burnham.

We wish to thank Alice Fuchs and Lucy Frisbee for their help and for their reading of the manuscript, and Mrs. Gail McComas for her cordial hospitality at all times.

Our thanks to Miss Caroline Driscoll for quotes from "Hold Fast Your Dreams" by Louise Driscoll; William Faulkner for quotes from *The Bear Story,* published by Random House, New York; Jack Foster, editor of the *Rocky Mountain News* for quotes from an editorial; Mrs. John G. Magee for quotes from "High Flight" by John Gillespie Magee; Colonel George Stewart (retired) for quotes from *American Way of Life;* the *New York Sun* for quotes from an editorial.

Appreciation to "A" Flight, 32nd Squadron, summer training group, 1958, for original song composition; and to these cadets for quotes from some of their original work: Cadets

David Carlstrom, D. D. Dillon, James Reed and Donald Sheppard.

To *Contrails*, *Chandells*, and *The Talon*, all publications at the United States Air Force Academy, for their co-operation and use of material published in their magazines, goes added gratitude.

Our thanks to the following cadets who gave generously of their time and knowledge: Cadets Robert Beckel, David Carlstrom, Jerry Caskey, Joseph DeSantis, J. C. Dinsmore, James Fletcher, Donald Madonna, John Melancon, John Milligan, Jay Mitchell, Gary Sheets, Brock Strom, G. D. Wilson and Victor Yocum.

Our particular thanks to Cadets Gerald Garvey and Bradley Hosmer who gave unstintingly of their time "above and beyond the call of duty" to follow this book through to its completion.

A very special thanks to our kind and patient husbands who have given us much inspiration and understanding in our writing projects.

Marian Talmadge
Iris Gilmore

Contents

WINGS FOR PEACE

1

Up in the Air

Cadet Frank Barton gazed about him in awe. The blue Colorado sky seemed to envelope him—above, beneath and all around. He felt a thrill of sheer, unadulterated joy surge through him as the plane in which he was riding soared effortlessly. This was the life, he thought—this was it. He'd flown before in other Air Force airplanes—T-33's, T-29's, T-28's. But this was his first experience in a glider—and it was wonderful!

The sensation was different from anything else in the world. Why, this was the true feeling of flight, he decided. No engine noise, no vibration—just that feeling of gliding along smoothly, of being a part of the plane, of being the master of the machine.

Lieutenant Harold Jenkins tapped him on the shoulder, and, as Frank glanced back, the officer pointed to the right and said, "Look over there. We've got company."

At first, Frank saw a long, narrow shadow wheel and dip.

Then a large bird flew in close and looked them over. The cadet started slightly as he recognized the bird as a falcon —could it be Mach One, the falcon he trained and cared for at the Air Force Academy? No, this was a wild falcon, he decided.

"That bird is really bugging us." Lieutenant Jenkins chuckled. "He thinks we're a queer-looking creature and he's probably waiting for us to flap our wings."

"I should think he'd be afraid of us," Frank replied. "After all, we're a lot bigger than he is."

"No, I've had lots of birds fly along with me like this when I was in a glider. They stay away from airplanes with engines—the noise apparently frightens them—or they can't keep up. But gliders seem to arouse their curiosity."

Frank watched the falcon as it turned and wheeled, then darted upward and flew in a great circle. Again it came in close and this time it hovered in mid-air. It was a picture of poise, relaxation and trust. Invisible hands seemed to bear it up. Its confidence in some Supreme Power appeared to free it from all thought of falling or danger. Frank pulled his thoughts back to the glider. Why, that's the way it is with us, he thought. We have to put our trust in a Higher Power, too. Then, we need to call on every ounce of ingenuity and skill in using our wings.

This year, more than last, he realized that he was training to be a good flyer, as well as a representative of his great country. In his small way, perhaps even he could help build for peace.

His instructor's voice broke into his reverie. "We're mighty lucky today. There are just enough thermals * to keep us aloft. Bear to the right, Mister."

"Yes, sir," Frank answered as he hauled over on the stick

---

* thermals—rising column of warm air.

and rudder, then asked, "How much longer do you think we can stay up, sir?"

"As long as we can get a breeze to soar in. Keep your eye on that bird. He'll pick out the thermals for us. Birds seem to have a built-in thermal sniffer that'll beat any variometer * you'll find in a glider. They know all the tricks of using the air currents to advantage."

"We can learn a lot from them, can't we, sir?"

"You bet we can. Actually, we can do practically anything in these sailplanes that they can do. After all, the glider is built to fly on the same principle as a bird—except for flapping its wings. But that falcon has one advantage over us."

"What's that?"

"He's logged a heck of a lot more flying time." Lieutenant Jenkins laughed, then directed, "Let's go over and latch onto his thermal."

Frank headed toward the falcon. Sure enough, as they got near him, the green pellet rose in the tube. The glider ascended two hundred feet per minute, then three hundred feet. They soared around for some time, following the falcon, until finally it turned suddenly and flew away rapidly in a direct flight plan to timberline.

"I guess he got tired of our company," Frank said. What adventure! What sport! he thought. To think he'd ever questioned the thrill of soaring. As they continued to seek out the thermals, the cadet went back over his afternoon's experience.

As a member of the newly formed Air Force Academy Soaring Club, he'd accompanied several cadets and two officers to the glider port at Buckley Field. There they looked with interest at the three Schweizer 2-22 gliders tied

---

* variometer—instrument used in a glider to show ascent and descent due to thermal activity.

down in a fenced enclosure. It was the first time that most of the cadets had ever seen a sailplane up close.

Major Willard Foster was in charge of the soaring program, assisted by Frank's favorite ATO,* Lieutenant Harold Jenkins. When they arrived in their jeeps, Major Foster said, "Pile out. Untie two of those gliders and we'll hook one to that pickup truck over there and the other to this jeep. Then it's just a short tow up the hill to the runway."

The cadets jumped out of the jeep and followed their orders. These men were now third classmen, back for their second year at the Air Force Academy, temporarily located at Lowry Air Force Base, near Denver, Colorado.

Frank's roommate, Pete Day, helped him untie the knots holding one of the gliders down. "What an experience!" Pete exclaimed with his usual enthusiasm. "It means getting into the air, which is what we all really want to do."

"Ye-ah," Frank answered uncertainly. "Only I wish these were power planes. That's what I'm anxious to fly."

"I've read some good articles about these gliders," Pete went on, "and they say everything you learn in them can be applied to flying in power airplanes."

"Well, maybe." Frank still didn't sound too enthusiastic. "At least, as you say, we'll be getting up in the air."

"I heard Major Foster say that, if the pilot of that private plane which crashed over on the Western Slope last week had known how to fly a glider, he'd probably never have wrecked his plane."

"How come?" Frank asked in surprise.

"He said that, if the pilot had understood more about air currents, he wouldn't have let himself get in such a dangerous situation."

They were interrupted by Major Foster's briefing, "You

---

* ATO—Air Training Officers who acted as upperclassmen for the first two years at the Air Force Academy.

can see, men, that a glider has only one wheel, in its center. Consequently, whenever it is moved on the ground, someone must hold up the wing so it won't be damaged. Mr. Shelton, you will drive the pickup truck. Mr. Barton, you and Mr. Day hold up the wings." He turned and instructed the rest of the cadets to untie the other gliders.

As they started up the hill, George Shelton gradually increased the speed of the truck until Frank and Pete were running on the double.

"Darn him," Frank panted out loud, although nobody could hear him. "He knows how h-hard it is to k-keep up with him and not d-drop this wing!"

"What's the matter? Getting weak?" George razzed, leaning out of the cab. "Thought you needed some exercise."

Frank didn't have the breath to answer. He let out a "Whew!" when they came to the runway. Then he looked down at his fatigues. His legs were covered with cactus spines and rough burrs.

"Leave it to old Knucklehead Shelton," he muttered disgustedly to Pete as the latter walked around the glider and joined him. "Ouch!" Frank cried as he pulled a cactus spine out of his finger.

"I'd like to roll old Shelton in a pile of cactus," Pete gritted between his teeth as he picked the longest spines and some burrs off his fatigues.

"Come over here a minute, men," Major Foster said. "I want to give you a few instructions and answer any questions. But remember, the more we talk, the less time you'll have in the air.

"One of the most important things in a glider operation is good ground coordination. It's absolutely necessary to keep the runways clear. Cadets must stay off the runways and keep vehicles off at all times. Remember this, when a sailplane is on final approach, the pilot is committed to a landing. He cannot go around again. And you're not going to be able to hear the glider coming in like power aircraft. Keep your neck on a swivel, look around you and stay on the ball.

"Another thing, you men all want to get in as much flying as possible. The less time a glider spends on the ground between flights, the more time you'll get in the blue. So let's try to snap things up on the ground. As soon as a sailplane releases from the tow plane, the tow plane will return to the field, pass low over the runway and drop the towline. One of you hop in a vehicle, drive out and get that towline. As soon as a glider lands, the pickup truck should start after it, to tow it in. Step lively and you'll get more air time. Lieutenant Jenkins, take them over to one of the gliders and brief them on it."

The young ATO climbed into the nearest glider and, while the cadets crowded around, he explained, "The instrument with the two tubes on the right side of the panel is called a variometer. It is used to tell when you're in a thermal. You'll notice that one tube has a green pellet and one a red pellet. When the green pellet goes up, we're in lift. When the red pellet goes up, we're in sink.

"We'll fly around searching until we hit lift. Then we'll circle, always trying to stay in the rising air. If we don't find any lift on this first flight, we'll glide right back to the field, and it will be a short flight. We may be lucky though, and have a long blast in that wild blue.

"You've all had some power time at the Air Force contract flight schools during visits there the past summer. The controls—the ailerons, elevator and rudder—on a glider work exactly the same as those on a power plane. You have been taught that an engine failure in a power plane is an emergency. That is true because you are counting on an engine.

The lack of engine thrust in a glider is not an emergency because you are not counting on it in the first place."

Major Foster came over to the glider and asked, "Do you have any questions?"

Pete responded, "Sir, how far can we fly from the field?"

"Don't fly any farther from the airport than the distance you will be able to glide back from your altitude. This is about two miles per thousand feet of altitude. The higher you are, the farther away you can go and still get back to the landing strip. Remember to keep your airspeed on final approach—no slower than forty-five miles an hour in the traffic pattern. If you think you aren't going to make the end of the runway, lower the nose, dive toward the end of the runway, and, with the added speed you gain, you may be able to level off a bit toward the end and get in. *Never pull back on the stick* if you're coming in low. You'll only settle in faster and drop it in short of the runway.

"You've each received a comprehensive briefing booklet on glider operation and, since you were supposed to have studied it before you came out today, you can give me your answers now, I am sure. Mr. Shelton, what is the purpose of spoilers on a glider?"

Frank glanced quickly at George Shelton. The big, blond cadet was always so sure of himself that he invariably seemed to rub Frank the wrong way. This time, Frank was surprised to see George color slightly, then stammer when he tried to answer.

"Well—uh . . . the spoilers . . . I—uh—they're just like flaps."

"What do you mean, 'just like flaps?'" The officer spoke sharply.

"Well . . . what I mean is . . . that is, they make the aircraft settle in faster if you're coming in high. They lower the stalling speed," George finished confidently.

"Lower the stalling speed! You didn't read the poop sheet, Mr. Shelton. The spoilers *raise* the stalling speed, and you should increase the speed a bit when you use them. If you're gliding in on the hairy edge and pull on the spoilers suddenly, you'll clobber it in for sure. . . . You'd better learn about spoilers, Mister. They're also used on the F-102 and the F-106. After all, soaring is preparing you to become one of the best pilots of the best planes in the world."

"Yes, sir. Thank you, sir." George made a sour face, then shrugged as the officer turned away.

"Lieutenant Jenkins," Major Foster continued, "you take Mr. Barton for his first ride. I'll take Mr. Henderson. The rest of you men listen and make yourselves useful wherever you can."

This was a real break, Frank thought. The young officer was his favorite ATO and Frank knew he was a good instructor, patient and interested in helping the cadets learn.

Lieutenant Jenkins said, "We check the glider out the same way that we check out a power airplane." He and Frank walked around the machine, making minute inspections.

"Get into the glider, Mr. Barton, and fasten your 'chute." Frank climbed into the front seat, settled himself awkwardly and went to work on his 'chute. The officer got into the rear seat.

"All right, Shelton and Day," the lieutenant shouted. "Stretch that tow line from the L-19."

George and Pete ran forward and got the rope. They attached it to the tow plane and stretched it toward the glider. Then George picked up the end and started to hook it on the glider.

"*What* do you think you're doing, Mr. Shelton?" the officer barked.

"Hooking up the glider, sir." George looked startled.

"Mister, don't come out here again without reading that briefing material," the lieutenant snapped. "The glider should never be hooked up until the glider pilot gives the signal to do so."

"Yes, sir." Meekly, George stepped back a couple of feet.

"Mr. Barton, check your shoulder harness and fasten your seat belt. Then check the controls."

"Yes, sir," Frank replied. And in a moment, "Harness and safety belt fastened, sir. Controls free."

"O.K., Mr. Shelton," Lieutenant Jenkins called. "You can hook 'er up now. Mr. Day, when I motion you to pick up that wing tip, that's the signal to the tow pilot that the glider is ready for take off. The tow plane will taxi forward slowly until the slack is out of the tow line. Then it will pause and begin a smooth acceleration. The glider takes off first. It will climb up about fifteen feet or so and then you must lower the nose slightly, to take the load off the tail of the tow plane.

"After the tow plane is off the ground, try to hold a position directly behind and slightly above the plane so that you'll stay out of the slipstream. We'll get a shaking up if you get in the prop wash. Try not to have any slack in the rope. This is hard to avoid on a rough day."

Frank gritted his teeth and tensed his muscles. The palms of his hands were wet. He kept trying to remember all that he had read and heard about gliding. Then, to his relief, he heard the officer say, "I'll be on the controls with you, to keep you out of trouble, since this is your first glider flight."

The lieutenant motioned to Pete to lift the wing. A few moments after the wing came up, the pilot of the tow plane gunned the motor and it taxied forward slowly. Frank felt a tug as the slack came out of the rope.

There was a little jerk when the glider started forward. The nose tried to go up and the tail down, but Frank moved the stick forward and the glider rolled along smoothly on its one center wheel. A quick glance to the right showed Pete running alongside the sailplane holding the wing tip.

As they gained speed, Pete dropped back and the glider skimmed down the runway. Frank used the ailerons to keep the wings level. Far sooner than he expected, the plane was off the ground.

"Climb it up a bit," Lieutenant Jenkins directed. "Whoa, there! Not so fast. You're pulling up on the tail of the tow plane. Be careful. He'll cut you loose before you wreck him. Ease the nose down a bit. Take the load off his tail or he can't get off the ground. That's it—no—don't dive it. You'll get too much slack in the rope. . . . Good! The tow plane's off—now keep directly behind and slightly above him."

Perspiration ran down Frank's cheeks. He felt tied in knots, but he managed to keep his wits about him as he followed orders. The tow plane started a turn to the left.

"There," the lieutenant said, "he's turning. Keep your flight path right behind his. Your nose should be slightly to the outside of the tow plane. This way, your turn covers the same radius the plane does. No, you're cutting inside on the turn. See that slack in the rope? Ease over toward the outside . . . there, that's better."

As the two planes straightened out of the turn, Frank drew a deep breath. Everything seemed under control. He turned his head carefully, as though it might crack off, and glanced swiftly toward the mountains. Yes, those snow-capped Rockies were still there, cutting into the blue sky.

He peeped over the side and saw the bomb range on the prairie below. The other glider and the cadets down there looked like so many toys. A feeling of confidence surged through him. It hadn't been too hard, he decided. He glanced ahead at the tow plane again and was surprised to see it suddenly gaining altitude.

"Looks as if he's struck some lift," his instructor said.

Frank pulled back on the stick and they climbed up to match the tow plane's altitude. Now they were back in proper position, and again Frank sighed with satisfaction—but too soon! The glider kept climbing, and Frank was far above where he wanted to be. He clutched the stick nervously.

"We're in the same lift area that booted the tow plane upstairs just now," the officer explained.

Frank dropped the nose of the glider and dived slightly toward the tow plane. An alarming amount of slack developed in the tow line. In a moment, the slack came out of the rope with a jerk, and the glider surged forward, developing more slack in the rope.

Lieutenant Jenkins spoke quietly, "If you let that slack jerk out too fast, you may break the tow line. I'll take the stick a minute." He yawed the nose slightly to the left. As the rope became taut, the nose swung to the right into position and things seemed under control again.

Suddenly, the tow plane rose again. The glider, too, entered the area of lift, and Frank watched the little green pellet of the variometer go up.

His instructor said, "I've checked the gliderport and other air traffic. Everything is O.K. This is a good place to release. I'll pull up somewhat sharply to signal the tow pilot, then ease the nose down a bit, to take tension off the tow line. Now, pull the red release knob . . . good . . . pull again, just to make sure . . . we're off! Start a sharp turn climbing to the right."

Frank watched the tow plane peel off to the left, as he banked to the right.

"Now circle back and we'll pick up that lift. . . . No, don't laze it around. Really rack it up." The officer kicked the plane around into a tight turn.

Frank noted that there was no response from the green pellet. The red pellet of the variometer was up.

"Looks as though we lost that lift," the lieutenant said.

"Well, keep it going straight ahead. Maybe we'll find another."

Frank noticed for the first time how silent it was in the plane. There was a slight whisper of the air against the glider, but that was all. He recalled that they'd been conversing in normal tones. Somehow, the clatter of an engine would seem a rude interruption here, he decided.

Just then he heard the sound of an airplane—a jet. He realized that this was the first time he'd ever heard another plane when he was in flight. It gave him an odd feeling. Over toward the right, he could see the jet, which had just taken off from Buckley Field.

Lieutenant Jenkins' voice interrupted his thoughts. "Let me have the stick a minute. I'll get us some altitude." The officer banked sharply and whipped the glider around in a tight turn to the right. Frank noticed the green pellet inching upward in the tube.

They'd gained two hundred feet, Frank realized as he looked at the instrument. The glider circled and kept going steadily upward. Frank held his breath. It didn't seem possible that they were going up and up *with no power*.

He was suddenly aware of a tremendous feeling of being alive and at one with space. He looked out at the long graceful wing of the glider and knew that this was a feeling he could get from no other type of aircraft. He glanced at the altimeter. They had gained fifteen hundred feet! Now the green pellet settled farther down in the tube. Soon it was at the bottom and the red pellet started to rise.

"Guess that's it," Lieutenant Jenkins said. "There's your first thermal. Rack it around now and try to pick up another one."

Frank eased the glider to the right until once more they found lift and the craft began to climb.

2

Downwind

Lieutenant Jenkins' voice brought Frank back to the present. "Better head her back toward the field now. We're getting a little low. Remember, you *never* play a thermal under five hundred feet. When you're down to five hundred feet, start coming in. If you encounter lift on final approach, put on spoilers and, if that's not enough, do S-turns to lose altitude. Never, *under any circumstances*, do a 360-degree turn on final approach."

Frank glanced at the variometer and saw the red pellet coming up fast. His altimeter showed just above five hundred feet.

"Fly a good downwind leg along the west side of the field," the officer continued. "We have five hundred feet now and the point we want to touch down on is about off the wing. I'll check with the tower." He spoke into the microphone, "91 to tower, coming in for a landing."

"Tower to 91. Roger. Runway is clear."

Frank grasped the stick more firmly. This would be a test.

14

At his contract base last summer, he'd had a chance to land a T-28 a couple of times with a civilian instructor. The thought of it always thrilled him. But now he was going in without an engine—nothing but his skill and the graceful glider to work with.

"Keep your air speed around forty-five," the lieutenant directed. "Better start your turn onto base now . . . that's it. Remember, this plane glides a lot flatter than a power machine. Line it up with the runway . . . you're a little high . . . drop the nose a bit and pull on the spoilers. Notice that we're settling faster."

They skimmed over the end of the runway.

"Now fly it onto the runway. Don't stall it in."

Just as they came down, Frank saw George run out on the runway with his camera, evidently planning to take a picture.

"You idiot!" Lieutenant Jenkins yelled, even though the cadet couldn't hear him. "Get out of the way."

Frank held his breath while the glider came in for the landing. His hands grew damp and sticky clutching the stick when he saw the runway come up fast toward him and the cadet standing there in the way. Beads of perspiration broke out on his forehead and his throat was so dry he couldn't swallow. The glider touched down lightly. Frank held the nose up a bit with back pressure on the stick as they skimmed down the runway.

"I'll take the controls," the officer said loudly. The wing brushed George, who looked up too late to see what was happening. It knocked him flat.

The plane settled down on the front skid with a crunching noise. It wavered a bit and the left wing dropped gently down on the wing skid. They came to rest.

Lieutenant Jenkins raised the canopy and scrambled out of the plane, followed by Frank. They both ran back to

George. Sergeant Gary, followed by a couple of cadets, hurried over from the control tower.

George got to his feet and shook his head dazedly. He touched his left shoulder gingerly.

"Are you hurt?" Lieutenant Jenkins demanded.

"I—I—no, sir," George stuttered. "I'm—I'm—I'm all right. Just shook up, sir."

The instructor gazed at the cadet for a moment, then said, "That'll be a Form Ten for you, Mister. You ought to know better than to get in the way of a glider when it's coming in for a landing."

"I'm sorry, sir. No excuse, Sir." George's voice sounded strained.

Frank picked up the other cadet's camera and handed it to him without speaking.

"You'll fly with Major Foster, Mr. Shelton." Then the officer turned to Frank and said, "You made a pretty good landing for the first time, Mr. Barton—particularly under the circumstances. Now lend a hand while I take Mr. Gregg up for his turn."

"Yes, sir. Thank you, sir."

Frank and Pete went over to the glider and helped Arthur Gregg push it back into position. After the two had climbed in, the officer said, "Fasten the tow rope to us, Mr. Barton. Mr. Day, handle the wing."

The two cadets followed their orders, then the L-19 started up and Pete ran along, holding the wing up, until the glider was moving faster than he could run. He let go and a great cloud of dust enveloped him and Frank. They coughed and rubbed their eyes as they turned away.

"Gosh, old Dumbwhack Shelton really goofed that time," Pete said. "This must be his unlucky day."

"Yeah, and it's a good thing Major Foster didn't see him.

The major would have gigged * him even more. Old George would have been walking the ramp ** until Christmas."

"How was your ride?" Pete asked eagerly. "Did you like it?"

"Like it! I'll say I did." Frank grinned happily. "Man! That soaring is for real."

"Didn't I tell you? I've read a lot about it and the fellows who go out for gliding really talk it up. What happened? Anything interesting?"

Frank told him of his experience and how they had followed the falcon to pick up thermals. When he finished he said, "Let's go over to the control tower and watch Sergeant Gary."

The two cadets went to the yellow truck, with its radio equipment, which was used as a control tower.

"Help yourself to some lemonade," Sergeant Gary offered. "I have to keep track of those fly boys up there." He pulled on his earphones.

Frank and Pete got some lemonade in paper cups. The slanting rays of the late September sun were still warm, so they sat down on the shady side of the truck, leaning against the wheels. As they talked, they glanced from time to time at the two gliders overhead.

"You know, we really are lucky to be here," Pete observed seriously. "There were plenty of times last year when I was pretty sure I'd be found deficient." ***

"Me, too, but here we are, third classmen in the United States Air Force Academy and going strong—I hope, I hope, I hope," Frank spoke equally seriously.

"Well, I don't know about how strong, but we're going."

---

* to be gigged—to receive demerits.
** walking the ramp—also called "walking tours." Marching in the area for a prescribed length of time to work off demerits.
*** found deficient—to fail or flunk.

Pete glanced up at one of the gliders soaring above the field. "There's old Meatball Shelton in that one."

Frank nodded. "Yeah, and I suppose he's telling Major Foster how to fly."

Pete chuckled. "I have to laugh when I think how surprised he was when the major asked him about the spoilers. I wonder how old Mr. 100% Shelton slipped up. You'll have to admit, no matter how obnoxious his ego is, he's usually well prepared."

"He said something about not getting time to read the poop sheet before we came out. That's once when he got caught flat-footed."

"Then to get knocked down by a glider . . . I'll bet he's chapped."

The two boys sat silent for a time, listening to Sergeant Gary give directions to the gliders. The officer watched the planes through his binoculars. They heard him say, "Tower to 69 and 71. You are at the same altitude."

The two cadets looked up quickly to see one glider swerve away to the north while the other started to climb.

After a time, Pete said, "I'm glad you were voted an Honor Representative * again. We need your type of fellow there to keep it rated high."

"Thanks, pal. You're really my press agent, aren't you? Remind me to raise your wages next Saturday." Frank leaned back on his elbows and chewed thoughtfully on a long weed. There weren't many sounds—a cricket sawed a monotonous tone nearby, and he heard the far-off drone of a T-29 heading toward Lowry Air Force Base.

Off to the north, he could see automobiles hurrying along the highway, but they were too far away to be heard. Suddenly he frowned as a worrisome thought wormed its way

---

* Honor Representative—Each squadron elects two Honor Representatives who make up the Honor Committee which implements the Honor Code.

into his mind. Ann's last letter bothered him. She kept talking about some fellow—what was his name? Oh, yes, Craig Brown. He sounded like a real gone goon, Frank had decided.

He sat up with a start and slapped at a horse fly that buzzed in close.

"What's the matter with you?" Pete asked. "You look like a dark brown thunder cloud."

"I'm just trying to dig Ann's last letter."

"What's the scoop—or don't you want to talk about it?"

"Oh, she said she had something important to tell me."

"Is there anything wrong with *that?* Sounds real good to me."

"It would have been all right if she'd stopped there." Frank rushed on without giving Pete a chance to say anything. "But she keeps mentioning some guy called Craig Brown."

"Aha! Sounds as if the green-eyed monster is creeping up on you. After all, man, you aren't married to Ann. She has a right to talk with other fellows down at Colorado College."

"Sure, sure. It's just that . . ."

Sergeant Gary's voice interrupted them. "Hey, you men, Major Foster is coming in for a landing. Time to get out there and help."

The two cadets sprang to their feet and hurried toward the runway, taking care to keep out of the glider's way. As it landed and came to a stop, the canopy opened and George Shelton crawled out.

"Thank you, sir. That was a good flight, sir." He hopped down and started away.

"Just a minute, Mister." Major Foster's clipped voice stopped him. "This glider has to be towed to the take-off position. Take a wing, Mr. Shelton."

When the glider was in the right position, the officer said, "Come on, Mr. Day. It's your turn."

At the signal from the major, Frank hooked the tow rope on the sailplane. The L-19's engine revved up, then the plane started forward. George ran along until the glider had enough speed so that Pete could keep the wings level. Then George let go and dropped back. Again those left behind were enveloped in a swirl of dust.

"Whew!" George spit out a mouthful of grit and rubbed his arm across his eyes. "That's the dirtiest part of this soaring business. But it really was a lot more fun than I expected. I think maybe Major Foster is right. We might learn something from these gliders."

"I should hope so," Frank answered as he picked up a stone and skimmed it across the prairie. "I'd hate to think we were out here wasting our time." He started toward the control tower.

"What's the matter with *you*, Plasterbrain?" George said sarcastically. "Aren't you getting a little uppish?"

"Nothing's the matter with me," Frank answered crossly. Then he was ashamed of himself. Even if he didn't like George very well, there was no reason for taking his spite out on him simply because he, Frank, was disturbed about Ann's letter.

"This is really good experience for me," George continued. "I've been taking private flying lessons out at the Skyranch Airport."

"Yeah—I know," Frank murmured. He ought to—old Dumbwhack Shelton bragged enough about it.

"I'm hoping to get my student pilot's license soon. That'll be one happy day for me."

As the two cadets reached the control tower, they heard Sergeant Gary say, "Tower to 69. Come on in, 69, the runway is clear. There is a wind shift to the southwest at fifteen knots."

He turned to the two cadets. "Lieutenant Jenkins is bringing in his glider. He said for you two to help tie it down."

Frank turned away disappointed. He'd hoped to have one more ride. He watched the glider float down effortlessly, with no sound except the whistle of the wind through its struts. He and George ran over and helped the officer and his student tie the glider to the pickup.

Frank went back to the tower for a moment, where he was startled to hear Sergeant Gary say sharply, "Watch it, 71! That's a strong crosswind."

Frank glanced up at the glider coming in for a landing and realized it was Major Foster's plane and Pete was with him.

The wind seemed to lift the glider and shake it rudely from side to side. Frank's nails bit into his palms as he strained forward, wishing he could help. The glider made a steep bank, then headed down the runway.

Frank drew a deep breath as it landed safely and came to a stop. He ran out to help and heard Major Foster say as he crawled out, "You did a good job, Mr. Day. That was a wicked crosswind we hit coming in, but we made it."

"Thank you, sir." Pete's voice sounded thin.

Frank glanced at his roommate's face and saw the freckles standing out sharply. He was white to his jughandle ears. He swallowed convulsively as he walked toward Frank.

"Are you O.K.?" Frank asked quickly.

"I'm just shook, that's all," Pete answered, the color beginning to come back to his cheeks. "I thought that wind was going to flip us over. It was real hairy."

"Come on, men," Lieutenant Jenkins' voice interrupted. "Tie this glider to the jeep and we'll head for the corral."

They towed the gliders back to the enclosure and tied them down. Then the cadets climbed into the jeep, which took them back to the Academy.

Just before they got out, Major Foster said, "As cadets, you are learning discipline and how to follow orders. At the Academy disobedience usually results in disciplinary action, you all know well. As future pilots, you must also learn aeronautical discipline. The results of disobeying one of the 'rules of the air' can be far more serious than disobedience at the Academy. There's an old saying among pilots that I think you ought to memorize. It applies to *all kinds* of aircraft—gliders, power airplanes, etc. 'Aviation in itself is not inherently dangerous. But, like the sea, it is terribly unforgiving of any carelessness, incapacity or neglect.'" The officer paused a moment to let his words sink in then said, "O.K., scramble."

The cadets hurried to their dorms. As Frank walked into the room with Pete, he said, "I'm going to jot down what Major Foster said about aviation not being dangerous. That quotation really puts the burden on the pilot, and I want to remember it."

"Yeah," Pete replied, wiping his forehead and face with his sleeve. "Whew! I liked that soaring business. It was real fun. But I'm tired."

Frank nodded. "I liked it, too. But it seems as if every silver lining has to have a dark cloud."

"Now what are you grumbling about?"

"Oh, I was just thinking that things are really piling up and this is only the beginning of the year. I'm glad I'm an Honor Representative again, but I worry about physics. I'm afraid it's going to give me a rugged time."

"There you go again, borrowing trouble."

"And I'm still worried about Ann's letter. I have a feeling . . ."

"You and your big, fat feelings. Skip it. Me—I'm going to sack out till chow."

Frank picked up the model F-86 on his desk and rubbed the shiny wings with his fingers. His brother, Joe, had given it to him several years ago, before he went to Korea. Joe hadn't come back, but he'd left Frank something important to live up to.

Stay on the beam, Joe had told him before he left, and you'll be all right. Frank had recalled his brother's advice many times in the past months, while he struggled through his first year at the Air Force Academy. And the admonition *had* helped him over some tough spots.

He walked over to the window and glanced toward the mountains etched against the western horizon. They looked like purple paper cutouts against the flaming sunset sky. Somehow, he never tired of looking at those mountains, he thought. They inspired him, too, as Joe's words did.

They were vast and endless . . . and beyond them was an even bigger world. The cadets had heard just yesterday in philosophy class how they could be an important part of that larger world—even help to make it a more peaceful one.

"Part of our job here," Colonel Oberg had said, "is to remember there's a power button which controls a lot of things. We want to train you men so that power button will never have to be pushed."

As Frank turned away from the window, though, the troublesome thoughts crowded back into his mind. Ann's letter and his struggle with physics.

Besides, he might have new military duties to fulfill. The non-commissioned lists would be posted soon and he both feared and looked forward to what he might have to do.

3

Shaping Up

When Frank's class returned to the Air Force Academy in September, they had found themselves in an unusual position. The ATO's were still there, acting as upperclassmen, but now some of the cadets were appointed as noncommissioned officers. The ATO's kept delegating more and more responsibility to them.

"That's the only way you'll learn," an ATO, Lieutenant Leonard Porter, said in a meeting one day. "After all, we can tell you what to do and how to do it, but until you take over some of the details, you'll never know what it means."

"Sure, sure," Pete grumbled later. "They want us to do everything—study, march, drill, walk tours, and now they want us to 'take over the responsibilities.' What does old Hard Nose mean?"

"He means we have to boss the doolies ° around like the ATO's did us last year."

° doolies—nickname for fourth classmen.

Pete's eyes gleamed. "That will please me. I'm just waiting to try out a little of that chewing routine on some poor
old broken-down fourth classman.* I'll bet he'll wish he'd
never heard of the Air Force Academy."

"Don't be so biggety. Remember how you resented it last
year."

"Just give me a chance." Pete rubbed his hands together
and screwed his face into a thousand scowling wrinkles.

"My, you really scare me!" Frank laughed. Just then,
they were interrupted by the buzzer, warning them it was
time for classes. "You'd better wait to see if you are put in
charge of anybody before you plan any dastardly tricks,"
he advised.

That evening after dinner, Pete went to the library to do
some research while Frank studied in their room. Later, the
door burst open and Pete dashed in, his eyes wide and his
freckles standing out in his excitement.

"Guess what?" he demanded.

"All right, give." Frank yawned and stretched.

"The non-commissioned ranks have been posted. You're
Flight Sergeant and I'm an Element Leader—me, an Element
Leader!"

"What?" Frank stood up so quickly his chair slammed
over on the floor. "Do you mean it? Are you kidding?" He
seized Pete and they scuffled around the room.

"No, honest. It's out there on the bulletin board."

"That's keen—it's just great!" Frank pounded his roommate's back. "I can't believe it, though. I never dreamed
I'd make one of the top ranks. Gosh, I'm proud . . . " He
stopped and looked thoughtful, then continued soberly,
"Oh, man, what a responsibility! I don't know if I can hack
it."

---

* fourth classman—same as freshman in other colleges.

"Of course you can, Meathead. The officers know what they're doing when they make these appointments."

"I hope so. And you're an element leader! You'll make a terrific one. That's super, Pete. All your hard work has paid off."

Pete grinned widely. "You jerk! You're the one with the important job. You're a Flight Sergeant. And when you are raised to a real rank of commissioned officer, I'll still be the perennial sergeant."

"Don't be so stupid! You'll be right up there at the top. After all, the men really respect you and that's what counts in the final analysis."

"We can't all be chiefs. Some have to be the 'Indians.' "

"Yes, but they're not spending all that money training us to be 'Indians.' "

"So they have to have sub-chiefs. I'll be one of those."

There was a quick knock at the door and George Shelton walked in with a smirk on his face. "Have you seen the bulletin board? I'm a Flight Sergeant for our squadron."

"Yeah, I saw it," Pete drawled. "Congratulations." Then he added, "You'll do all right, George."

"Thanks. I hope I can fulfill the confidence the officers and you men—put in me. It's a big challenge."

The words were all right, Frank thought, but the smug tone belied them. Why did he always react this way to George, he wondered.

"Seems as though you and I will be working mighty close." George looked directly at Frank.

"Well, yes, I guess we will." Frank felt awkward. He said quickly, "Congratulations, George. I know you'll do a good job." He could say that in all honesty.

"Thanks. I expect to. Congratulations to you, too," George added as an afterthought. "What did you get, Pete?"

"Oh, I'm an element leader," Pete answered breezily.

"They know where to put me to get the most for their money."

George shrugged, then said, "Confidentially, I'm looking toward the future. My goal is to be Wing Commander when we're first classmen. Just watch my smoke!" He gave the door a small slam as he swaggered out.

Frank looked at Pete for a moment, then said ruefully, "I'm in a real tough spot to have to work on this level with George. Why are we always together, will you tell me that?"

"Because you're so much alike," Pete jumped aside as a pillow flew through the air, barely missing him, but upsetting his books all over the floor. "I'll thank you to leave my books alone," he grumbled in mock indignation.

"I'm sorry, Pete. Here, let me fix them." Frank stooped to pick up the books and put them back in an orderly row. "It's going to be a real test, any way you look at it, working with my buddies and gaining their confidence."

The next day, the Squadron Commander called a meeting of the Flight Commanders and the Flight Sergeants. He told them how he expected them to run their respective Flights and ended by saying, "Treat your men like people—they're intelligent and will respond to correction if you show them where they need it. Don't degrade them in front of their classmates. Don't use physical punishment such as 'run your chin in,' but use intelligent, rational posture correction." He paused a moment, then continued, "Above all, never let yourself get emotionally involved and show a fourth classman that you are angry."

As Frank and Pete started toward the dorm, George caught up with them. "They sure put the burden on us, didn't they?" he questioned.

"Yes," Frank answered, "and now it's up to us to show that we can hack it."

"Well, I'm not so sure on all that old palaver about treating the doolies like people—they aren't people—they're doolies and should be made to know their place."

"I think the Commander is right. He has the same idea my dad always had about dealing with my brother Joe and me. Dad always said you could catch more flies with sugar than with vinegar."

George laughed shortly. "That's O.K. some places. But in a military institution such as this you have to show them who's boss. Before the year is over, my men are going to think I'm a regular old hard nose."

"You mean you're going to be another Lieutenant Porter?" Pete's voice rose slightly.

"So what? He made pretty good men out of us, didn't he?"

"Yes, but he did it the hard way, as far as I'm concerned," Frank retorted. "I'm going to try Colonel Cassman's idea—I like it."

"Well, you treat your Flight your way and I'll treat mine the way I want to." George's tone was flippant. "And may the best man win." He ran up the dorm steps ahead of the other two cadets.

"Maybe he's right," Frank said as he and Pete went into their room, the old feeling of indecision suddenly overwhelming him. "When the cadets are so close to your own age, it's a little hard to make them obey unless you get a little tough."

"Don't cross your bridges till you come to them," Pete advised. "And, for gosh sakes, don't get in a swivet yet. You haven't even met your Filght for the first time. And since I'm one of your Element Leaders, I'll help all I can."

"I don't know what I'd do without you, Pete." Frank looked at the tall, skinny cadet fondly. "You're my little ray of sunshine."

"Cut the corn and come on. We have to drill the socks off those doolies."

They went out to the parade ground, where Frank had his chance to handle some fourth classmen. He was assigned a squad to drill. But before he took them through their paces he said, "Give me your attention!"

He tried to keep his voice steady, but there was a queer sensation in the pit of his stomach, and he felt almost dizzy. He took a couple of deep breaths, then continued, "First of all, I want you to know I mean business. When I give an order, I mean it. And it's to be done right. Maybe you men will consider me hard—I don't know. That's all right with me. I will be hard and tough on you, but I promise that I'll always try to be *fair*. I won't ask you to do things I wouldn't do myself."

His voice sounded unusually loud and harsh in his ears. He paused and looked at his men as they gazed straight ahead. Gosh, he thought, did he ever look that *young?* Why, they seemed like high-school kids. Well, that's what they were, practically—most of them were just out of high school. In his newly-assumed authority he forgot completely how very recently he himself had been a high-school graduate.

Frank swallowed and took another deep breath. He was shaking slightly. This was really an emotional thing—taking over these cadets and working with them. He hoped his voice wouldn't tremble when he gave the orders. "I intend to treat you like intelligent men. In return, I expect you to react intelligently." He stopped, then ordered, "Forward, march!"

He drilled and worked with his squad for over an hour, until it was time to report to another duty. As he dismissed the cadets, and they double-timed toward the dorms, he stood for a moment looking after them.

Dear God, he prayed silently, *make me a good leader, kind and patient.* These new cadets were really swell kids. He wanted to encourage them all he could.

On his way back to the dorm, he gloried in the fact that *he* no longer had to run every place as he'd had to when he was a fourth classman.

That evening, Pete burst into the room, eyes sparkling and a box tucked under his arm. Strange sounds issued forth.

"What's cooking?" Frank asked as he looked up from studying.

"Man, this is it! I found out Lieutenant Porter doesn't like cats."

"So he doesn't like cats—what do I care?" Besides, I don't particularly care about Hard Nose Porter, either."

"That's the point. Here's a chance to play a trick on him. Look, I found this kitten in the area." Pete lifted the lid, and Frank saw a small tiger-striped kitten crouched back in the corner.

He started to lift him out, but the spunky little animal spit at him and lifted its paw menacingly. "Boy, he has plenty of spirit!" Frank chuckled. "What are you going to do with him?"

"I heard old Hard Nose say he had to report for some orders and wouldn't be back till just before taps. I made this sign down in the laboratory." He held it up.

Frank read aloud, "BEWARE OF THE TIGER."

"We'll tack the sign on his door. Then we'll put the kitten in the box on his bed. That ought to chap him."

"Yeah—and you'll be gigged if he finds out who did it. Oh well, go ahead—have fun. Me, I have to finish this chapter on Physics. Man, that chaps me more than any old cat!"

Pete went out . . . and returned in a few minutes, saying,

"Everything's under control. Now we'll see where the chips land."

A few minutes before taps, Pete and Frank heard Lieutenant Porter's determined footsteps hurry up the stairs. Both boys stopped what they were doing and peeped out the door. They saw the officer halt and read the sign, then shrug. He opened the door and went into his room.

There was a short silence, then a roar and finally a summoning shout, "Burke! Elspy! Barton! Shelton! Day! All of you taxi in here!"

Frank and Pete hurried across the hall and stood in the doorway at attention. Lieutenant Porter had his back against the wall. He was breathing heavily and pointing a shaking finger. The kitten was backed up on the bed, spitting and mewing angrily.

"Take that—that—animal—one of you," Porter ordered. "Get it out of here at once."

"Yes, sir," both boys answered. They almost knocked each other down rushing to the rescue. But the kitten wasn't easily caught. It dodged them as they raced around the room, knocking down chairs and setting papers flying. Every time the kitten came near the officer, he let out a bellow.

Finally, it scrounged back under the bed and Frank got down on his stomach. "Keep quiet—can't you?" he muttered, knowing the little creature was frightened out of its wits. He edged in nearer. The kitten was still spitting and clawing. After a while, he managed to grab the little thing, but not before it left a long scratch on the back of his hand.

Frank wiggled out and stood up, clothes disheveled and breathing hard. By now, the doorway was filled with cadets, and he could tell at a glance that they were holding back the laughs. Pete's eyes were brilliant, and he wiggled his jug ears comically. Frank suppressed a grin.

He glanced at the lieutenant. His brows were puckered and his narrow lips set in a hard line. "Get rid of it—I don't care where—just get it out of my room," he ordered. Then he noticed the other cadets crowded in the doorway. "The rest of you meatheads get back to your quarters!" he barked.

The cadets faded away while Frank ran down the steps and carried the kitten out into the night. He finally decided to take it to the Security Flight Room * and see if someone there could take care of it. Poor little thing, he thought, as it clung to his clothes frantically.

When Frank returned to the dorm, Lieutenant Porter called from his room, "Thank you, Mr. Barton. I appreciate what you did." His face still looked grim. "I don't like cats —and if I catch the cadet who put him in here—well, he'll walk the area." Then he noticed the deep scratch on Frank's hand. "Mr. Barton—did you get scratched?"

"Yes, sir."

"Do you think you should go to the dispensary?"

"No, sir. It'll be all right."

"Well, I want to be sure." The officer's voice seemed a little less hard. "I'll put some iodine on it—then it'll probably be O.K."

Frank held his hand out, and the lieutenant swabbed the scratch. It stung a little, but that was all.

"Take your shower and hit the sack." The officer sounded more like himself. As Frank turned to go, he called after him, "Thanks again, Mr. Barton."

"Yes, sir." Frank hurried to his room.

"Now," Frank said to Pete, "I know I'm back at the Academy and the year has really started."

"Why?"

"Because you're up to your usual monkey business. Just

---

* Security Flight Room. The nerve center for the whole Academy.

let me give you a little advice—lay off Hard Nose or you'll be walking the ramp."

"Thanks, pal. I've had so much advice in my life I could lean against it like a wall."

Frank could not help laughing. "O.K., O.K. I'll button my lip, but don't say I didn't warn you!"

Fall activities were soon posted and the cadets spent some time discussing their preferences and signing up for various sports and clubs. This year, for the first time, the Academy would be represented by varsity teams in many sports—football, basketball, baseball, soccer, track, fencing, gymnastics, skiing, judo, wrestling, boxing and swimming.

"I'm going out for soccer again," Frank announced as he signed the list.

"Me, too," Pete added his name.

"I learned plenty last year and I'm anxious to get started."

And on every nice Sunday afternoon Frank and Pete joined other cadets in the Soaring Club, where they flew in the gliders located at Buckley Field.

"I'm glad we decided to join the Soaring Club," Frank said one Sunday evening after the two friends had been out all afternoon. "That way, we really log some flying hours and it's wonderful to get up in the air."

"Yeah," his roommate replied, "that's one thing I don't like here. We just don't get to fly as much as I like. I've heard that some of the cadets are taking lessons out at one of the airports."

"Old Meathead Shelton is one. He's always talking about his experiences. It costs dough, though, and I don't think I could afford it. My dad's still having a rough time with his business. And Mom writes that he hasn't been feeling very well. I wouldn't want to ask for any more money."

"I know it . . . but it would be nice."

"Right now, I'd better be making my plans for our navigation mission tomorrow night. That's when we're to go, isn't it?"

Pete looked at his schedule. "Un-huh. And it looks as though Hard Nose Porter is going with us." He made a face and wiggled his ears. "I hope I'm on my good behavior."

"Oh, goody!" Frank exclaimed sarcastically. "Hard Nose will add so much to our flight."

"Probably add a Form Ten and a few extra walking tours for your pleasure. Ouch!" He whirled away as Frank grabbed him by the shoulder and pommelled him a couple of times. "You quit picking on me, you big bully."

If He Can Hack It

One evening soon after academics started, Bob Elspy came into Pete's and Frank's room and threw himself on a bed. Bob had been Frank's roommate when they first came to the Academy a year ago, and they were still good friends.

"Frank," he said earnestly, "I've got a suggestion for you and I hope you'll agree."

"Go ahead." Frank clasped his hands behind his head and looked fondly at the other cadet's serious face. His square-built frame was solidly packed, Frank thought, like a small tank.

"I wish you'd decide to come out for football—now wait a minute before you object."

"What!" Frank exploded and his chair came forward with a bang as he gripped the edge of his desk. His face showed complete surprise as his eyebrows shot up.

"Yes, I mean it—you've gained a lot of weight since you came to the Academy. Besides, you're tall and you're quick on your feet."

35

"I think he's right," Pete agreed. "Why don't you?"

Frank still stared at Bob in disbelief. "Me? In football? How crazy can you get?"

"I don't think it's so crazy." Bob's voice sounded a little annoyed. "Let's put it this way—we need some more men if we're ever going to build ourselves up to a big time team."

"But I haven't had any experience. I'm raw stuff—I—well, I just don't think I'm football material." Frank didn't add that the thought of playing football gave him a queer feeling in the pit of his stomach.

"You did all right in soccer last year," Pete reminded him, "and it's plenty rough. I'd like to remind you that the coach says you're one of our best players."

"But soccer—that's different. And, anyway, it's not as important a sport as football. Gosh . . ." Frank's voice trailed off.

The soccer coach had been quite enthusiastic about their team this year. If he, Frank, went out for football, he'd have to give up soccer, where he'd built a solid place for himself on the team.

Bob eyed him narrowly. "You aren't scared, are you? You don't still have that fear of bodily contact, do you, that bothered you last year?"

Frank looked down at his clasped fist. Was he scared? Did he still shrink at the idea of meeting heavy bodies at full speed? "No—no—I don't think— No, I don't feel that way any more. Soccer and boxing got me over that last year, thank goodness!"

"Then what's the matter, Muttonhead?" Pete chimed in with his usual enthusiasm. "You've told me plenty of times what a great player your brother Joe was. Why can't you be a good player, too?"

Frank thought of Joe—his brother who'd been shot down over Korea. Yes, Joe had been a top notch football player.

He'd been captain of the team at home and had played at KU until he joined the Air Force. It had been because of Joe's death that his mother hadn't let him play rough games. So when he came to the Academy last year, he'd been really handicapped in the physical contact games. But he'd worked hard all year and had finally overcome his feeling of fear.

"I'd never be the player Joe was if I played a thousand years," he answered. "And I'd have so much to learn."

"So what?" Bob demanded. "You *could* learn if you'd try. And nobody expects you to be as good as your brother was. The coach just wants every fellow to be at his best. Besides, we need the men. Our team hasn't any depth," he added flatly.

"You learned a lot about dexterity last year, Frank," Pete said. "Not only in soccer, but in handling the falcons. Look how you finally mastered graphics—and all because you were willing to work with your hands."

Frank looked down at his hands and flexed his long, tapering fingers thoughtfully. He could almost feel the rough texture of the pigskin ball. Gosh, it would be fun to try. He'd like to toss some passes, if he had a chance. Then he shook his head.

"I just don't know if I could take that much time to practice. I'm finding Physics plenty rugged and I need all the time I have to bone up on it."

"You're just making excuses," Bob said disgustedly. "You could do it if you wanted to. Well," he got up and started for the door. "Think it over, Meatball. I'm not asking you for your own glory and honor, you know. I'm asking you because we need men on the team and you have the size and weight and could really help us. That is—if you think you could spare the time." He went out and slammed the door.

"Well, I take it our friend is a little irked with you," Pete said. "And I can't say I blame him much. You might show a little more enthusiasm—or at least act as if you are interested in helping."

Frank was silent for a moment, then said, "I can't make up my mind that fast and you know it. Besides, that's a big undertaking, to go out for the football team. Here I am a third classman with no freshman football behind me—not even any in high school."

"You act as though they are planning to put you on the first string. Brother, don't be so big-headed!"

"I hadn't thought of that," Frank said slowly. "They need plenty of fellows on the team—even fellows who never get to play in the big games. That's what we lack on our team —depth—everybody knows that."

"Is light beginning to dawn in your little old lame brain?"

Frank stood up suddenly. "You know, funnyface, I think Bob has the right idea. Maybe I should go out for football— at least it will give the first team something to practice on."

"Don't be so modest. You might develop into a real player."

"I'll never be that good. But let me tell you something, Mister. This is going to mean a lot of extra work for me. It will mean late lights to study Physics." He stopped suddenly, as if he remembered something.

"What's the matter?"

Frank sank down in his chair, his shoulders slumped forward. "It will mean I'll have to give up training the falcons." This would be hard, he knew. He'd developed a great love for the sleek birds who flew so swiftly and were such brave, clean fighters.

"You could work with them after football season," Pete suggested.

"Yeah, but that's not the same thing. It was such a thrill

last year to fly them at the football games. Remember how Mach One would soar up over the stands, and there would be that silence as he swooped down? That was for real."

"Well, you can't have everything," Pete opened a text-book as he continued, "Me, I've got to study. You have to make up your own mind."

The next day, Frank reported to the soccer coach and told him he was quitting soccer and going out for football.

Coach McConnell, a thoughtful and understanding man, listened gravely, then asked, "Frank, why are you making this change?"

"They need depth on the football team, and I'm deep—between the ears." Frank tried to make a joke of it. This was really harder than he'd thought it would be.

The coach took a long pull on his blackened brier, before he said, "I think I know what you mean, Mr. Barton. We're all trying to build an Academy 'in depth.' I've watched that football team and I predict that it will be a top-rated team—maybe even by the time your class graduates."

"Do you think so, sir? That would be wonderful."

"Yes, and you might become the star quarterback, in spite of your lack of football experience. Stranger things have happened in the sport's world. You're fast, strong and smart."

Frank's face reddened with embarrassment as he stuttered, "That—that couldn't be, sir. Excuse me, sir. I don't mean to contradict you, but I'm not that good."

"Maybe not—but as I say, stranger things have happened. The point is, though, I'll really hate to lose you. You've been one of our best players and I'd hoped that maybe we could build a pretty good team—we might even get to a national championship in a couple of years."

Frank squirmed uncomfortably and did not answer.

"Of course, soccer doesn't get the publicity that football does, but it's just as important in our battle here at the Academy for all-around excellence."

"I know, sir. That's all the more reason why I don't want you to think I'm letting you down." Frank stopped for a moment, then went on, "Frankly, I'd rather stay on the soccer team. I think I'd have a much better chance in every way. After all, I'm on the first team. And, selfishly, I'd love to be on a team which won a national championship. It would mean so much to me, Coach."

"Well, Mister, the decision is up to you. If you choose football, you have my best wishes for success."

"Thank you, sir. Right now, I feel that I must try out for football because they need extra men. But I want you to know, sir, that I appreciate all you've done for me in soccer and I'll never forget it."

The coach clapped his hand on Frank's shoulder. "Mr. Barton, I'm afraid I'm a little selfish, too. I hate to lose you. But you've made your decision. Now I want you to know that, if the football tryout doesn't work, we want you back with us in soccer."

Frank swallowed hard. Coach McConnell was a real gone guy and he was going to miss his quiet, encouraging manner. "Thank you, sir. You've been swell to me. And I hope you understand."

"I do. Now scram."

Frank hurried over to the Field House where he checked in his soccer suit and checked out some football equipment. Then he reported to the coach and said he wanted to go out for football, if they could use him.

"Sure, we can use you, Mister." The coach grinned at him. "We can always use a big fellow like you. Report over there to Lieutenant Porter. He'll give you a workout."

Frank's heart sank. He hadn't realized that the ATO was

helping with the football team this year. That made things a little tougher. He still didn't think that Porter liked him too well, and, no matter how hard he tried to like the officer, Frank always seemed to be ill at ease with him, and he had to work hard within himself not to bristle when the lieutenant corrected him.

He was further dismayed when he heard a familiar nasal voice say, "Well, well, well, if it isn't Mr. Muttonhead Barton himself reporting for the team. I suppose you think you'll save the day for good old Siwash."

Frank frowned, then said quickly, "I'll try to save the day for the good old Air Force Academy, if I ever get a chance. That'll be my job." As he turned away, he felt the old feeling of inadequacy welling up in him. What was he doing here, anyway? Why was he out here on the football field?

He felt an arm settle across his shoulders and turned quickly to see Bob grinning at him. "I knew you'd do it, chum. I knew you'd decide that we really need you out here."

"Sure we need him," George said sarcastically.

"Don't pay any attention to that meatball," Bob said good-humoredly. "He's just worried that you'll give him a run for his money. And I hope you do."

Frank wasn't so sure as they lined up for practice. Lieutenant Porter tried him in several places—end, guard, fullback and finally halfback.

"You're fast on your feet, Barton," the officer said sharply, "but you're clumsy as a bear cub with the ball." His gray eyes glinted coldly. Frank felt the old sense of antagonism toward the ATO sweep through him. He'd show Hard Nose Porter that he wasn't clumsy, he vowed. He'd make Pete practice throwing the ball with him until he, Frank, could handle it smoothly.

A couple of hours later, he was back in his room at the dorm.

"Well, Red Grange, how went the football practice?" Pete grinned widely.

"O.K., O.K.," Frank said impatiently. "But you've got to help me."

"Whaddaya mean? I've got my own problems. Nobody helps me," Pete teased in a whining voice.

But Frank paid no attention. "I'm going to show old Hard Nose Porter that I'm not as clumsy as a bear cub." He slammed down a book. "I'll make him eat those words yet."

"Good for you! I don't know what you're talking about, but if it has to do with Lieutenant Porter, I agree with you."

"He said I was as clumsy as a bear cub with the ball," Frank explained. "He did say I was quick on my feet, though—thanks to that soccer experience last year. But I'll show him."

Suddenly he sat down. "I'm bushed," he said wearily. "That workout was something. I think I'll sack out till dinner. Don't let me sleep through."

"O.K.," Pete promised.

Just before he dropped off to sleep, Frank had a sinking feeling. He wasn't sure how good he was. He didn't know if he could show Lieutenant Porter anything. He felt all shaky inside and not quite as sure of himself as he'd tried to let on to Pete.

After class the next day and before he reported for football practice, Frank hurried over to the falcon house to talk with Captain Linstrom. This was a difficult job, too. After all, he loved working with the falcons and found it a real sacrifice to give it up.

"Sir, I've come to tell you that I can't work with the falcons this fall."

"What's the matter, Mr. Barton? Are you falling down in your grades?"

"No, sir." Frank smiled slightly. "It's not that bad. The thing is, I've decided to go out for football and that means no time for falcon training."

"Good for you!" Captain Linstrom grinned. "I'll miss you around here—and so will Mach One, I'm sure." He picked up one of the falcons and smoothed its feathers. "But we need men on our team and I'm willing to sacrifice you over here, if you can help on the team."

"I have no illusions about myself, sir. I'm not going to be an important or big player. But you know our team is pretty shallow, sir. And I figure if I can do my part in helping back them up, then that's where I belong."

"Aren't you on the first string soccer team, Barton?"

"Yes, sir—I was. But I've talked it over with Colonel Mc-Connell. He released me."

"Well, I'm glad and sorry. I'm glad because I think you'll help our football team. And I'm sorry to lose you here and to lose you on the soccer team. They stand a good chance at a championship, from what I can see. And you'd get to be on a winning team. Your chances aren't too good to be on a winning team in football. After all, we're a pretty young school. Nobody expects us to be winners so soon."

"No, sir." Then Frank grinned widely. "But you know we might just fool them, sir." He stopped, embarrassed. "Not because I'm going on the team—but because the men really have determination—a determination to win that they're building up."

The captain laughed. "Yes, I think I know what you mean. Well, good luck, Mr. Barton. And when football season is over, Mach One and I will be glad to welcome you back here—if you have time."

"Thank you, sir. I hope I'll have time." As Frank ran

toward the Field House, he felt a warm glow inside him for Captain Linstrom and for the soccer coach. Gosh, they really are swell guys, he thought.

But many times during the season Frank had cause to question the wisdom of his decision to play football.

"I'm the best bench warmer on the team," he grumbled to Pete after the third game. He still hadn't even substituted for a few minutes.

"What did you expect?" Pete was very unsympathetic. "A berth on the first string? Who do you think you are, Tom Harmon?"

"No, dopey," Frank answered crossly. "I know I'm green as grass. It's just that football practice takes a lot out of a guy. And it would be fun to get a chance to play *just once*."

"Well, you knew when you chose football you had about as much chance playing this year as a snowball has down on the equator."

"You're a fine roommate. You really boost my morale."

"I'm sorry." Pete's voice changed. "I know it's tough. But you won't regret you are playing—wait and see."

"It might not be so bad if old Hard Nose Porter weren't on the coaching squad."

"Has he been riding you again?"

Frank shrugged. "I'm never really sure. Sometimes I think he deliberately makes things tougher for me."

"Such as?"

"He always manages to put me into the roughest playing spots."

"I suppose he's trying to toughen you up."

"Could be—well, it's my choice and I'll stick to it if it kills me."

"Oh, you'll live—unfortunately—to torture me." Pete tried to dodge a well-aimed pillow, which socked him on the side of the head. "Cut it out—I had my bed made real smooth," he complained.

"Sorry," retorted Frank, who didn't sound the least bit repentant.

"By the way," Pete went on, "how are you and Knucklehead Shelton getting along on the team? I haven't heard any gripes lately."

"Pretty good. The thing is, we're both more or less in the same boat—and we're both trying for the same position—halfback on about the third string. He'll probably get it—you know how cocky he is and sure of himself. And he really knows how to butter up old Hard Nose."

"There you go again. Where's your self-confidence?"

Frank smiled sheepishly. "Thanks, roomie. I need a little jacking up. Just light that fire under me whenever I begin to sag."

"Golly!" Pete grabbed his cap and started for the door. "I almost forgot—I'm drilling my element in three minutes. Watch out, doolies, here I come!"

After Pete left, Frank stared out the window. The pressures were really beginning to bear down, and there never seemed to be a split second to draw a deep breath.

It was nothing but study—particularly Physics, which racked him—football practice, classes, drilling his troops and performing his military duties as a Flight Sergeant.

And to top it all off, he hadn't heard from Ann since that last disturbing letter, although he'd written her a couple of short notes.

He sighed as he changed into his fatigues. Well, at least he'd see her after the game with Idaho State this Saturday. But somehow the idea of seeing her again didn't make him as happy as it used to. He was worried, he had to admit. Darn that Craig Brown! Why did he have to spoil everything?

5

What Is Courage?

A couple of evenings later, Frank looked up from the theme he'd just completed and exclaimed, "There—that's finished, thank heavens!"

"What's finished?" Pete asked.

"My theme on *The Bear*. You know, Pete, it really makes me feel a little better. I think the boy in the story had to face some of the problems that we face here."

"Such as?"

"Listen to this." Frank picked up his paper and read, "'The theme of *The Bear*, a short story by William Faulkner, is concerned with a growing boy's search for truth. The moral is presented by the father at the close of the story, when he addresses his son as follows: "Courage, and honor, and pride . . . and pity, and love of justice and liberty. They all touch the heart, and what the heart holds to becomes the truth, as far as we know truth."

"'To derive the meaning of truth as stated above requires a great deal of thought. In the story a young boy matures

46

very slowly as he acquires the meaning of truth. I believe that Faulkner is trying to tell us that truth is found only through experiences. People come to know the truth as they experience it, because it creates an inner warmth which cannot be mistaken. The boy had this experience many times.' "

As he stopped reading Frank glanced toward his friend, to see his reaction. "It gives me a lot of food for thought."

"Me, too," Pete answered seriously. "Let's ask Colonel Thorn to discuss this story in class tomorrow."

Next day, in their English class, Pete raised his hand determinedly and said, "Sir, Mr. Barton and I have been talking about the underlying theme in *The Bear*. May we open it to class discussion?"

"Certainly, Mr. Day. That's a good idea. Who wants to lead off?"

"I do, sir," Pete answered. "I started it, so I'd like to have my say first. In the story, the boy's father mentions several things: courage, and honor, and humility, and pride, and love of justice and of liberty—all these must touch the heart if we are to know the truth. It seems to me that's a pretty big order."

"But remember you don't discover them all at once, Mr. Day," the professor answered. "How about it, men?"

Jerry Nolan replied, "Sir, I think in the story the boy learned the truths one by one. For example—he learned courage first when he came to accept the forest as a challenge."

"And he learned honor and pride when he got his first deer and bear, sir," Bob Elspy added. "He really was proud of himself at that time."

"Yes," their professor answered, "and, as the Bible says, 'Pride goeth before a fall.' What did the boy have to learn next?"

"Things got much harder for him then, sir," Pete broke in, "particularly after he learned the truth of these three values. He hadn't learned the truth of humility, yet, and, having experienced pride, humility was very difficult for him to acquire."

That was right, Frank thought to himself. He could follow a little of this pattern in his own life. He'd touched upon the truth of courage last year when he'd overcome his lack of confidence and feeling of insecurity. He'd had both honor and pride when he'd been elected as Honor Representative, and when he'd finished his first year at the Academy.

But what about humility? Had he, Frank, learned anything about humility? He squirmed in his seat.

The officer's voice broke into his reverie, "How did the boy learn humility, Mr. Barton?"

Frank thought for a moment, then answered, "Sir, by going into the forest without his gun and compass. In this way, he felt he was giving the bear and the wilderness a fair chance. And, sir," Frank's voice became more eager, "that led him immediately into the truth of justice. For the first time, he really knew the value of justice."

"And then?" the colonel prompted.

"Why, then, sir, he learned the truth of pity," Pete said in an awed tone, as though suddenly realizing another point in the story, "because he made his first great sacrifice. He had left behind his gun and now endangered his life in front of the bear to save the life of a mongrel dog. This is when he learned the truth of pity."

"In what way did he pity the dog, Mr. Day?"

"Why, sir, he pitied the dog because it lacked the sense to realize the futility of attacking the bear."

Frank replied thoughtfully, "The boy could have gone home for his gun and then shot the bear, sir. But he had learned the truth of freedom. He respected the freedom of the bear as though it were his own. The bear seemed to have a deeper meaning to the boy now because, to him, it really represented the wilderness. And the boy knew, deep down in his heart, that he didn't want to destroy the liberty of this wilderness."

"Thank you, Mr. Barton. It seems to me that some of you gentlemen have learned something of the essence of this story. Let me assure you that, in real life, it isn't this easy. We read something like this in a story and we think that we can start right in and do the same thing. But we can't—any more than the boy could.

"In summary, we might say, the boy did not acquire any one of these values and then proceed to the next one, but each seemed to strengthen the validity of the others. If you will think back over the story, or re-read it, you will find that courage seemed to be the most difficult truth for the boy to maintain.

"Near the end of the story, if you remember, the boy considered this again. He pitied the mongrel, but he also respected its courage in attacking the bear. This was really a much different courage from any that he had ever encountered.

"He had actually come to know courage as his knowledge of the forest increased and, because he had gained this knowledge, he lost his fear of the unknown. He became courageous because he found confidence. But to display courage when the odds were entirely against him was completely different. It was in his last experience with the bear that he learned true courage.

"Gentlemen, it seems to me that this story has real meaning for those of us who have dedicated our lives to the defense of our country. I'm sure that you will find, over and over again, that courage *is* the most difficult truth to maintain. None of us knows until he is put in a precarious position, how he will react to danger and what he will do. But when we are under great emotional stress, sometimes we come through with a phenomenal show of courage. On the other hand, the *real* courage is to stick by our ideals—to believe that we are right in choosing to maintain the peace. You'll find our aims here at the Academy questioned many, many times. You'll be asked to answer for them. You'll learn that you must keep your courage high under all circumstances. Gentlemen, you are dismissed."

As Frank fell into formation and marched back toward the dorm, he felt a tingle go through him. Colonel Thorn was really an inspiring professor and he, Frank, always found the English classes very stimulating.

He thought about some of his own problems—how he sometimes lacked confidence and was insecure, how he had a hard time making up his mind. Courage—did he really have courage, he wondered. He'd have to work on this business of courage, he decided.

While getting ready for chow, the two boys discussed the English class meeting that day.

"Colonel Thorn certainly knows how to make you think," Frank said as he gave his shoes a last flick of the cloth.

"Those were important points he—and all of us—brought out from the story," Pete said thoughtfully. "But they're a little hard to live up to and even to see in your own life sometimes."

"I can see some of it pretty plain in my life," Frank said. "Particularly that part about 'pride goeth before a fall.'"

"Such as?"

"Well, I was pretty proud and set up when I was elected to the Honor Committee again this year."

"You should be. What's wrong with that?"

"Nothing in particular, except that I must remember to

be humble, too. I need to realize that I'm not always right. I'm even going to work on trying to like George a little better and understand him."

"That won't be humility, Frank. The word is 'miracle'!"

"Well, I'll try. Until he pulls another of his tricks and then I'll be ready to scalp him."

"Gosh," Pete lowered his voice, "but that stuff about courage—that really scares me sometimes when I think about it. Suppose—just suppose we were in a plane and the enemy were attacking us. What is courage then? Where is courage?"

"I know what you mean. Thinking about it and actually having it happen to you are two different things. I'm going to work on it, though."

"How do you work on courage?"

"I really don't know, Pete. Maybe one step is to face every single problem and try to work it out—don't put it off."

They were interrupted by a fourth class minute caller announcing dinner formation.

The next Sunday, Frank, Pete, George and several other cadets went out to the gliderport. It was a bright, sunshiny day, with just enough wind to make soaring real fun.

Each cadet had had one flight and there was still time for a second one before they had to return. George had had previous power time before coming to the Academy, so he'd been one of the first cadets to solo in the glider.

He never let Frank and Pete forget that he was ahead in logging flying time and had soloed. In addition, he was taking flying lessons, which gave him another chance to crow over them.

But he occasionally slipped, in spite of all of his bragging, and today was one of these times. He had taken the pickup truck and gone out to get the tow rope which the tow plane had dropped. He drove down the center of the runway.

"Omigosh, look at Knucklehead Shelton!" Pete exclaimed. "He's barreling down the center of the runway."

"Probably thinking of how good he is," Frank said . . . then he yelled, as he saw a glider coming into land, "Get out of the way, Shelton!"

There was a swish as a glider zipped past to the left of the truck and had to land in the rough area next to the runway.

Frank and Pete ran over as George turned the truck around and headed toward the glider. The two cadets got there in time to see the canopy on the glider pop up and Major Foster emerge from the rear seat with a bounce.

"Head up and locked as usual, Mr. Shelton," the officer roared. "Get that blasted truck off the active runway and keep it off! When a glider's on final, I don't want any vehicles or any cadets anywhere near the runway. You should know that by now!"

"Yes, sir." George's face was pale and his lips stiff.

The officer and the cadets examined the glider. The end of a stout weed stalk had ripped the fabric on the under side of the right wing.

"Looks as if you've knocked this one out of commission for today, Mister," the officer said grimly. "One more stunt like this, and you'll be grounded."

"Yes, sir." George's voice croaked slightly.

"That means those cadets who were scheduled to soar in this glider won't get another flight."

"Wouldn't that be our luck?" Pete groaned as the officer walked away. "And it's all your fault, Plasterbrain," he said to George, giving the latter a scathing look.

"Gee, I'm really sorry," George said, looking meekly at the cadets. "I guess I was just goofing off."

Frank and Pete walked away in disgust, then came back as Major Foster directed them to help tow the glider back to the enclosure and get ready for the trip back to the Academy.

A few days later, Frank had a chance to test his theory on courage, at least in a minor way. The cadets were attending a navigation class which most of them found quite interesting.

"As you know, men," Colonel Barnard of the Navigation Department said, "we'll take you on a lot of different kinds of missions before you are graduated from the Academy. For example, there are map-reading missions, radar missions, dead-reckoning missions, grid missions, pressure-pattern missions and celestial missions.

"In your senior year, you'll go on two of the most difficult kinds of missions—flying over water and over an icecap. These two kinds can be very, very hazardous and the navigator must be ever alert."

"Sir," one of the cadets asked, "why is it more difficult to navigate over water or ice?"

"Because so often you have no landmarks—nothing below which will help to tell you where you are," the colonel replied. "That's why these missions you will fly are so important. They are celestial missions and must be flown at night. As you know, you'll take fixes on the stars and compute your location from them.

"The man who is taking the fix stands on a small platform or pedestal beneath the astradome. One word of warning: Always be sure to fasten the strap there to your 'chute belt before taking a fix. The airplane is pressurized, as you know. If anything should happen to break the dome, you'd shoot out through the hole like a pea squeezed out of a pod if the strap wasn't attached."

Later, as Frank and Pete got ready for their mission, the former checked his kit with its equipment. There were a computer, a Weems plotter, a pair of dividers, navigation maps, log forms, an Air Almanac, star tables, stop watch, triangles and some pencils. He found the kit in order, so he tucked in some scratch paper on which to figure his problems and closed it securely.

A bus took the six cadets who were to participate in the training exercise to the flight line at Lowry, where they lined up by the right wing of the T-29. In front of them stood the crew—two navigation instructors, two pilots and a flight engineer. The aircraft commander faced them, giving the last-minute briefing.

"Check your parachutes, fit your harnesses," he ordered. Then he instructed them on bail-out procedure, crash-landing procedure and cabin-fire procedure. He ended by saying, "One more thing, I expect the aircraft to be left clean and in order. All right, let's go."

The crew climbed in, followed by the cadets, who took their places at the seats in front of the tables. These were equipped with instruments and paraphernalia used for flying navigation missions.

"Did you see who one of our navigation instructors is?" Frank murmured to Pete just before take-off.

"Yeah—old Hard Nose Porter. He'll probably give us a raunchy time."

"I'm going to watch my step," Frank said. "Maybe I can please him for once."

"I won't live that long," Pete muttered. "If I sprouted wings, Porter would say they were the wrong color."

Frank grinned as he turned in his seat and spread out his equipment.

The take-off was smooth. It was a moonless night, and the stars pricked the heavens like so many bright candles.

Soon Denver was left behind as the T-29 winged its way on course. Each cadet busied himself with the problem of navigating the plane, although only one—George Shelton—had the assignment to direct their course for that particular leg of the mission.

About an hour out of Denver, the cadets were startled to hear the bail-out warning bell. They jumped to their feet, tightened their straps and snapped on their parachutes.

Frank tightened his straps easily but he had trouble snapping his 'chute in place. As he struggled with it, perspiration broke out on his forehead and his hands began to shake. The harder he worked, the worse things became.

He had visions of leaping from the aircraft with no parachute. That would be curtains for him, he thought wildly. Suddenly, he was aware that Pete had come back and was standing beside his seat. "What's the matter? Can I help?" he asked quietly.

Frank shook his head. "No—go on and get in place or they'll chew you out." Although his fingers seemed all thumbs, unexpectedly the stubborn clip snapped onto the strap and his equipment was in order. He hurried to take his place in the line, completely shaken, just as Lieutenant Porter announced that it had been only a bail-out drill.

As Frank turned, still nervous and tense, George said, "You're getting pretty clumsy, Barton. If that alarm had been the real McCoy, you'd have been out of luck. Why don't you get hot?"

Frank didn't answer. He was still too upset from the experience and he didn't trust his voice.

As Pete returned to his seat, he stumbled and accidentally pulled the D ring on his parachute. Yards and yards of nylon immediately billowed out all around him. He struggled and threshed his arms about, trying to extricate himself.

Lieutenant Porter came up and snapped, "Well, Mister,

you did a pretty good job of messing up that 'chute. Get busy and fix it. I wonder if some of you ever will be first class cadets!"

Abruptly, he turned to Frank and demanded, "What was the matter with you, Mister? What took you so long to get ready for bail-out?"

Frank swallowed hard before he answered, "I'm sorry, sir, I had trouble with the snap on my parachute. Something didn't work right."

Lieutenant Porter's gray eyes fairly glittered as he said, "Some of you men are going to have to do a little extra work around here, I can see that. Mr. Barton, you and Mr. Day report to me at 1530 hours tomorrow and we'll go over some parachute procedure."

Later, as Frank bent over his work papers, George stopped by again to remark, "What you two dumbwhacks need is some extra training with some really sharp cadets. You act like a couple of gross doolies."

"Dry up!" Pete muttered. "We all make mistakes once in a while."

"Not me." George grinned. "I'm up on my toes all the time."

Darn him, thought Frank. The trouble was that George *was* good. He really didn't make many mistakes. Some people certainly were born lucky!

As they flew on through the night Frank's thoughts wandered back to his recent panicky experience, and he thought of *The Bear* and the class discussion about courage. Actually, what was courage? Had he completely lost his in that short episode back there? How did you develop courage, anyway?

His reverie was interrupted by Lieutenant Porter's voice announcing over the intercom that Mr. Shelton was to get into the dome and take a fix on the stars.

Frank watched as the other cadet stepped into the dome and got on the pedestal. Then he noticed that George failed to follow one order. He didn't fasten the strap to his 'chute harness as Colonel Barnard had warned them they should do whenever they stood on the pedestal to take a fix.

Frank saw the big, blond cadet deftly using his instruments to get the fix. Everything seemed to be going well until the aircraft veered suddenly, then started to dive down.

George swayed to one side, then the other. He reached out and tried to grab something to steady himself, but he missed, and, the next thing Frank knew, he was sprawled in the aisle by Frank's seat.

"George, you O.K.?" Frank asked in alarm.

"What in the devil is going on here?" Lieutenant Porter roared. "What happened to *you*, Mr. Shelton?"

George struggled to his feet and shook his head groggily. Then he answered shamefacedly, "Sir, I—I fell off the platform when the airplane started down."

"Fell off! What the—how did *that* happen?" the officer demanded.

"Sir, I suppose it was because I didn't have my safety strap fastened."

"Oh, I see! A smart guy, huh? Well, let me tell you, Mister, you learn to obey orders around here. Serves you right. Maybe that fall will teach you a lesson. Now get back up there and take another fix. And, this time, *do what you're supposed to do!*"

"Yes, sir," George answered meekly.

As George prepared to mount the platform again, Pete leaned out in the aisle and said, "I thought you were always on your toes, Mr. Shelton. Looks more like you were standing on your head."

"Go jump in the lake!" George retorted.

"Maybe you ought to join some of the gross doolies," Frank suggested smugly. "I'm sure you'd add a lot to the group."

George didn't answer as he stepped up on the pedestal. This time, Frank saw him carefully attach the strap to his 'chute harness.

A few hours later, the flight was almost over. Frank could see the lights of Lowry sprinkled below them. The cadets and crew had eaten their box lunches with a satisfied feeling that they had had a good flight after the excitement of the early evening. Even Lieutenant Porter seemed satisfied and didn't say any more about the mistakes made earlier.

Frank's thoughts wandered back to his experience with his 'chute and the panic that had gripped him when he thought he couldn't get it fixed. He thought again of the story of *The Bear* and he and Pete's discussion of courage. This was something he was going to have to work on, he decided.

Then the thought of Ann came to him and he remembered that he was going to see her this weekend after the Idaho game. His spirits lifted for a moment. It had been so long since they'd had a date. The only trouble was, he frowned, as he gazed out at the airport coming closer to them as they swung in for a landing, there was that matter of Craig Brown to settle with her.

He, Frank, wasn't jealous—at least, he didn't think he was. And he wanted Ann to have friends down at her college. But somehow he'd taken a violent dislike to Craig Brown and he didn't even know him.

Well, he thought, he and Ann would settle that on Saturday.

6

~～～～

The Misunderstanding

The game with Idaho had been uninspiring and disappointing. The Academy lost and this didn't help Frank's spirits. He got out of his football uniform and into his civilian clothes as fast as he could.

Ann had said she couldn't come to the game, but to pick her up at home later. When Frank said good-by to Pete after the game, the latter advised, "Don't look so gloomy. The world isn't coming to an end. Ann won't want anything to do with that picklepuss of yours."

But Frank turned away without answering and took a bus to Ann's house. She must have been watching for him, he decided, because she opened the door almost as soon as the doorbell rang. She had her coat on and didn't even ask him to come in and speak to her parents, which was most unusual.

"Hi, Frank! It's so nice to see you." Ann's voice sounded crisp and almost alien.

Frank swallowed painfully before he said, "It's been a long

59

time. I thought we never would see each other this fall. Shall we catch a bus and go on downtown?"

"Why don't we take a swing around Cheesman Park first? I really need the exercise and I'd like to get the cobwebs out of my brain. I've been studying all afternoon for an exam on Monday." Her voice sounded deliberately gay.

"O.K. by me." Frank tried to match her tone, but he stole sideways glances at her, puzzled by her manner. When he tried to take her hand, she quickly tucked both hands in her coat sleeves like a muff.

"How was the game? I was so surprised when you wrote that you'd gone out for football. I didn't know you were interested in playing."

Frank felt she was making conversation and suddenly a determination filled him. He'd find out what was the matter —but quick. "We lost," he answered flatly. Then, ignoring the rest of her remark, he plunged on, "But right now that doesn't seem to matter. What does matter is that there's something wrong between us. I don't know what it is—if I've hurt your feelings or done something I shouldn't, I'm sorry. But please tell me. I don't know why you're acting this way."

Ann stopped and laid a hand on his arm. "Oh, Frank, I'm sorry! It's all my fault. I'm all mixed up. But my parents said I was old enough to work out my own problems now."

"What's bothering you, Ann? You just don't act like your-self." There was enough light left in the western sky for him to see large, unshed tears in her eyes.

She shook her head, then walked ahead slowly as they started on the circle road around the park. "It's—it's awfully hard to explain. No—no, don't say anything. Let me sound off before you ask questions."

She took a deep breath, then went on in a rush. "I told you that I'm mixed up. That's putting it mildly. You see,

Frank, I do like you—very, very much. But I've met somebody else and I like him, too." She paused.

Frank was stunned when he heard her actually say the words. He had to admit that he'd been suspecting something like this. He forced himself to walk on and say nothing.

Ann continued, "I've written you about Craig—Craig Brown. I haven't tried to hide anything. You know he's in my Philosophy and World Affairs classes. We've had a lot of interesting talks—mostly at the drug store over cokes. You'd like him, Frank—really you would."

Frank grunted, but didn't answer. Like him, he thought. The only thing he'd like was to punch that Brown fellow in the nose.

"Well, Craig has set me to thinking in a whole new area I'd never even dreamed about. You see, he's a pacifist and he thinks we put too much emphasis on arms and fighting and . . ." Ann stopped, suddenly at a loss.

Frank walked on, still not saying anything. He could feel his face flush. Well, she'd asked him not to talk before she'd told her story, so let her tell it. He'd keep still until she asked him a question, he vowed.

Ann took her handkerchief out of her pocket and began kneading it between her hands. "Craig said—well, he said that he disapproved of everything you stood for—that the whole military system was archaic—something out of the dark ages—and that I was blinded by your uniform." She finished in a rush.

They scuffed through the leaves and Frank thought he'd always remember that sad, crunching sound and the dry, decaying odor.

Ann stopped and again put her hand on his arm. "Do you understand at all what I'm trying to say?"

Frank looked down at her hand—delicate, with long, nar-

row fingers and he yearned to take it in his and tell her not
to pay any attention to that big dumb dope in Colorado
Springs. But he didn't. He just looked at her and answered,
"Yes, I understand what you're trying to say. You're trying
to say that you don't approve of what I'm doing, where I'm
going to school and that you like this—this Craig Brown
better than you do me."

"Oh, no, Frank—I don't like him *better*. I like him—and
what he says seems reasonable. I'm really mixed up."

"In love with a uniform—why, heck, you've seen me
plenty of times when I've been out of uniform. How crazy
can he get?"

"It isn't that, Frank. It's just—it's just that what he says
about war and peace seems to make sense."

"What kind of sense does it make? Just tell me that and
put it in one-syllable words so I can understand it." Frank's
voice was rough with feeling and shook slightly.

"You'll have to admit that you're preparing for war.
Everything you do at that—at that Academy is to get you
ready for war. You study all that stuff—military maneuvers
and strategy. You're learning to fly those jet bombers and
fighters. Next you'll learn how to handle guided missiles.
You have to do all that dumb marching and drilling. Even
you gripe about the military discipline and say that it's
stupid and out of style."

Frank reddened and found his breath coming quickly. He
used every effort to keep control of his voice because he was
afraid it would break. If he could just get mad enough, he
thought, maybe he wouldn't lose control. But he wasn't mad
at Ann—it was that jerk—that Brown guy. If he had him
here now, he'd knock some sense into him.

He gritted his teeth, then said slowly, "Yes, Ann, I've
griped plenty about military discipline. I'll admit it. But
deep down in my heart I know why we have it. It has made

men out of the boys who came to the Academy last year. It has been the thing that has whipped us into shape from a bunch of raw, green recruits into a Wing of pretty good men."

"There are plenty of good men who aren't in military academies."

"Yes, I grant you that. But for the type of preparedness that our country has to have now, we still need men with military discipline." He stopped a moment, almost praying for something to help him show her what he meant. Then he remembered a book he'd read recently for English class. "So many of the things I don't quite know how to say have been said for me in a book I made a report on for English. It's called *Tale Of Valor* by Vardis Fisher. I wish you'd get it in the library and read it."

"What's it about?"

"It's a story of the Lewis and Clark expedition and, believe me, if it hadn't been for military discipline, those men never would have made that four-thousand-mile trek through wilderness and come back with only one man missing."

"But that was a hundred and fifty years ago. Times have changed since then."

"Times have changed, but not true values, Ann. We still have to have men who love their country and who are willing to sacrifice their lives for her. Men who understand discipline and know why they must do what they are told."

"Now you're waving the flag—that's what Craig says. He told me you'd bring in the old chestnut about love of country and the willingness to sacrifice yourself for the grand old flag."

Frank stared at the girl. Could this be *Ann*—could these words be coming out of *her* mouth? He shook his head in disbelief, then tried another tack. "But we must be prepared, Ann. And we must be strong. Colonel Oberg says it's only through strength at this time that we can stay a free nation. If we let down our fences for a moment, we could become just another satellite country. And I'm not talking about the outer space kind!"

"You sound like somebody trying to scare me with a boogie-man." There was a slight trace of sarcasm in her voice now, and Frank stiffened with anger. "Craig says we should turn the other cheek."

"Turn the other cheek—hah! You don't deal that way with madmen and unprincipled enemies. And that's what we have to deal with. You can't expect people to behave honorably when they have no honor."

"But we can negotiate and show them that we are willing to go the long mile. We don't always have to be showing them our muscles."

Frank thought for a moment, snatching for some kind of answer. Finally he said slowly, "That's where you're wrong, I think. Nobody picks on a big fellow because he knows he might get hurt. And I think we should keep ourselves big enough and strong enough to scare any nation which thinks it can conquer us."

"You're thoroughly indoctrinated, aren't you, Frank? I never truly realized it before because—well, we just never talked about these things. I guess I was pretty ignorant and didn't appreciate that there was another side."

"I suppose there are several sides. There should be. Do you think your—this side that you're presenting is the right one?"

"I don't know. All I know is that I don't want another war because, if one comes, we'll probably all be destroyed."

Frank stopped and stared at her open-mouthed. "You don't think for one minute that *we* want another war, do you? If there's another war, it won't take three guesses to know who'll go first—us—the Air Force Academy men—and

West Point and Annapolis. You ought to see the list of casualties at those two Academies for only the year 1950—those classes were graduated just in time for the Korean War. Major Foster was stationed at West Point then, and he said the flag flew at half-mast several times each week. Then there was my brother Joe—oh—what's the use!" His voice cracked slightly with emotion.

Ann was silent. Finally, she said, "That's exactly what I'm trying to tell you. See what terrible sorrows war brings?" She stopped again, then continued in a hopeless tone, "We're not getting anywhere in this discussion, Frank. I guess I'd better go home."

Frank felt his throat tighten and he found it hard to control his voice. "What do you want me to do, Ann? Resign from the Academy?"

"Of course not, silly! You wouldn't anyway—at least not for me."

Now anger welled up in him as he retorted, "No, you're darned right I wouldn't resign for you or for anybody else. I believe in what I'm doing and I certainly haven't had any evidence at that Academy that we're—we're war mongers."

Ann answered sharply, "Nobody called you war mongers. It's just that Craig has shown me another picture and, right now, I'm interested in doing a little more investigation on the subject. Come on, I really must go home. I've a mountain of studying to do before I go back to school tomorrow."

They walked back to her house in silence. Frank couldn't think of a thing to talk about. Finally, Ann broke the silence by asking, "How did you say the game came out?"

"The game? Oh, you mean the football game this afternoon?" He had completely forgotten about it, and it seemed a million years ago since they'd played. "They beat us this time, but don't worry, our day is coming. After all, this is only our second year. Just give us a chance." He clenched his fists and lengthened his stride.

"Well, you needn't bite my head off. Of course, your team will start winning one of these days."

"You can just put that down in your book. We are building in ourselves a determination to excel, and I know we will. Why," he drew a deep breath, then continued, "I wouldn't be afraid to bet that in 1959, when I'm a first classman, we'll win more games than we'll lose."

"You have plenty of confidence in your team, haven't you?" Ann said softly, more like her old self. "Well, keep it, Frank. They'll probably need it."

They had reached her home by now, and she ran up the steps lightly. Frank followed slowly.

At the top, Ann turned and said, "I'm awfully sorry, Frank. I really *am* mixed up, and you'll just have to give me a chance to work this out for myself. If it makes you feel any better, Mother and Dad are on your side. They're sure I have softening of the brain. But, bless them, they think I'm a big girl now and must work out my own problems."

Frank wasn't so sure that she was a big girl. She looked tiny standing there—and a little wistful. Why, oh why, did things like this have to happen? Especially to him and Ann?

He cleared his throat, then asked slowly, "What about another date? Can we plan one now?"

Ann shook her head. "Not now, Frank. I really have to work this out and I can't think straight when I'm with you and writing to you. Let's not see each other for a while. That should give me a chance to think things over."

"Not see each other?" Frank's voice croaked. This was awful!

Big tears welled up in Ann's eyes and her voice shook as she said, "Good-by, Frank. Thanks for a wonderful friendship." She stood on tiptoe and kissed his forehead, then turned quickly and ran into the house, the door slamming behind her.

That slam had such a sound of finality, Frank thought, as he walked down the steps. Automatically he took a bus for the base. There was no point in staying out now, when he had no date with Ann. He was so upset he hoped that Pete would be at a movie or someplace so he, Frank, wouldn't have to tell his friend about his misunderstanding with Ann tonight.

But the light was on and the door open when he got back to the dorm. He heard voices in the room. If only he didn't show the way he felt! George was there, talking with Pete. The two cadets looked up as he came in.

"Well, if it ain't Romeo himself," George said, bowing low with mock deference. "Aren't you home early? What's the matter? Did you and Ann have a fight?" He sounded as if he hoped that were true.

"Yes, we did," Frank answered bluntly. "And if you'll excuse me, I'm going to hit the sack."

George shrugged, then stood up and retorted caustically, "Well, I certainly know when I'm not wanted. *Pardon me.*" He walked out.

Pete got up and closed the door, then blurted, "For gosh sakes, what's the matter? Why did you have to tell him you had a fight with Ann?"

"He asked me point blank, didn't he? What did you want me to do? Lie?"

"Well, no—that is—well, you know old Meatball, he just took a shot in the dark."

"It was a good shot—a real bull's eye."

"Want to talk about it?"

"No." Frank hung up his uniform and put away his clothes in neat piles, as he'd been doing for over a year now. Silence hung in the room like a heavy cloud.

Pete sat down at his desk and made a pretext of reading, but Frank knew he wasn't. As Frank crawled into bed, he began to feel very much ashamed of himself. Finally he said, "I'm sorry, Pete. I was just taking my spite out on you, and that isn't fair. Yes, I'd kind of like to talk about it and get it off my chest. Then we'll skip the whole thing, if you don't mind."

"Gosh, Frank, what happened?"

"Ann and I are finished—kaput—broke up. Does that sound natural? It seems to me I've played this record before, only with another name," he said bitterly. "Last time it was Nancy back home and her 'Dear John' letter. There really must be something the matter with me—all my girls break off. What's wrong? Won't even my best friends tell me?" He tried to make a joke of it, but his voice shook slightly.

"Why don't you begin at the beginning and clue me in?"

"You know that feeling I've had about that jerk in Colorado Springs that Ann's been writing about?"

Pete nodded, but said nothing.

"Well, he's filled Ann up with a lot of junk about pacifism and how we're living in an archaic world at the Academy. Doing nothing here except preparing for the next big war to exterminate the world."

"I hope you set her straight." Pete glared.

"What could I say? I told her how we feel about it—we don't want to fight. But I couldn't think straight, and I don't believe I got to first base with her. At least, we're not seeing each other for a while."

"Not seeing each other?" Pete's voice made it sound ominous. "That's a dangerous technique, man! You leave that character down there an open field, and he might persuade her to marry him."

"I know it—but what could I do?" Frank asked. "Hit her over the head and carry her off to a cave?"

Pete shook his head. "Women!" he exclaimed. "I'm glad I'm not tied to anybody. They're really big trouble."

"Right you are. Just don't get mixed up with any—take my advice." Frank rolled over and pulled the covers above his head. He kept thinking about what Ann had said—about war and the Academy and the archaic military discipline. Were they wrong here? Was the system archaic? Were they really preparing for war? Doubts began to gnaw at the edges of his mind. He was going to have to think about all these questions. And, somehow, he was going to have to find the right answers.

Finally, he fell into a troubled sleep, tossing and sighing loudly. He dreamed he was flying a glider over the site of the new Academy, down near Colorado Springs. Another glider soared in close with an unknown fellow piloting it.

The fellow shouted, "I'm Craig Brown. Want to duel with me?"

"I'd love to duel with you," Frank yelled as he sat up in bed.

"What did you say?" Pete asked sleepily from the other bed.

"I was talking to myself," Frank murmured. "The first signs of insanity. Think nothing of it."

Frank found the next few days a terrific let down. He seemed to feel some of his old fears of lack of confidence and insecurity creeping back into his consciousness. Had he made the wrong choice in coming to the Air Force Academy? Was the military system archaic? Were they being trained for war only—not for peace? There was the age-old question, "What is truth?" These were the questions that kept whirling through his head until he felt depressed and unhappy.

Pete went around muttering half aloud about how some people moped and wouldn't talk—sure made a happy place to study and work.

Then, after a week or so, Frank found himself getting wrapped up in his studies. Football practice used up any excess energy he might have had. He found little time to think of Ann. He was back in the groove.

One day in English class, though, he was caught up short by a quotation from *Henry V* which they discussed at length in class.

> "In time of peace there's nothing so befits a
> man as modest stillness and humility——"

Major Foster ended the class by saying, "That's the kind of man we want to produce at the Academy—a peace-loving gentleman, but one who is willing to make the supreme sacrifice."

That evening, Frank sat at his desk and thought about the quotation for some time. Finally, he asked Pete, "You remember what Major Foster said today about a peace-loving gentleman?"

"Yeah." Pete looked up from his book.

"I'm keeping that in my little black book as ammunition for Ann. The next time I see her, she's going to get plenty of answers from me."

But he sounded more confident than he felt. He didn't even know when he'd see Ann again. It was her move next, he thought stubbornly. Let her get in touch with him.

7

They Pass in Review

But Frank didn't hear from Ann, and now Christmas leave was approaching. Excitement permeated the Academy halls.

"Just think! It's our first Christmas at home since we came to the Academy," Frank exclaimed as he jammed shoes, socks, and books into his B-4 bag.

"You said it," Pete's voice shrilled higher as he hurried from his locker to his bed, which was buried under a mountain of clothes, scrapbook material, snapshots and books. "Our three weeks' leave last summer was O.K., but it'll be fun to be home for Christmas."

"Remember last year?" Frank's voice sounded husky. "We went to Ann's house. That good dinner and her family being so nice to us really added up to a Merry Christmas."

Pete glanced up. "Have you heard from Ann?"

"No—but then I didn't expect to. Anyway, remember our lesson in English about the bear? I've decided that this is my chance to learn the truth of humility. I've had a crack at courage and pride and honor. Maybe I need to be re-

71

minded that a little humbleness in my life will make a better man of me."

Pete was silent. Finally he asked, "What about Nancy? Will you see her at home this Christmas?"

"Sure," Frank answered brightly. "But then I saw her last summer, too. I'm not interested in her any more."

The day before leave was to start, Frank received a small package from Ann. "I wonder what it is," he muttered. "Surely she isn't sending me a Christmas present."

He opened the package quickly, and a tiny set of wings fell into his palm. He looked at them for a moment, then swallowed hard. They were the wings he'd given Ann last year on Recognition Day! For the first time, the break with her seemed so final.

A note was tucked in the box and he read it carefully.

Dear Frank,
  I'm returning the wings which you gave me last summer. I just don't feel right about keeping them under the circumstances.
  Do have a happy time on your first Christmas leave at home. We had fun last year, didn't we?

                                        Sincerely,
                                            Ann

Frank crushed the note in his hand, then changed his mind and smoothed it out again. He folded it neatly, together with the small silver wings, and tucked it into his desk drawer.

He walked to the window and looked out toward the mountains. Today they were like a cardboard silhouette pasted against the blue sky. He remembered the chaplain saying in his sermon a few weeks ago, "I will lift up mine eyes unto the hills from whence cometh my help."

That's what he, Frank, needed to do. He was determined

that he was not going to let this incident spoil his first Christmas vacation home. He drew a deep breath as he picked up his B-4 bag and hurried out to the bus which would take him over to Lowry, where he was catching an airplane ride home.

Home! Prairie View, Kansas. The snow-covered prairies looked good to him as they circled the small town and came in for a landing. He thanked the pilot, then caught a taxi.

He sighed as he looked out the window, thinking toward the holiday ahead. Would he be able to fit in easily with his old gang of friends? How would it seem to see Nancy and Doug again—Nancy, his old girl, pinned to his best friend?

"How does it feel to be home?" Mr. Barton asked Frank after supper the first night. "Has anything changed?"

"No," Frank answered, "everything looks swell to me. And Mom's cooking is as good as ever."

"Don't soft-soap me, young man!" His mother smiled happily. "I'm sure I can't feed you as well as they do at the Academy. I've read all those letters you've written about the wonderful food."

"Oh, Mom, you know they don't cook the way you do. The food is wonderful, I'll admit. But after all, Mom's food is the best. Besides that, you're my best girl."

"Speaking of girls," his father looked at him questioningly. "What about Ann? You haven't mentioned her."

Frank was silent a moment, then replied, "Ann and I have agreed to disagree for the time being."

"I'm sorry to hear that," Mrs. Barton said. "She seemed like a very nice girl. What about Nancy? Does she interest you at all any more?"

"No, Mom." Frank breathed a sigh of relief as he realized his parents weren't going to ask him a lot of questions about

Ann. "I knew last summer, after I saw Nancy again, that everything was over between us. She couldn't compare with Ann . . ." His voice trailed off.

"Well, let's not worry about girls now." His mother picked up the conversation. "This is Christmas time, and we're going to have fun."

And they did. It was wonderful to sleep late, have leisurely breakfasts and meet old friends.

After the traditional carol sing at church on Christmas Eve, Frank and his old gang went to Nancy's home. While the girls made sandwiches and popped corn, the fellows sat around and talked.

Doug reminisced, "Do you remember the time, Frank, that you, Fred and I were the Three Wise Men in the Sunday School pageant? I'll never forget how you strutted down the aisle and barked out, 'Frankincense to offer have I.' Your voice was changing and it sounded horrible—first deep, then high and squeaky."

Frank laughed with the others and reminded Doug, "You weren't so smooth yourself, old man. Remember how you stumbled and fell, ripping your costume?"

For the first time since he'd gone to the Academy, Frank felt at ease with his old friends. Nancy, his one-time best girl, still flirted with him when Doug wasn't around. Frank decided that she was pretty shallow and he wondered how he could ever have thought she was so hep.

His thoughts went back to Ann. If only things were right between them! Would everything work out for them?

And then Christmas leave was over, and once more Frank was back in his room at the dorm, unpacking his B-4 bag. "There are mighty good things about going home on leave," Frank said to Pete, "but I'm glad to be back at the Academy."

"You can say that again," Pete answered. "I'm full of resolutions about this place. I'm going to shape up and be a better cadet."

"So am I." Frank spoke very seriously. "You know, Pete, I realize more than ever how important our Honor Code is to us here."

"So do I," Pete quickly agreed. "Why, back home I certainly noticed that most of the fellows didn't mind playing around with the truth. Take speeding, for example. One of my friends was stopped by a cop, and Tom said, 'Why, officer, I didn't realize I was going over sixty.' All the time he knew he'd been touching seventy-five."

Frank frowned and exclaimed, "Now, wait a minute! You don't think we have a corner on honor, do you?"

"No," Pete hastened to assure him, "of course not! But the thing that racked me was hearing some of my old crowd who go to other schools tell how in their fraternities they write research papers for some of the pledges. And one guy said he writes themes and class papers for two dollars per paper. Gosh!"

"I know—I heard things like that, too. Well, we have our Honor Code which outlaws that kind of thing. I'm glad, too, because I think it's better for us to do our own work."

"I really got put in my place, though, by a couple of fellows I met. You know how it is here—our cadets all seem so clean-cut, the All-American boy type—posture straight, haircut short, clothes neat. You get so used to seeing them that some of the men in other schools look strange. They don't always cut their hair very short and some of their clothes are pretty sloppy."

"I know exactly what you're going to say. You felt plenty superior and looked down on them. I did, too."

"I found out I was wrong. Some of the men I talked with were really sharp. I found myself forgetting how they looked and listened to their ideas instead. I guess we get a little too smug around here."

"Well, I certainly got taken down off my high horse," Frank said. "Jack Billings is a fellow I knew at home. His dad was president of the bank, of the school board, and on the church governing board. The family always drove big cars. They had the biggest house in town, and both Jack and his sister went to boarding schools in the East. Well, last fall a big scandal popped when the bank got into trouble. Then Mr. Billings had a stroke and subsequently died just before he was to go to prison for mismanaging the funds of the bank."

"This sounds like a soap opera," Pete said.

"It happens to be real life stuff." Frank assured him. "Actually, with the father dead, there was no financial obligation as far as the family was concerned. But Jack stopped school. So did his sister. They sold all their property. Jack is working with a construction gang on public roads and his sister is clerking in a drug store at home. They intend to pay back every cent to the creditors, even if it takes them years."

Pete was silent a moment before he answered, "We're not the only people with honor, certainly, but I'm glad we have the Honor Code to keep the standard high."

As Frank finished putting away his things, he exclaimed, "Great guns! Have we ever turned into two wacky philosophers. Look at this Calculus lesson on page eleven assigned for tomorrow. Whew!"

"Wait a minute. What about Nancy? Any heart throb there?"

"Heck, no! That's over for good. I couldn't even dig how she nearly cracked my heart into splinters last year. A fellow can sure be a sap where girls are concerned. If I had it to do over, I'd never go steady through high school again.

It's as dumb as going into a store and buying the first thing you see."

"O.K., O.K., break it up! No sermons, please." Pete picked up a book. "Calculus—here I come." Soon he was chewing on a pencil and breathing heavily as he dug into $x + y = z$.

That evening, Frank burst into the room. "Good news!" he yelled. "We're going to Washington, D. C."

"Are you crazy?" Pete asked. "We just got back from leave."

"It's out there on the bulletin board. The whole Wing of Cadets is to march in the President's inaugural parade this month."

"That's great!" Pete jumped up. "Won't we have fun?"

But it wasn't at all fun before they left. Since there wasn't time for extra drilling, the officers decided that the cadets would have to get up at 0500 hours every morning.

When Frank was roused before dawn the next morning, he looked sleepily out the window and exclaimed, "Man, look there! It's dark as pitch!"

"Are you sure that's the right time?" Pete spoke protestingly as he picked up their alarm clock and shook it.

"I heard the squawk box. Shake a leg."

"Oh, boy, getting up this early every morning will get me down!" Pete moaned.

"It better get you up," Frank retorted. "It'll be worth it, though. We all need this extra drilling so we'll look sharp in the inaugural parade."

Pete was wide awake now and hurrying into his clothes. "That's for sure. We're babes in arms in comparison to Annapolis and West Point when it comes to parades. And we've got to outshine 'em, that's all."

"That's the old spirit. We want our Flight to be the sharpest in the parade. And it won't be long now until we're taking off for Washington."

And it wasn't long until the day when the huge C-124 Globemasters transported the entire Wing of Cadets to Andrews Air Force Base, near Washington, D. C.

"I hope I'll not be the only cadet to trip on my shoestrings while we're parading right in front of the President," Pete muttered as they boarded a bus which took the cadets to Suitland Hall, their headquarters.

"Just keep your eyes front and don't bump into any monuments." George spoke in a condescending tone. "My, it's good to be back in Washington! Of course, I've been here many times and it's really old stuff to me."

"Well, it isn't old stuff to me," Frank replied pointedly. "It's something pretty special and I hope it always will be."

"Me, too," Pete agreed. "I can't wait to see the Declaration of Independence and the Lincoln and Jefferson Memorials."

On Sunday, most of the Cadet Wing attended the Chapel of the Air. During the sermon, the chaplain quoted from a poem called *High Flight*. He said it was the official poem of the Royal Canadian Air Force and had been written by a young pilot who later had been killed in the service. He quoted the last stanza:

> Up, up the long, delirious, burning blue
>   I've topped the wind-swept heights with easy grace,
> Where never lark, or even eagle flew—
>   And, while with silent, lifting mind I've trod
> The high untrespassed sanctity of space,
> Put out my hand and touched the face of God.

There was a hush as he finished, then the closing hymn rolled forth. Frank decided that that poem certainly gave the cadets something to think about.

Later, Frank said to Pete, "I understand the reception tonight is to be the biggest bib-and-tucker affair we've ever graced. We wear our full dress uniforms, you know."

That evening, as Frank and Pete stood in the line leading into the elegant reception room, Pete whispered, "My back teeth are chattering. I'm going to drop down the nearest fire escape. I can't face my public."

"You'd better plan to meet them, for here they come now. That's Mrs. Party-fixer herself, with two helpless, unsuspecting debutantes to be saddled with us for the evening."

They were attractive girls, Frank thought. He liked Shirley Allen, his date, a pretty girl with brown hair and blue eyes. Before long, they were chuckling over Pete and his date.

"Patty Peterson's my roommate at Mt. Vernon Seminary," Shirley told Frank. "She's a straight 'A' student, but full of mischief and always getting into scrapes."

"Then she has met her match in Pete, my roomie. He's certainly not a straight 'A,' but he has been in plenty of scrapes. He's the life of our dorm. He says he has walked hundreds of miles on the area. We call his stomach 'the Mammoth Cave' because he stashes away so many thousands of calories."

"I've noticed. Isn't that his fifth trip to the buffet?"

Frank laughed as he watched Pete approach the table, lavish with shrimp, miniature meatballs, sausages, long trays filled with cheese, small cream puff shells filled with lobster and crab. Down at the end were trays of pastries.

The room was a dazzling picture, Frank thought, as he looked about. There were girls of every description and size —tall girls, slim girls, plump ones, little ones. There were short bobs, long bobs, page-boy bobs. Their gowns were every color of the rainbow and the cadets in their bright blue uniforms seemed to accent the bright dresses.

Frank and Shirley watched their two friends as they moved closer to them. Pete and Patty seemed unmindful of their surroundings and almost completely absorbed in each other.

They heard Patty say, "Here, Pete, hold this bag a minute. My bracelet came unfastened."

Pete gingerly took the bulging gold mesh bag. He nervously played with the catch while Patty fastened her bracelet. Just as she held out her hand for the bag, the catch flew open and the entire contents of the bag seemed to explode into the room.

Out fell a lipstick, a compact popped open, the mirror splintering as it struck the floor. A small silver comb, a lacy handkerchief and several silver coins scattered in every direction.

Pete lit out as if he were in a football scrimmage, first left, then right, trying to retrieve the fallen articles. He darted between the legs of an astonished cadet, just missed stepping on a red taffeta skirt and scrambled under an end table. He reached for the lipstick and backed out, then started to straighten up. His crew cut struck the bottom of a full punch cup in the hand of a very surprised officer.

"I—I'm sorry, sir." Pete's face was as red as his hair as he automatically stiffened his spine. He looked furtively at the tall officer who muttered between his teeth, "Watch what you're doing, Mister."

By this time, Patty had joined him and he whispered to her, "Where's the infirmary? I feel sick. Wouldn't I pick on a two-star general?"

"Oh, Pete, I want you to meet my father," Patty said saucily, as she looked up at the tall officer. "Father, this is

Cadet Peter John Day of the United States Air Force Academy. He just rescued my lipstick."

"Good—good evening—s—s—sir," Pete stammered.

As the officer turned away, Frank overheard Patty say, "Don't let Father frighten you. Of course, everybody is scared to death of him—except me. He loves to bark, but he never bites. See this little finger—how crooked it is? Well, that's from wrapping him around it for nineteen years." She giggled.

After the two cadets had gone to bed back at Suitland Hall that night, Pete said dreamily, "Patty thought I looked so cute under that table—you know, just before the uprising —the one that jiggled the general's punch cup?"

"How could anybody miss seeing you? I thought you were going to wreck the place. Well, you'd better look cute marching down Pennsylvania Avenue tomorrow morning."

Frank wondered if the rest of the Wing were as excited as he was as they marched in the parade the next day. He felt as though every eye of the thousands of onlookers lining the pavement were on the Air Force Cadets.

He recalled their Commandant back at the Academy saying, "We must do our best. This is our biggest parade occasion so far, you might say our debut. West Point and Annapolis are old-timers at this. But we must let the public know there is an Air Force Academy Wing!"

They won't forget us, Frank thought, as he glowed with pride. Bursts of applause and loud cheers followed them as they swung along.

When they came to the President's reviewing stand, the cadets looked to the left and saluted the President. There he stood with the First Lady, her arms filled with pink carnations. Frank remembered reading in the paper that they were the famous Colorado carnations.

Then he recalled a little over a year ago, when the President had visited the Academy, and he, Frank, had escorted him to his seat in Chapel on Sunday morning.

Back in their room, Frank and Pete discussed the parade excitedly.

"I love a parade," Pete piped wearily.

"I like the way we strutted our stuff," Frank boasted. "We certainly stood up and were counted."

"Stood up! You said it!" Pete groaned as he rubbed his feet. "My poor number twelves! Nobody told me I'd have to march in the Air Force. I thought they were supposed to fly every place."

"You'd have cause for griping if you'd joined the infantry," Frank reminded him. "Come on, let's go over to the Smithsonian and see all the airplanes on exhibit."

"That's for me," Pete agreed, hustling into his overcoat.

"I want to see *The Spirit of St. Louis*," Frank continued, "I've dreamed about it many times and now I'll see it 'in person.' "

At the Smithsonian, Frank was surprised to see that almost the entire Wing was on hand, looking at the airplanes. Even some of the officers and ATO's were there, too.

Lieutenant Jenkins came over and spoke to the two friends. "Well, I see you men know the right place to come in Washington. How do you like the aircraft exhibit?"

"This is for real, sir," Frank answered earnestly. "And my favorite airplane is *The Spirit of St. Louis*. My dad knows Lindbergh. I hope I get to meet him some day."

8

Sometimes Alert, Sometimes Bored, Always Trying

After their return from the inaugural ceremonies in Washington, the cadets settled into the routine of classes, drilling and the general let-down following leaves and exciting experiences.

"Same old stuff," Frank grumbled one morning as he and Pete were getting ready for breakfast. "I wish something would happen to break the old routine."

"I don't need any breaks of that kind," Pete answered. "What I need is a break in Calculus, before it breaks me."

"Another thing," Frank continued, "we've got to do something about getting our men in better shape. Old Shelton's Flight has nosed us out twice this month."

"I know it," Pete replied. "And the way he rides those doolies, you'd think they'd do anything except try to please him."

"Sometimes I wonder if it pays to be too nice to fourth

83

classmen. 'Treat them like people,' old Hard Nose is always saying. 'They're intelligent and will respond to correction if you show them where they need it.' You know we've tried that way and still haven't placed first."

"I have a pretty good memory and I don't remember Lieutenant Hard Nose Porter treating us like people last year when we were doolies. I always felt as though he thought we were something that had escaped out of *Dracula*."

The buzzer for breakfast interrupted them and they hurried out to join their formations.

As Frank marched his men toward the dining hall, he tried to size them up. They were a swell bunch, he thought, and usually cooperated pretty well. But they weren't real sharp yet. He knew he'd have to do something about that. Yesterday, George's Flight had won the shoe-shine contest for the third time because his Flight had the three best pairs of shoe shines.

That evening as Frank studied the record of his Flight, he said to Pete, "You know our men are coming along. You've helped a lot, Pete. 'A' Flight is slowly creeping up on 'B' Flight."

"How do you figure?" Pete asked.

"Well, we've come up in general military bearing and dress when in ranks. Also, in marching to meals competition."

Pete studied the report. "But they are still ahead of us on best rooms and dormitory for inspections. We're going to have to crack down on our guys."

"Maybe a few 'hard nose' tactics are in order." Frank frowned. "But somehow that kind of discipline rubs me the wrong way. You know how much we resented Porter last year. I vowed then I'd never handle any men under me harshly. I still think our method is the better one. At least, we'll go on trying it for a while."

"You are probably right," Pete answered thoughtfully, "but if we don't show more improvement pretty soon, maybe we had better start cracking down on them."

A few days later, Lieutenant Porter stopped Frank and said, "I want to see you in my room at 1615 hours this afternoon."

"What do you suppose I've done wrong now?" Frank asked Pete as he shined his shoes before keeping the appointment.

Then he went to the officer's room, knocked on his door and was told to come in.

"At ease, Mr. Barton," the lieutenant said. "I want to talk over something with you. Your Flight has been showing some improvement over the past month or so. But not as much as it should." He leafed through some papers. "Your shoe shines aren't very good; there have been too many errors in marching to meals; and I've heard a lot of complaints that your doolies aren't up on their freshman required knowledge."

Frank flushed, swallowed hard, then said, "I'm sorry, sir. Do you have any suggestions, sir?"

"Yes, Mister, I suggest that you work on them a little harder. If you don't, they'll work on you. And that's fatal to an officer in charge of men. You must teach them to respect you. That's all. Post."

Frank said, "Thank you, sir." When he got back to his room, he slammed the door and yelled at Pete, "That old so-and-so Hard Nose. He just tries to make things harder. And I'm *not* going to be like him—not if I lose out entirely."

"Calm down." Pete looked up from his book. "You'll burst a blood vessel. I thought our Flight was improving."

"So did I." Frank sat down and held his head in his hands. "I guess I'll just have to chew them out tonight."

After his Flight had lined up for dinner formation that evening, he said, "Men, I've been looking over the records. We've been showing a gradual improvement for which I'm grateful. But we have to do even better. It's time we showed 'B' Flight that we're much superior. You know my theory—I think you're intelligent men and should be treated accordingly. I'm just not the type to ride you and punish you constantly . . . but maybe I'm wrong. Maybe I should start cracking down."

He studied the faces of the cadets in his Flight. They were a nice bunch of men, he knew, and he really liked them—even young D. G. Allison who reminded him of Pete—always getting into trouble.

"Now, let's march to dinner without one single error tonight. Remember, if 'A' Flight makes *no* error, the squadron *can't* lose. Get on the ball! Look sharp! You can do it! Forward, march!"

As they marched toward the dining hall, Frank watched them out of the corner of his eye. They seemed to be marching better and he hoped they'd show more improvement each day.

Later that week, after reading the ratings on Flights and Squadrons, Frank grinned gleefully at Pete and exclaimed, "We finally made it! For the first time, 'A' Flight has won over 'B' Flight. Now it's our job to keep them on their toes and inspired to stay on the top."

A couple of days later, Frank came into their room and threw a magazine on the table. "I'm really griped," he announced. "I don't know why some of the newspapers and magazine writers are always harping on the Air Force Academy's 'lack of tradition.' "

"Well, after all, we're pretty young," his roommate answered. "We haven't had much time to build tradition."

"Yes, but the Air Force itself has plenty, which we're carrying on. And you know we're building tradition here every day of our lives."

Pete examined his schedule and said, "Maybe the General will have something to say about tradition in the Wright Memorial lecture he's giving us Friday."

The next day in their history class, when Colonel Farbee assigned the lesson, he suggested that each cadet write a biography on some pilot who had made flying history and tie the assignment in with the coming lecture on Friday.

The following week, in the history class, Colonel Farbee said, "Gentlemen, today our class will discuss the Wright Memorial lecture which the Chief of Staff of the Air Force gave last Friday. As you all know, this talk commemorated the fifty-third anniversary of the first successful powered flight."

The professor paused a moment, then continued, "Let's discuss some of the points brought out in the lecture. Who wants to start?"

Bob Elspy raised his hand and when acknowledged said, "Sir, I remember the general made a decided point against the idea of the Air Force being referred to as young—without history or tradition. He said that, on the contrary, we were old—for age is properly measured in terms of experience."

"Good point, Mr. Elspy. Anyone else? Mr. Shelton?"

"Sir, the general also said that, in terms of experience, we have both history and tradition. Although the Air Force has legally been a separate service only since 1947, we have been independent in spirit and in nature of work since the Army first purchased an aircraft for use in its observer corps."

"That's true," Colonel Farbee nodded. "You remember, he reminded us of the momentous accomplishments of Wilbur and Orville Wright, too."

Pete raised his hand, then said, "And, sir, when he mentioned the Air Force 'greats,' his roll call sounded like the Academy's Hall of Fame, where the oil paintings hang—Mitchell, Arnold, Spaatz, Rickenbacker, Doolittle."

"Sounded familiar, didn't it, gentlemen? This brings us to our biographies. We'll have time for just one brief report today. Does anyone think he has written about someone from flying history whose life illustrates what we're discussing—tradition, making of air history, our particular kind of discipline? If so, make a short summary—the high points of your study."

Frank raised his hand quickly. This was the kind of assignment he enjoyed.

"Mister Barton."

"Sir, my study is about Charles Lindbergh. I think his life illustrates what we've been discussing."

"Go ahead, Mister."

"I'll start my report, sir, with a quotation from one of your lectures, because it bears on almost everything I read about Lindbergh. 'He may have to make a long journey by himself and find his way back.' You quoted that last year when we were discussing discipline, sir."

There was a friendly outburst of laughter among the cadets and the professor joined in. "You flatter me, Mr. Barton, to remember my 'pearls of wisdom' for that long."

"Well, sir, probably most of you recall an article which appeared in the *Talon* * last month. It's about our kind of discipline—how we're different from other branches of the service by the very nature of our work with aircraft.

"For instance, it's extremely important for Air Force men to learn discipline—to obey without question—even more than the average man in the Armed Services. This is because often we're alone up in the air. Not only our own

* *Talon*—School magazine published by the Air Force Academy cadets.

lives depend upon our ability to obey instantly, without question, but maybe thousands of other persons' lives—maybe our whole country—rely on this kind of discipline.

"Also, there is a certain aloneness—some men call it lone-liness—that goes with our way of life. This calls for even more discipline, sir. We don't have the comradeship the infantryman experiences or the close association which exists on a Navy carrier. Many times we're up in the air alone, faced with decisions—even with our own conscience some-times. That's what makes our training here at the Academy invaluable.

"Lindbergh's lone trans-Atlantic flight in May, 1927, called for this kind of discipline. The quick dash to Paris was a daring feat of bravery, unheard of at that time, and it cap-tured the imagination and admiration of the entire world. I have never read a finer tribute about flying than the one from the New York *Sun,* printed on May 21, 1927. When I read it, I pictured Lindbergh as a young man—just like us here—cadets—about our age. I believe Lindy will always seem young to boys. This is what the newspaper said:

LINDBERGH FLIES ALONE

Alone? Is he alone at whose right side rides Courage with Skill within the cockpit and Faith upon the left? Does soli-tude surround the brave when Adventure leads the way and Ambition reads the dials? Is there no company with him for whom the air is cleft by Daring and the darkness is made light by Emprise? True, the fragile bodies of his fellows do not weigh down his plane; true, the fretful minds of weaker men are lacking from his crowded cabin; but as his airship keeps her course he holds communion with those rarer spirits that inspire to intrepidity and by their sustaining potency give strength to arm, resource to mind, content to soul. Alone? With what other companions would that man fly to whom the choice were given?"

Frank laid his theme on the professor's desk and sat down, trying to act quite casual, even though his heart was thumping pretty fast. It usually did when he recited on this type of subject. He wanted to make a good impression. After all, Colonel Farbee was one of his favorite professors, and he knew his classmates were sharp cadets.

"Thank you, Mr. Barton. You have opened a wide area for discussion which, unfortunately, we can't take up today." The colonel glanced briefly at the report. "Mr. Barton has undoubtedly given many pertinent details about Lindbergh —his training, the unusual acclaims and honors given him. As you probably know, he received the Distinguished Flying Cross from our country and a commission as Colonel in the Army Reserve Corps.

"Then the French decorated him with their Legion of Honor. England and Belgium gave him trophies of silver and gold. But the amazing thing through all this publicity was Lindbergh's complete absence of self-acclaim and his refusal to commercialize and capitalize on his accomplishment." The officer paused, then closed his classbook, saying, "He's a challenging example for all of us. Gentlemen, you are dismissed."

As he joined his formation to march back to the area, Frank thought suddenly of Ann. All this discussion about aloneness in a flyer's life gave him a feeling of loneliness. It had been so long since he'd seen or even heard from Ann. He found himself sinking into a mood of despair.

That evening, as he sat at his desk, trying to study, Frank found his thoughts turning again to Ann. What was she doing tonight? Was she out with that stupe, Craig Brown?

He jabbed his pencil into the paper on the desk before him so hard the point snapped off. He threw it down irritably.

"What's the matter, Meathead?" Pete looked up from his book.

Frank frowned. "I was just thinking about Ann."

"All right, give. You've looked like a junior grade thundercloud all evening. What's on what you laughingly call your mind?"

Frank took a small box from his desk drawer. From it he lifted the wings which Ann had returned last fall. He gazed at them for a long moment before answering, "I'm trying to decide if I should swallow my pride and write to Ann. I vowed last fall I'd let her make the first move, but, man, I'm weakening."

"Sometimes, Mister, I think you have the brains of a mental midget." Pete's voice showed disgust. "Go ahead and write. Let her know you're still alive and kicking."

Frank took a deep breath. "O.K., here goes. I'll do it right now, even if I have to ask for late lights to finish my Physics assignment."

He spent the next thirty minutes laboriously composing what he thought was a neutral kind of letter to Ann. After many sighs and erasures, he finally announced, "There! I've asked her for a date on the first week end she comes home. I've promised not to discuss the Academy and its purposes, if she doesn't want to."

Pete snorted, "Why not?"

"Oh, I have plenty of ammunition ready. I think maybe I could convince her now that our purpose here is to prepare for peace—that the military man is really the ultimate pacifist. But *I'm* not going to force the issue."

He signed the letter and stuffed it in an envelope. Then he opened his Physics book and began to study. From time to time, though, he'd stop and stare off into space. Did he really have a lot of ammunition—facts—to put before Ann? Was he, himself, really convinced that they were being trained for peace? He squirmed and tried to find a more comfortable place on his chair.

"You're as nervous as an old witch," Pete complained. "Why don't you sit still?"

"I'm sorry, Pete. I'll do my best."

The next week went by so quickly Frank hardly had a chance to think about an answer from Ann.

On Friday, he asked Lieutenant Jenkins for an appointment. When they were in the officer's quarters, Frank said, "Sir, I need some advice. I don't feel that my Flight is measuring up as it should."

"What do you mean, Mister? In what way?"

"Maybe I'm too easy on my men, sir. Mr. Shelton seems to think so. He says I'm too soft—that I treat them like babies."

"What do *you* think?"

Frank frowned. How should he tell the officer how he felt? "Sir, I've tried a few hard-nosed tactics, but I'm not very good at them. I keep recalling how I resented that kind of stuff last year. I've been trying to work with my cadets as you and some of the other ATO's have suggested. I hope I treat them like intelligent men. Somehow, I'm just not very good at chewing them out or getting too tough."

"What makes you think Mr. Shelton's Flight is superior to yours?"

"They've made quite a few more points than we have—although I'll admit our scores are getting a lot closer together. We even won last week."

The young officer looked thoughtful for a moment, then said, emphatically, "Mister, discipline is not to be measured by the stiffness of a fourth classman's spine or by the lustre of a shoe shine."

"No, sir." Frank was a little startled by the ATO's intensity.

"There's a lot more goes into making a good cadet besides emphasizing physical courage, endurance and posture. That's why I believe in treating the doolies like intelligent men. After all, the military man isn't the only one who must practice discipline. Look at some of the professions—most doctors, dentists, ministers, and lawyers have to be disciplined men to carry out their assignments."

"I think I know what you mean, sir. Engineers, architects, musicians, accountants—yes, even scholars would know what we're talking about."

Lieutenant Jenkins gazed at Frank earnestly before he declared, "I've been mighty proud of your progress, Mister. Keep it up."

"Thank you, sir."

"As to your Flight—well, it might interest you to know that Mr. Shelton is beginning to have his troubles. The morale in his Flight is getting a little low. That's bad. Mr. Shelton is going to learn a very dear lesson—it seems some people always have to find out the hard way."

Frank didn't know exactly what to say, so he remained silent.

"What I'm getting at is this, Mr. Barton. You keep plugging away with your men the way you've been doing. Your Flight is shaping up well. The morale is high. Your men like you. Maybe the shoe shines aren't always the brightest, but, as I said before, that isn't the only thing that counts."

"Yes, sir. Thank you, sir."

"Anything else, Mr. Barton?"

"No, sir. Except . . . thank you very much for helping me over some rough spots since I've been at the Academy. I appreciate it, sir."

The lieutenant smiled slowly. "We need conscientious

cadets such as you are, Mr. Barton. We try to encourage them. But don't wear yourself out. After all, you have two more rugged years before you graduate."

"No, sir. I won't, sir."

As Frank hurried back to dorm, a feeling of confidence and well-being surged through him. He really was improving with his Flight! Lieutenant Jenkins approved of him. The Academy was a wonderful place to be, he decided.

He walked into his room and the first thing he saw on his desk was a letter from Ann. He tore it open hurriedly and read:

Dear Frank,

How nice to hear from you after this long time. You seem to be getting along pretty well with your school work. Evidently the life there agrees with you.

I'm sorry, Frank, but I don't think I ought to plan to see you yet. I still haven't made up my mind on this whole subject that we discussed last fall. I'm working on it, though, and I expect to come up with the facts I need one of these days.

I hope Academics don't get too rugged before the year is over. Say "hello" to Pete for me.

Your friend,
Ann

P. S. This is such a terrible letter that I hate to send it. I've written it a dozen times and it always comes out wrong. I do want you to know that I still like you very, very much. I'm just mixed up, that's all.

Frank sank down in his chair and stared at the letter. He had been so happy when he saw the envelope, but the note inside was so disappointing. He looked at it again, and read the P. S. which he thought was the best part. The rest was so stiff and formal—totally unlike Ann.

He noticed the word "like" had been erased and written over. That made him feel a little better. Then his spirits sank again. He wasn't going to see Ann, after all! That took all the enjoyment out of his talk with Lieutenant Jenkins. He'd been so set up by that talk—and now this!

He went over to the locker to change his clothes. As he opened the door, his eye caught the card his dad had given him last year, which he'd pasted on the door. *"To thine own self be true,"* he read silently. He squared his shoulders. That's what he'd have to be, in spite of Ann or anything she had to say about the Academy.

9

Good News, Bad News

Again Frank found himself in the swing of class and outside activities so that he scarcely had time to think about Ann and her letter. There was always the pressure of Academics to keep him busy studying.

He had been helping to train the falcons again, although, now that spring football training was starting, he'd have to give them up. It was so good to work with the sleek birds. But he still felt that he was needed in football, so once again he told Captain Linstrom he would have to quit.

A letter from his mother worried him, too. She wrote that his dad had had a slight heart attack and the doctor said he'd have to take it easy—and above all, his dad would have to quit worrying about the business.

"Gosh!" Frank exclaimed, with a stricken look in his eyes. "If anything should happen to Dad—why, I just couldn't take it, that's all."

"Easy there man. The doctor knows what he's doing and,

if your dad follows his orders, he'll be all right. There are plenty of heart patients walking around."

Yes, Frank thought, that's true. But it was different when it was your own dad. Then another thought struck him. "If Dad is sick, maybe I'd better decide to take my leave at home this summer and not go on the European tour."

The Academy had scheduled a four-week European tour for those cadets who were willing to give up their home leave and take the trip instead. The brass had made it very clear that this was not a pleasure jaunt, to be taken at the expense of the taxpayers. While there would be some week ends for pleasure and sight-seeing, the cadets were going for one purpose only—to learn something about the Air Force's activities in Europe and the great challenge to American diplomacy which faced the overseas personnel at all times.

After writing to their parents, both Frank and Pete had agreed to go on the trip. Now, thought Frank, this news changed everything. What a disappointment it would be! He shook his head. Still, his dad meant more to him than any trip at this time in his life.

"Not go on the European tour?" Pete stared at him aghast. "But we've already signed up. Besides, it wouldn't be any fun without you."

"I hate like the dickens to even think about giving it up, Pete, but my dad comes first. And if I can help at home— even for four weeks, I've got to do it."

Pete nodded in agreement. "Of course you do, Frank. I'm sorry I spoke out the way I did. You know me—always talking when I ought to be listening." He attempted the feeble poke at himself, hoping it would raise Frank's spirits.

But his roommate didn't answer. He sat down at the type-writer and started a letter home.

The next Sunday, however, while Frank, Pete and several

other cadets were out at the gliderport, something happened to Frank which made up for a few of the disappointments of the past weeks.

He had just finished a flight with Lieutenant Jenkins and had made a good landing. The glider had been towed to the end of the runway, and the tow plane was in place.

"Go ahead, Mr. Barton. Get in the plane," Lieutenant Jenkins directed.

Frank looked at him in surprise, then obeyed. He fastened his shoulder harness and seat belt, then waited for the officer to get in the back seat. There was some delay and he glanced back. He was surprised to see the ATO standing beside the glider, tying up the rear seat belt and shoulder harness.

"O.K., Mr. Barton. She's all yours this time."

Frank couldn't believe his ears and he stared wide-eyed at the lieutenant, his mouth open.

"If you hit a thermal," the officer continued, "ride it up, but don't get too far from the gliderport. Keep your air speed up in the pattern and don't try to stretch your glide on final. Good luck."

A thrill went through Frank. Why, he was going to solo! Somehow he hadn't expected to do that just now—not on this flight, anyway.

Pete grinned at him and said, "Happy landings, feller. Hope you find some green air."

Frank swallowed a couple of times, then signaled to a cadet to hook up the tow rope. Pete stood beside the wing, waiting for his signal. Frank finally managed to raise his hand—and saw it tremble. Gosh, he hoped nobody else could see that!

He waved at Pete, who lifted the wing. The tow plane revved up and they started down the runway. Just before

Pete dropped back, Frank waved again. Then he was too busy with the controls to do anything else except pilot the glider.

He hit lift almost immediately after the tow plane cut loose and found himself going up and up and up! Somehow, in a very special way, this seemed like a *real* flight. Everything that had gone before—all the instruction from Lieutenant Jenkins and Major Foster; all the practice and learning and flying dual—seemed like make-believe now, as though he had been merely pretending to fly. Now there was no one to offer advice, no one to turn to, no other judgment to lean on but his own. It was *his* aircraft, *his* flight!

As long as there had been an instructor with him, he'd been only a co-pilot. Today, at last, he was a *pilot!* For a moment, he had a feeling of being immersed in the air around him, as a swimmer is immersed in water—a sense of being part of the element.

Suddenly he realized that this was a feeling he would never quite achieve in any power plane, with the engine noise separating him from the intimate sense of flight. A shiver of half-fear, half-delight thrilled through him. This was a moment he would never forget. *This was his first solo flight!*

He knew that in the future he would fly bigger aircraft— tons bigger—faster, farther, higher—aircraft beside which the 2-22 would be a mere toy. But he was sure that nothing in the future would ever quite match the feeling of his personal "Kitty Hawk."

It was as though he'd achieved a tremendous goal. He realized he could never admit his feelings to his friends— even to Pete. But he knew that, after he landed, he would walk a little taller, hold his head a little higher, because today he had soloed for the first time!

Instinctively, he thought back to the cadets' trip to Washington and the services at the Chapel of the Air. He could almost hear the Chaplain saying,

. . . I've topped the windswept heights with easy grace
. . . while with silent, lifting mind I've trod
The high untrespassed sanctity of space,
Put out my hand and touched the face of God.

Frank felt a kinship with the young pilot who had written those lines. Yes, and he felt a kinship with every pilot who had ever guided an airplane through the "wild blue yonder."

After his solo flight, the days seemed to zip by for Frank until, suddenly, the end of his second year at the Academy was drawing to a close. There had been some good times and some good things had happened to him. He'd made the football team. True, he wasn't on the first team, but he was still in there plugging. He'd soloed in the glider, too, and whenever he thought of that experience a thrill went through him. The Sundays after that had been glorious ones because, almost every time, he'd had at least one or more chances to take the glider up alone.

Even George Shelton seemed to treat him with a little more respect.

Then, yesterday, Lieutenant Jenkins had said, "Your Flight has really come up to a high level. I'm proud of you, Mister."

So, all in all, Frank had a pretty good feeling about his military improvement and his Flight.

There were only a couple of things to spoil his outlook at this point, he thought—well, maybe three. There was his father's illness, coupled with the fact that he, Frank, wouldn't be able to go on the European tour. Then, he hadn't heard from Ann again.

Pete hurried into their room from the library one evening and tossed a letter on Frank's desk. "Gosh," he exclaimed, "only a week until school is out! I can hardly wait."

Frank picked up the letter and looked at it curiously. It was postmarked from his home town, but he didn't recognize the handwriting.

Pete watched him in amusement for a moment, then said, "Well, if you want to know what's inside, why not open the letter and read it?"

Frank promptly followed his friend's suggestion. Soon he was grinnig from ear to ear. "Why that's great! It's spectacular!" He jumped up and pounded Pete on the back.

"Lay off!" Pete backed away. "Pick on somebody your own size. What's so spectacular?"

"This letter is from our family doctor. He says that Dad is getting along O.K. and that he—you know, the doctor—just heard from Mother that I was planning to give up the European trip. He says it's very foolish because that would worry Dad more than if I went."

Pete's freckled face broke into a wide grin. "You mean you can go? Whoopee!" He grabbed a chair and danced around the room with it. "Paris—here we come!"

At long last, the finals were over and both boys found they had passed in all their Academic subjects.

"Don't tell anybody," Pete muttered as he studied the grade list, "but I still don't understand how my name got so far up on the Calculus list."

Frank stared unbelievingly. "Hold me up, Pete. I can't believe my eyes." He pointed to the bulletin board. "I've made the Dean's list. Wait till my dad hears about this!"

There was one more surprise waiting for Frank as he picked up his mail. A card from Ann was tucked among several letters.

Dear Frank:

I just read your name in the paper in the list of cadets who are going to Europe for three weeks. I hope you have a wonderful time. Why don't you write me a card from over there?

As ever,

Ann

What a day! Frank hadn't been so happy since he'd received the news he'd been accepted by the Air Force Academy.

"I just can't believe these things are happening to me," he told Pete. "I'm sure something terrible is about to descend on me. I'll probably break my leg tomorrow as we climb into that C-124."

"Why not just accept the good things and forget about everything else?" Pete suggested.

10

Operation Red Eye

Frank and Pete picked up their B-4 bags and climbed into a C-124. Other cadets followed until five of the six huge planes were filled. Frank glanced at his watch as they took off from Lowry Air Force Base.

"It's just 0900 hours," he said to Pete. "We're right on time."

A few hours later, they landed at Tinker Air Force Base, near Oklahoma City. A blast of hot air hit the cadets as they got out of the plane, so that a swim in the pool at the Officers' Club was a most welcome activity a little later.

That evening, the Air Force personnel entertained the visitors at a dance, bringing in a handpicked group of future Miss Oklahomas as their dates. It was fun, with their own band, the Airmen of Note, playing for them.

Just before they hit the sack that night, George came into the room assigned to Frank and Pete, followed by several cadets.

"Listen to this, fellows," George's high nasal voice rang with authority. "I've got a real slick idea."

103

"It better be slick," Pete answered, "because I'm dead on my feet. I need some shut-eye."

George ignored him as he continued. "You know how it is on these trips. When we have these dances, some of the men get stuck with some real 'beasts'—you know, girls who can't dance, or who look like something out of *Frankenstein*."

"Oh, it's not as bad as all that," Frank protested. "Most of them are pretty nice gals."

George fixed him with a withering glance. "You don't have to join in the 'Ghoul Pool,' if you aren't interested."

"The 'Ghoul Pool'?" Frank and Pete chorused.

"Yeah—that's what we've decided to call it," Bob replied. "George's idea is that we all contribute fifteen cents apiece and make up this 'Ghoul Pool.'"

"And then the fellow who gets stuck with the worst 'beast,'" Tom explained with a chuckle, "will still play in a little luck. He'll collect the cash at the end of the evening."

"But I don't understand—who will decide which one is the 'beast'?" Frank asked.

"We'll appoint three judges," George answered. "They'll circulate during the evening and decide which one of us is really stuck."

"Then they'll take a vote," Bob piped up, "and decide which fellow wins the pool."

"I have an idea," Pete said, getting into the spirit of the game. "The judges can dance by and tap the poor fellow on the shoulder and say, '1675' or whatever the amount is, to cheer him up. That is the magic number which shows him he wins."

The cadets laughed and agreed this would be the method. Frank didn't like George's idea one little bit, but he didn't have the courage to say so when the other fellows were so enthusiastic. He hastily looked at his watch and exclaimed, "Scram, you guys! It's almost time for taps."

Next morning, the cadets visited the Air Materiel installment at Tinker. It was a real eye-opener, they all agreed.

"Gosh," Pete said, as they hurried along from exhibit to exhibit, "isn't that Univac spectacular? It's a regular seven-headed monster, the way it keeps track of everything."

"It's almost unbelievable," Frank agreed. "When I think that an order can come in from any place in the world—say, Japan. Somebody there needs a part for one of the jet planes. As soon as the order is received, that little old machine goes to work. It figures out the nature of the request, orders it from the right department, sends a notice to the packing room, directs how the object will get there, how it should be sent, sends a message to Japan as to when the part will arrive . . ."

"Yes, and, best of all, it only takes about ten seconds to do it." Pete shook his head. "To think that I used to read science fiction and thought it was wonderful! This beats anything I've ever even dreamed about."

"Why, man," Bob interrupted, "it would be hard to make the average American citizen believe you if you told him. He'd just laugh and say you were making it up."

"It gives a fellow even more respect for the Air Force when he sees this place functioning," Frank added.

"Even old leadhead George is impressed," Pete reported. "He said the operation astounded him and he was a Math major."

Just then, the cadets walked into a mile-long repair depot where the AOC * started briefing them on additional mechanical details.

＊　　　＊　　　＊

* AOC—Air Officer Commanding, now in charge instead of ATO's.

Next day, the Academy group embarked once more in their C-124's, this time headed for Wright-Patterson Field in Dayton, Ohio. As they circled the field, George leaned over Frank's shoulder and pointed out the window.

"I know this area real well," he said in a cocky tone. "I've been here plenty of times. In fact, I expect some of my friends may be waiting to meet me. Look," he pointed again, "there are lots of civilians on hand."

The huge plane touched down like a feather. As the door opened and the cadets climbed out, they were greeted by a blare of trumpets and a roll of drums. A brass band began to play the Air Force Song and everybody sang "Off We Go into the Wild Blue Yonder—"

A wonderful feeling thrilled through Frank. This was a terrific experience. Several civilians pushed forward and soon some of the cadets were surrounded by relatives and friends.

"What a way to be greeted," Pete said wistfully. "A brass band, your folks, your best girl . . ."

"And the heat," Frank added, as he wiped the perspiration off his forehead.

"I don't care about the heat. I just wish we'd landed in Portland, Oregon." Pete looked a little unhappy.

"Come on, droopy." Frank tugged at Pete's arm. "Let's get to our quarters. Maybe we'll get another chance to swim."

And they did. In addition, there was another reception and dance for them that evening. In the meantime, the agreed Ghoul Pool collection had been taken up among the cadets. It amounted to $16.75. Bob, Tom Lansing and Dave Henderson were selected as judges.

Before the evening was over, they tapped Bill Samanski on the shoulder and said the magic number: 1675. Frank saw the cadet grin widely, lift his hand over his partner's head and make the O.K. sign with his thumb and forefinger.

"I think it's a kind of raunchy trick," Frank admitted to Pete later in their room. "Talk about gallantry! It makes me squirm."

"I know," Pete answered, "but it really is all in fun."

Just then, George stuck his head in the door and asked, "It worked, didn't it, fellows? The only trouble is, if you can't get the cutest-looking gal in the room, your next best bet is to go for the 'beast.'"

"Sure, sure," Pete replied, "but you might just get fooled, Mister. You might get the second worst 'beast' and still no money." He laughed. "That would really serve you right, Mr. Shelton, for dreaming up this dirty trick."

"Watch my smoke next time," George promised confidently. "I'll have either the prettiest or the ugliest girl in the room."

Wright-Patterson Air Force Base is the home of the Wright Air Development Center. Here the cadets were introduced to specifications and mock-ups of just about everything that is being planned to come for the airman and the Air Force, from space gondolas to the newest in "hard hats." *

It was a very impressive exhibition, followed by a "fly-by," which gave the visitors a sample of what different airplanes could do. Again, the cadets were wide-eyed at the display of air power before them. All went well until an F-84, flying on the wing of an F-86, came in for a landing. During the turn onto final approach, the F-84 stalled out.

A groan sounded from the crowd as they realized what was happening. The F-84 hit a group of trees and the external tanks were torn off.

---

* hard hats—crash helmets.

"The plane's disintegrating!" Pete yelled.

The fuselage struck the ground in flames. Frank stared in horror as he realized that the pilot was still in it. He hadn't had a chance to parachute.

A young woman standing directly in front of him screamed hysterically then sobbed, "It's Daddy—it's Daddy!" The two children with her clutched her skirts and started to cry. Suddenly, she ran down the steps, the children stumbling behind.

"Come on," Frank shouted at Pete, "we'll help her." He picked up one child while Pete snatched the other. They followed the woman until she ran up to the colonel in charge of the show.

"Do something, do something!" she moaned over and over. "Can't you *do* something?"

The officer put an arm about her shoulders and tried to calm her. Bob Elspy ran up, shouting, "They got him out, sir! They got him out!"

Frank looked toward where the accident had happened and saw two men with their clothing afire, dragging the limp body of the pilot from the flaming wreckage.

The colonel kept saying over and over, "This is most unfortunate. This is most unfortunate." He summoned a young lieutenant, who took charge of the woman and her two children.

The cadets walked slowly back to their seats. What a horrible thing, Frank thought, shuddering. The stands were tensely silent. Everybody was staring in fascination at the still-burning wreckage. Firemen sprayed it with foam and angry black smoke poured skyward.

"That's the way the ball bounces," Pete said through stiff lips. "I guess we all have to face it—all of us who will be pilots know it could happen to us."

Frank only nodded in reply. When he finally did speak,

his voice shook slightly. "It's just a part of the business of flying. We learn we're expendable."

Back at their quarters, the cadets were relieved to hear that the pilot was still alive and was being flown immediately to San Antonio, Texas, where the Air Force maintains the best hospital service for treating severe burns.

Next day the cadets flew on once more, this time to Maxwell Air Force Base, in Montgomery, Alabama. At first they were somewhat subdued, the pall of the accident still hanging over them, but after a while they began to talk among themselves, and eventually their spirits came back.

The Air University Command is located at Maxwell, and here the cadets dug in for a week of concentrated study on an atom and nuclear weapons course. At the end of the week, they were given a test which they had to pass in order to receive their navigator's wings in the future.

A welcome break came during the week end, however, when they scattered to go swimming, golfing, water skiing and skeet shooting.

Here at the Air University, the cadets were briefed on the latest in the Air Force's scientific research program, including such fascinating subjects as photography, missile planning, aircraft development, aircraft design and other areas.

Again there was a reception and dance held in their honor. And once again the "Ghoul Pool" was taken up, this time the amount coming to $18.00.

As Frank and Pete walked into the reception hall, they saw George hurrying across the floor to choose a partner.

"I think he's trying to win the pool tonight," Pete said out of the side of his mouth. Then he stopped and his mouth fell open in amazement.

Frank looked and saw Patty Peterson, the girl Pete had

dated in Washington and had been writing to ever since. Frank gave his friend a push and said, "Hurry up and get Patty before somebody else does."

Pete stumbled forward like a sleepwalker as Patty came toward him, saying, "Hi, Pete! I thought I'd give you a surprise."

But Pete was too stunned to answer. He just put his arm around her, as the music started up, and they danced away.

Frank chuckled until a hostess motioned for him to come over and meet one of the girls.

Later in the evening, Frank watched Art Grigsby maneuver around and tap Tom Lansing on the shoulder, murmuring, "1800." Frank saw George dance toward Art and say, "Surely, my friend, there is a mistake somewhere." But Art shook his head and grinned wickedly as he turned away.

George flushed angrily, then swung his partner and danced toward the nearest exit.

That evening, while the cadets were getting ready for bed, Pete rushed in at the last minute, still starry-eyed and bubbling with excitement.

"Calm down," Frank said, "or you'll pop and splash all over the place."

"What-an-evening!" Pete exclaimed for the umpteenth time. "Can you imagine? Patty engineered this whole deal herself." He spoke with pride. "One of the girls in her dorm lives here in Montgomery and, when she heard we were coming here, she wangled an invitation."

"Lucky dog!" Frank smiled at his roommate.

"Say, I almost forgot!" Pete ran out in the hall and yelled, "Come on, men. I've got some real dope."

Several cadets hurried out into the hall and surrounded the red-head. "This is the best—but the best!" Pete laughed uproariously.

"Let's have it, meathead," Bob said threateningly, "or I'll heave you out of the window."

"This is but good," Pete continued. "You know our 'Ghoul Pool'? Well, Patty told me the girls had one, too. Only they didn't call it that. They had a deal fixed up like ours so that, whoever got stuck with what they considered the drippiest cadet that girl would win the prize."

"No!" Bob exclaimed in amazement.

"I don't believe it," George added.

"You're spoofing, Pete," Tom said.

"No, I'm not," Pete protested. "Honest. And guess who—guess who got the prize?"

Several of the cadets grabbed him and began to shake him, tossing him from one to the other.

"Cut it out," Pete threatened, "or I won't clue you in."

"Give," Bob ordered as he grasped Pete's neck in a vise-like grip.

"Well, you asked for it," Pete gasped. "The cadet who had the honor winning the prize for least likely to succeed was none other than—" He paused dramatically, then bowed and said, "Mr. George Shelton."

George colored and pressed his lips together. "I don't believe it," he repeated angrily this time. "You're making that up."

"No, honest." Pete wiped the tears of mirth from his eyes. "And you'll have to admit, George, the joke is on you. Weren't you the wise guy who dreamed up this 'Ghoul Pool'?"

George turned without an answer, stalked to his room and slammed the door. The other cadets laughed and shouted as they went back to their quarters.

There were three more days of intensive study and work before they finally took their examinations.

"They almost finished me," Frank groaned. "I know I didn't pass."

"Nonsense!" Pete replied. "They were plenty stiff, but I'm sure we'll pull through. At least I'm not going to worry about it until we get back to the Academy. They won't kick us out here."

Next the cadets flew to Eglin Air Force Base, in Florida. One of the first places they visited was the climactic hangar where tests were being conducted for arctic conditions. From an outside temperature of 105 degrees, the group went into a temperature in the building of 65 degrees below zero.

"*Br-r-r-r*," Pete rubbed his hands together. "It wouldn't take long to freeze to death in here."

"Look," Frank exclaimed, "there is a kind of snow on the ground formed by the frost!"

"How about that!" Pete said, his eyes glinting. "Here's my chance to get even with Mr. Dumbwhack Shelton for doubting my word the other night." He stooped quickly and picked up a handful of snow, forming it into a snowball.

"Lay off," Frank warned him. "You're going to get into trouble."

But Pete paid no attention and, just as the visitors stopped before another exhibit, he called softly, "Hey, Mr. Shelton, look at this."

George turned around, then ducked as he saw Pete throw the snowball at him. The AOC was directly behind George and the snowball hit him in the neck with a resounding smack. There was a sudden silence, then a slight murmur went through the cadet group.

The officer turned, his face red with anger. He reached up and wiped the remains of the snowball off his neck, demanding furiously, "What smart guy did that?"

Frank glanced at Pete, who had turned so pale, his

freckles were standing out. His ears seemed more conspicuous than ever.

Pete saluted and said in a high, squeaky voice, "I threw the snowball, sir. I—I'm sorry, sir."

"What's your name, Mister?"

"Cadet P. J. Day, sir."

"Well, that will be a Form 10 for you, Mister Day." The officer turned and went on with his lecture as though nothing had happened.

Later, a chastened Pete muttered to Frank, "Serves me right. I'll learn some time—maybe—not to show off that way."

That afternoon, the AOC handed Pete the Form 10 which read: "28 June, Eglin Air Force Base, Florida. Cadet Peter John Day, Second Class. Hitting officer with a snowball. Fifteen demerits, 20 punishments."

"You'll have to admit," Pete sighed ruefully, "that it isn't everybody that can hit an officer with a snowball in Florida in the middle of summer!"

The episode was soon forgotten, however, as the cadets went out to the field for the scheduled fire power show. Eglin Base is known as the fire power center for the Air Force and the cadets had looked forward to this demonstration.

As they took their places in the stands, the loud speaker came to life, announcing that the show would start with a regular count down, as in most types of testing and missile firing.

Suddenly, the sound of planes was heard and the voice over the speaker said, "Ten, nine, eight, seven, six, five, four, three, two, ONE."

When the jet planes above went through the speed of sound, a terrific "BOOM! BOOM!" hit the stands. Everybody jumped. Then they heard the voice of the pilot say, "I'm at 45,000 feet and I'm rolling out."

In only a few seconds, it seemed, the famous Thunderbird Acrobatic Team cut through the low overcast, flying in perfect formation, roaring, dipping and going into its amazing acrobatics.

Frank was reminded of the first time he'd seen those planes perform, two years ago, on Dedication Day at the Academy. Again he was thrilled and overwhelmed by their precise and exact formation.

The announcer continued, "And now, on your right, an F-102 is firing missiles, on target. Next comes a B-36, dropping its bombs. Here comes the most advanced jet, the F-104."

So the show continued. There was a parade of B-52's, B-47's, B-66's, and KC-135's, flying in perfect formation.

As they winged over, the announcer said, "Here you see the most modern and advanced jets in the Air Force."

After a short pause, the loud speaker blared, "Next we give you a review of every machine gun that has been used in the armed services over the years. Each one will fire one hundred rounds of ammunition."

"This ought to be interesting," Pete said. "I'll bet the contrast will be something."

The first machine gun was fired. *"Boom—boom—boom!"*

"This gun, one of the first models, is still being used by some units of the army," the announcer reported. "It takes about sixty seconds to fire one hundred rounds."

From there, the demonstration went through the whole series of machine guns, until the cadets saw the latest Air Force gun to be developed. When it was fired, it seemed to go: *"Brrrrt!"* and it was over. The hundred-round burst was so short it sounded like one huge hiccough.

"Gosh," Frank muttered to Pete, "that's what I call fantastic! Imagine shooting a hundred rounds of ammuntion in such a short time." He glanced around and saw other cadets exclaiming or shaking their heads in disbelief.

"And now our final demonstration," the announcer said. "Over to the right, you will see a mock-up army anti-aircraft emplacement and a tank platoon. Coming in from the left is a whole squadron of F-100's. As you know, that's sixteen planes. Let's see what they do to this land-based outfit."

The cadets watched wide-eyed as the F-100's swooped in and totally demolished the emplacement and platoon.

"That's hairy," Pete said in an awestruck voice. "I'm really shook."

"I know what you mean," Frank's voice trembled slightly. "What tremendous power our Air Force holds in its hands! And just think, these were only TNT weapons. Imagine what one F-100 with a tactical atomic bomb could do to this whole base! With destruction like that available, it's even more important than ever that we keep peace in the world."

When the exhibition was over, the cadets marched back to the hangars, where they emplaned for Denver.

Frank and Pete found seats together and, as they sank into them, Pete said, "This trip has been for real. My head is fairly bursting with all we've seen. But now I'm getting in some sack time." He pulled up his knees and closed his eyes.

"Yeah," Frank answered, glancing out the window at the earth far below. "What a show we've had! But the best is yet to come. Think of it—in a few days, we'll be on our way to Europe!"

11

"Innocents Abroad"

As soon as Frank returned to the Academy he telephoned his mother to ask about how his dad was feeling, and if she thought he ought to take the European tour.

"Yes, indeed, Son," his mother said firmly. "Your dad would never forgive himself if you missed this chance. He says it's an important part of your education. Really, he looks and feels so much better. You mustn't worry. Have a wonderful trip. Don't try to write letters—postcards will do."

When Frank hung up the receiver, he breathed a sigh of relief. He was so happy that his dad was feeing better. Now he could *really* enjoy the trip.

That evening, those of the cadets who were going to Europe gathered in the auditorium to be briefed on their forthcoming expedition.

General Saunders mounted the platform and said, "Gentlemen, you are about to embark on an important educational trip, the primary purpose of which is to increase your professional knowledge. The business part of your journey is to see how the Air Force operates in Europe. For this privilege, you have voluntarily exchanged your leave time at home. To me, this is a very significant part of your experience as cadets. You're going to see your Air Force and its sister services trying to sell democracy in the toughest market in the world. One of the first things you'll notice is that our men are ready to fight, but, thank God, they also pray for peace.

"You're going to get a bird's-eye view, so to speak, of what your future life will be. You're going to be exposed to the social, economic and political aspects of foreign nations. Remember, you, as future air commanders and representatives of our nation, are today's ambassadors, too. How you conduct yourselves, your attitudes, your conversation—everything you do will add or detract from what the people in these lands think about us.

"You won't have much free time—after all, this isn't a pleasure junket to be taken at the expense of the taxpayers. This is an important part of your education, as I said before. But in your free time, I would suggest that you avail yourselves of the best that each country has to offer. And, believe me, men, each country has *much* to give you—far more than you have to give to any of them at this stage in your education.

"What you bring back will depend entirely upon the individual man. But I hope that our two years of training here hasn't been in vain. I hope that, in addition to the souvenirs, ticket stubs and other gay reminders of happy week ends, you'll also bring back an appreciation of other people—their ways, their cultures and their beliefs. Also, that you'll be very mindful of what your own parent—the Air Force—is doing to help maintain peace in the world.

"Gentlemen—fill your eyes, fill your minds, fill your pockets, but, above all, fill your hearts! You are dismissed."

The next day, on the flight line at Lowry, Frank said to Pete, "Gosh, what General Saunders said last night was really inspiring. I hope I can live up to at least part of it during this summer tour."

Later, when the big airplane had left McGuire Air Force base and was soaring northeastward, Frank exclaimed, "This is it! We're actually on our way to Europe."

"Yeah, and, believe me, I'm going to soak up everything I possibly can." Pete settled back in his seat. "Don't bother talking with me," he said a minute later. "I'm going to get as much sack time on this flight as possible so that I can stay awake every minute we're over there."

"Sure, sure," Frank replied. "I can just see you staying awake all the time. We'll be lucky to keep you awake during the briefings." He too settled back as the huge C-118 winged its way out over the Atlantic.

A brief stop at Gander in Newfoundland and again the plane was on its way northeastward.

"It's funny," Frank murmured many hours later, "but I don't think it ever got really dark. Isn't that the sun coming up again?"

"That's because we're so far north—and it's summertime. Where's all that navigation you learned last year?" Pete tried to find a more comfortable position.

"Of course," Frank muttered and went back to sleep.

A few hours later, the voice of Major Foster who was in charge of the group, came over the intercom, "You men had better wake up now and start stretching. If you watch closely on the port side, you'll soon see Scotland. We'll land at Prestwick and be met by three C-54's, which will take us on to Germany."

Pete leaned toward the window, straining his eyes toward the horizon. "Can't see a thing," he muttered.

"Yes," Frank pointed excitedly, "see that place which

looks like the top of a wave. Watch it a minute. It's getting bigger."

"Sure enough." Pete picked up the excitement from Frank and the other cadets watching from their window.

"There's a ship down there," Bob announced, and they all strained to see it.

"There's land—I see Scotland!" Frank was sure now.

Less than thirty minutes later, the plane set down smoothly on the Prestwick landing field and the cadets piled out. After a hearty lunch, they divided into three groups and climbed into the waiting C-54's.

Now they were winging over the English channel, filled with barges and small ships. Then they could see the low countries—Holland and Belgium. They watched for the canals, also holding their small boats and barges. There were windmills whirling in the breeze, and the countryside appeared to be laid out very precisely.

"We're too high to see any wooden shoes, though." Pete sighed. "And I hoped to see some pretty Dutch girls."

Now they crossed the Rhine River, which they recognized because of its size, and saw toylike castles clinging to the high banks. A few minutes later, they came down to the landing field at Rhine/Main, near Frankfort on the Main, and the first lap of their journey was over.

Next day, the cadets boarded a Navy patrol boat and sailed down the Rhine to Bonn, capital of free Germany.

"This is like a dream to me," Frank said as he and Pete leaned over the railing, watching the beautiful countryside. "I've read about the romantic Rhine River, but I never expected to see it."

"Look at that castle over there—I'll bet that's where Rapunzel let down her hair." Pete chuckled.

"Or where the Prince discovered Sleeping Beauty." Frank entered into the game. "You know, the Grimm Brothers who wrote all those fairy tales were from Germany. I'll bet this is the part of their country they were writing about."

"The forest is really thick, isn't it?" Pete glanced to the other side. "Hey, look over there—what are they raising?"

"Grapes," Frank answered. "See, they make those fences and the grape vines climb over them. You know Germany is famous for its Rhine wines."

They were interrupted by a voice over the intercom, announcing that they were approaching Bonn and would soon land.

The cadets went to the American Embassy at Bonn, where they were briefed on the work of the Embassy personnel and USAFE.*

The American Ambassador said, "I hope you will be particularly impressed by the ambitious nature of the German people while you are here. You have but to look around you to see the vigorous skyscraper cities which have sprung up with almost incredible speed from the rubble they were twelve years ago.

"No one knows the full answer to the fantastic drive which made all this happen, but you can count on the fact that part of the miracle is in the old German tradition of hard work. It's enough to make us evaluate our own initiative in the modern world.

"But don't think of Germany only in the sense of modern buildings. It's also one of the best places to get the feeling of what the Middle Ages were like. When you visit some of the older cities which weren't bombed during the war, you'll be fascinated with their gingerbread houses, like stage sets, and a *Meistersinger* atmosphere.

"The thing for which we are most grateful, though, is the general feeling and acceptance of democracy by the Ger-

---

* USAFE—United States Air Force in Europe.

man people. They have accepted it and grasped it as though it were something they have always wanted and desired. And the interesting thing is, it's working."

The next day, the cadets spent a great deal of time at an airfield with German fighter pilots. Many of these men had seen action in World War II.

"Just think," Pete whispered to Frank, "these fellows used to be our enemies, and now they are our allies."

Frank nodded. "Yes, a kind of first defense line between us and the Iron Curtain."

The cadets also visited an American Air Force Base and saw their planes in constant readiness, in case of a tense situation or a crisis, such as the Berlin Blockade of a few years ago.

After three days, the cadets boarded their C-54's once more and flew to England. Here they called at the Embassy in London and were briefed on what was being done in that area.

During their free time, they visited many of the famous landmarks of England which they had studied about in their History and English courses. One which particularly impressed them was the Tower of London.

"This I've always wanted to see!" Pete exclaimed. "I can almost imagine the ghosts of all the people who have been murdered here—Henry VIII's wives, Mary Queen of Scots—you know—all the rest."

Later, the cadets watched the changing of the guard at Buckingham Palace and Frank said, "It wouldn't be hard for us to take over those guard jobs. We certainly know all about bracing and caging our eyes."

Pete gazed at a big soldier with his tall shako. *"Uh-huh,* but I wouldn't go for those hats. It's bad enough to walk the ramp—that's really what they are doing—without balancing that heavy thing on your head."

From London, they flew to Cranwell, the British Royal Air Force Academy, where they were entertained by the English cadets.

"Seems like home," Pete said a little wistfully. "I almost feel homesick."

"For what?" Frank asked in surprise. "I thought you were the one who liked to get off the base and have fun."

"Oh, I don't know—all that formation and spit and polish —it just seems so natural."

In the afternoon, the United States Air Force Academy cadets played athletic games with the English cadets. It was fun to learn something about how to play cricket and to join in a rousing game of soccer.

That evening, the English cadets entertained the Americans at what they called a "dining in" party. They had an hilarious time, capped by the English cadets showing their guests how to joust. Two cadets mounted the shoulders of two other cadets, took long poles and proceeded to try to knock each other off to win the game.

"What fun we've had!" Frank exclaimed as the weary Americans got ready to hit the sack. "I'll never forget this visit. I feel we've made some real friends."

"Me, too," Pete answered. "And we're going to try that jousting business when we get back home. That's real fun."

Next morning the cadets flew to a SAC * base, where they were briefed on the importance of SAC in helping to keep peace in Europe.

"SAC, as you know," Major Foster explained, "is always on the alert. Those planes out there can be in the air in less than fifteen minutes, if there is any kind of emergency."

Later, the major said, "I'm sorry, men, but we've just had orders to give you polio shots. As you know, our next stop

* SAC—Strategic Air Command.

is Spain, and we've been notified there's an outbreak of polio there."

"Wouldn't you know it?" Pete grumbled. "My arm already feels like a pin cushion from the shots we took before we left."

"Quit griping," Bob said. "You ought to be glad to have a chance to see Spain."

Six hours later, they landed at the airport near Madrid and were whisked into town to the Embassy, where they were briefed on the American air bases and the Embassy work in Spain.

That afternoon, they were given free time to see the sights in the Spanish capital.

Next day, they drove to Toledo. That night, in Madrid, most of the cadets saw their first bullfight. It was a colorful, exciting affair—with certain reservations in the feeling of these American boys unaccustomed to this kind of entertainment.

Their next stop was in France, at the Salon de Provence, home of the French Air Force Academy. Here they attended the graduation exercises of the French cadets and stood at attention during the ceremonies.

From there they flew to Paris, which was one of the highlights of the trip, most of the cadets agreed. Here they visited SHAPE * headquarters and met General Newsome, who gave them an excellent talk.

He then explained the function of SHAPE. As Frank sat quietly with the other cadets listening to this dedicated man speak, he studied the general carefully. What a thin wisp of a man he was, Frank thought. He had strong, fine features and, although he was tanned, he had a tired look, especially around the eyes.

---

* Supreme Headquarters Allied Powers Europe.

"General Newsome has a notably brilliant mind," Major Foster had told his charges earlier, "which most people say, in low speed, goes at least one hundred and fifty mental miles per minute!"

Now Frank believed the major. He sensed that the general's mind was always several jumps ahead of what he was saying.

"Gosh," Pete said later, "how that man can talk! I've heard some good speeches, but never anything like that one."

"Most speakers have a point or two to make and that's about it," Frank agreed. "But every single thing General Newsome told us was significant. He didn't waste a word."

The next two days were free for the cadets to see the sights of Paris. There were the Louvre, Montmartre, the Arch of Triumphe with the eternal flame burning beneath, the bookstalls on the Seine, Notre Dame Cathedral and the Eiffel Tower. At night, they visited some famous night spots, including the Piagalle, the Folies and the Lido.

"We never could stand this pace if we weren't in such good physical condition," Frank said to Pete as they tramped from one sight to another, sometimes taking cabs, other times walking.

"Even at that, my poor dogs are beginning to scream," Pete complained. "I'm for stopping and getting some lunch."

"You and your dogs!" Frank exclaimed in disgust. "All right. Let's go in here and you can try out your high-school French."

The two boys sat at a sidewalk table and the waiter brought them a menu. "I can't read this," Pete sputtered. "I can read French printing, but not French script—writing—or whatever it is."

"You're always bragging about how much French you

know. Get hot." Frank studied the menu. "This might as well be Sanskrit as far as I'm concerned."

Pete managed to stammer out a few French words, then looked questioningly at the waiter. The latter grinned good-naturedly and said, "You may order in English, M'sieur. Here, I will help you with the menu."

The next week end, the cadets flew to Garmish-Partenkirchen, in the Bavarian Alps of Germany, where they had a wonderful time hiking in the mountains.

As they were resting by a sparkling mountain stream, Frank said to Pete, "You know, this looks just about as German as Aspen, Colorado. Anyway, it has the same kind of spectacular mountain scenery."

"Yeah," Pete answered, "and you can tell by all the ski tows that they have good skiing here. Remember what fun we had skiing at Aspen a year ago, when we were doolies?"

On Saturday evening, there was a dance in the middle of the square, on a wooden platform put up for the occasion. The townspeople came dressed in peasant costumes and it was a gay party.

Several of the girls kept waving at Pete, Frank and Bob, who stood off to one side, watching the gaiety. *"Bitte, bitte,"* they cried. "Dance! Dance with us!"

Finally Bob said, "Well, I'm game if you fellows are. I guess that's a waltz or polka they're doing. I've never done it—but I'll try, if you will."

"O.K. with me," Pete agreed. "Come on."

Frank felt something of his old shyness slip back on him. It was always a little hard for him to join in fun spontaneously, as Pete and Bob could do. But he trailed the pair up the steps and as several girls rushed towards them, he found himself grabbed and whirled off to the strains of an accordion and fiddle by a partner with a merry smile.

It was gay fun and Frank found that, by concentrating

hard, he could follow the steps. Once he glanced up to see Pete swing by with a plump girl in his arms.

Pete's freckles stood out on their stems and he was laughing gaily. His jug handle ears were red to the tips, and his red hair seemed to pick up the glow from the lights overhead. His partner's blonde braids stood straight out as he whirled her more and more swiftly.

Then Frank saw Bob, who was also enjoying himself. He and his partner were doing some intricate polka steps. Frank was satisfied to stick to plain steps, but, by now, he had entered into the spirit of the dance and was thoroughly enjoying himself. His partner did not even attempt to talk to him, but her happy smile more than made up for that.

The three cadets spent the rest of the evening dancing with girl after girl, until, suddenly, Frank looked at his watch and realized they had just ten minutes to get back to the base. They bid their partners a hasty good-by and hurried away.

On Monday, the cadets flew to the Berlin airport, where Major Foster, who had accompanied them during the entire trip, briefed them.

"After our scheduled inspection here in Berlin, you may tour the city on your own. You have special passes which will allow you to visit the Russian sector—East Berlin. I know probably most of you are very eager to get a look at that Communist world across the street.

"West Berlin, you will find, is an island of freedom in a Communist sea. Every time I've been here, it seems to me, the air has been electric—not with tension or fear, but with energy. These West Berliners appear to be certain of ultimate victory. The typical Berliner has a fortitude and an ironical humor that shows the city's determination to survive—and to survive in freedom and independence.

"One thing more—when you go over into the Russian sector, be very, very careful. We don't want any international incidents, please." He paused and laughed. "I'm not forbidding it, you understand, but if I were you, I wouldn't try to take any pictures over there."

Several cadets joined Frank and Pete and took a cab into the city of Berlin. They strolled along the Kurfurstendamm and the Tauenzienstrasse, the latter being a combined Fifth Avenue and Broadway.

"Gosh, these people have a good time," Pete said, gazing about. "Why don't we get something to eat?"

They found a small sidewalk cafe where George took over the ordering, since he said he wanted to show off his German. Pete particularly enjoyed the smoked meats and sausages, and the crusty bread, which he declared were the best he'd ever tasted. All of them drank cups and cups of black coffee, with blobs of whipped cream on top.

Finally, the group decided to break up. Frank suggested, "Come on, Pete. Let's go over to the Russian sector."

George, who had been undecided about what to do, said, "Hey, I'd like to go with you. There's strength in numbers, and you might need it."

Frank frowned and murmured to Pete, "Why does he want to go with us? I'd just as soon he'd choose somebody else to latch onto."

"Well, he'd better behave, or I'll punch him in the nose," Pete promised.

The trio took a bus to East Berlin. George kept up a steady stream of conversation about what he had read and heard concerning this area. But Frank didn't pay too much attention. He was interested in studying the people who rode the bus. Most of them seemed subdued—quite a contrast with the ambitious, happy people they'd met in West Berlin and western Germany.

When they got into East Berlin, Pete exclaimed, "Hey, look, everything is different here! Why, they haven't even rebuilt those buildings which were bombed out during the war."

"Not only that," George gazed around, "but the rubble is still here. Look at those people picking around in the ruins. I suppose they're still trying to salvage things."

"Even their clothes are different," Frank added. "See how poorly they're dressed. It's the human element that I think is tragic."

The three cadets strolled along the street, looking in the shop windows.

"Things are much more expensive here," Frank said. "They don't have the nice merchandise in their stores that we saw in the other sector."

"I really feel sorry for these people," Pete declared. "You know how enterprising we thought the German people were in West Germany—over around Bonn. Why, they'd done wonders with restoring and rebuilding their part of the country."

"Everybody knows they're the most ambitious people in the world," George replied. "But the Russians don't give them a chance over here, do they?"

"It's too bad," Frank said. "Berlin never should have been divided this way."

"Come on," George started across the street. "Let's look at this monument over there. I think those are Russian soldiers. Maybe they'll talk with us."

"Just be careful, Meathead," Pete warned as he followed George across the street. "Remember what Major Foster said. We don't want any international incidents."

"Why, this is called the Garden of Remembrance!" George exclaimed. "I've seen pictures of it. It's a memorial to the

Russian soldiers who were killed during the capture of Berlin."

The three cadets studied the monument in silence for a minute, then George walked toward the soldiers and said, "Hello! Do you speak English?"

The three Russian soldiers looked the American cadets over carefully, then one shook his head and answered, *"Nein."*

"Sprechen sie Deutsch?" George tested his German.

"Yah—yah," one of the soldiers, a tall, dark fellow answered.

Then he and George carried on a somewhat halting conversation in German, mixed with English and Russian. This seemed to amuse the other Russian soldiers, and they became a little more friendly.

Finally Pete said, "Say, George, ask them if they'd trade the emblems on their caps for the ones on our caps. Aren't theirs the red star with hammer and sickle? I'd like to have one of theirs for a souvenir."

"Do you think we should?" Frank asked doubtfully.

"Why not?" Pete replied. "Our cap emblems belong to us —we paid for them. Besides, we can replace them at the commissary in West Berlin."

George passed on Pete's suggestion haltingly, pointing to the emblem on his cap.

"Nein—nein!" The Russian soldier shook his head and looked a little less friendly.

"Darn!" Pete exclaimed. "I think it would be something to go back with one of those emblems."

"So do I," Frank agreed. "I'd sure like to have one."

George tried urging again and, this time, one of the other soldiers said something to the first one, pulling an object out of his pocket. The first soldier spoke to George.

"What did he say?" Pete demanded impatiently.

"He said they had some old emblems in their pockets. We could have those."

Pete grinned triumphantly. "Fine! Let's trade with them." He started to take the emblem off his cap, but the Russian soldier stopped him. "*Nein, nein,*" he said to George and rattled off some more German.

"He says they will give us their emblem," the cadet translated, "but they can't accept ours. They might get into trouble if they did."

"That's all right with me," Frank said. "I'm glad to get theirs."

The three cadets thanked the soldiers, then the latter walked away.

"You know they seem half human," Frank observed, as if he had just discovered something.

"What did you think they'd act like—the big bad wolf?" George asked sarcastically.

Frank shrugged as they started toward the bus station.

"You fellows go on, I'll be with you in a minute," George said, turning back.

"Come on, Mister."

"We'd better stick together," Frank called over his shoulder. "I don't think we should separate."

"Oh, all right, I'm coming," George answered impatiently. "I just wanted something here."

Frank turned around just in time to see George slip the small camera out of his blouse pocket and take a quick picture of the three soldiers as they walked away. Not satisfied with one, he quickly turned the film. As he took another, the Russian soldier who had done all the talking turned around and saw him.

The soldier yelled something and ran back. He sputtered some German at George, holding out his hand.

George shook his head and kept saying, "No—*nein*. I didn't mean anything by it."

Frank felt the hair on the back of his neck rise. He was breathing rapidly and his heart pounded. He glanced around wildly, to see if there were any friendly-looking people about. But there were just the six of them—he, the other two cadets and the three Russian soldiers. Snatches of stories he'd heard and read about people being arrested in East Berlin flashed through his mind. Siberia—the Salt Mines—concentration camps—that's where prisoners sometimes disappeared behind the Iron Curtain.

He glanced briefly toward Pete, who stood with feet apart in a semi-belligerent attitude. But Frank noted that the color had drained from his face and his freckles stood out, a sure sign that he was perturbed.

"What's he saying?" Frank demanded in a husky voice.

"He wants my camera—said I didn't have any business taking their picture. They could get into trouble."

The Russian advanced menacingly, still holding out his hand and talking in a threatening tone. George backed up until the three cadets stood side by side.

"You'd better give it to him," Pete advised. "Remember what Major Foster warned. We don't want any trouble. Besides, they could slap us in jail—might even end up in a concentration camp." Pete's voice rose to a high squeak.

Again the Russian soldier said something and, this time, his face reddened angrily.

The fellow really meant business, Frank decided. Then he had an idea. "Give him the film, dumbwhack," he said to George. "That's all he wants, anyway."

George spoke quickly to the soldier, taking the camera from his pocket, but holding fast to it. The soldier snatched it out of his hand, however. George raised an arm to strike him, but Frank grabbed it and hung on, saying quietly, "Don't antagonize him. Let's see what he does."

The soldier yanked the camera open and tore out the film, waving it about in the sunlight. Then he handed both the film and the camera back to George, bowed slightly, turned and walked away, his back stiff.

"Wow!" Pete let out his breath. "That was a close call. Honestly, Shelton, sometimes you do the dumbest things. I ought to smack you on the nose."

"Well, I didn't think they'd see me." George sounded a little worried. "That was a lucky break."

"Better than you deserve," Frank told him. "If you don't watch out, you're going to lose your big, fat nose one of these days, sticking it in other people's business. Come on. Let's go back to the other sector."

The three cadets hurried to a bus and jumped aboard. Frank could not resist looking furtively over his shoulder, expecting that they would be hauled off unceremoniously at any moment.

When they came near the customs border, where the West German police were checking the cars and busses, Frank glanced curiously toward a huge gate which towered above and threw a giant shadow over them. Then he recalled what the cadets had been told that morning about the Brandenburg Gate. It was considered by East German refugees as the Gate of Freedom.

He drew a deep breath and muttered to Pete, "I know exactly how people who are escaping from behind the Iron Curtain feel when they see that Brandenburg Gate—*it's really a gate to freedom!*"

12

Back in the Groove

Frank sat down, drew a deep breath and picked up the miniature airplane on his desk. He looked at it for quite a while, smoothing the wings thoughtfully. Then he put it down, rolled a clean sheet of paper in his typewriter and began tapping out a letter.

Dear Mom and Dad,

It hardly seems possible that I'm beginning my third year at the Air Force Academy. Just think, I'm now a second classman and our ATO friends have departed—but not all in peace. That is, some of them have been sent to other assignments. Some are still here—Lieutenant Jenkins (who was promoted to Captain) is in the thermo-dynamic department and still helping with our soaring program.

Lieutenant Porter—the one we always called Hard Nose— is still here, too, and he's in the physical education department. I really think I'm getting used to him and, now that I'm an upper classman, I don't mind him so much.

I missed coming home on leave this summer—now I realize

it more than ever—but our European trip was really great. I'm sure you got that idea from my cards, which I tried to keep coming, although I never did have time to write a letter. The rest of the things I have to tell you will have to wait until I see you on Christmas leave.

As you know, the Wing Officers are reshuffled every semester, to give us a chance to serve in different capacities as leaders in our squadrons. And we're still chosen on the basis which I explained before—that is, we're rated by our officers and by our fellow cadets. Then some of the cadets, according to their scores, get the higher ranking officers' jobs. However, that isn't always true, because the officers want to try out all the cadets in jobs and test their abilities. This time, I came up with First Sergeant, although Captain Jenkins told me my rating was much higher. He said they have to shuffle the men around in order to give all of them a chance.

I'm in charge of sick slips, announcements, administration of squadron duties and that type of work. Of course, I still have to help drill, make inspections, etc.

There's a new cadet this year—fourth classman, of course —by the name of Steve Clark that seems like a pretty solid chap. He's in my squadron and both Pete and I like him.

Duty calls, so I'll close. I hope you are feeling better, Dad. Mom, *please* write and tell me how he really feels.

Love,
Frank

Just as he sealed and stamped the envelope, there was a knock on his door and George Shelton walked in.

"Come on, Meathead," the big blond cadet said, "you and I are to do the Inspection today."

"O.K.," Frank said. He got his cap and followed George.

They went from room to room in the dorm, assuming the duties that the ATO's had discharged when the two cadets were fourth classmen. There were such matters as dirty water glasses, dust on the molding, clothes in messy piles, beds not neat enough.

Frank sighed as he wrote out the demerit slips, recalling how he'd hated this Inspection business his first year. Now he didn't mind it, since neatness and order had become second nature.

The pair went into the last room, which happened to belong to Steve Clark and Lee Wells.

As George glanced around the room he said, "This is Dumbwhack Clark's room. I don't care much for his attitude and I intend to make things plenty rugged for him."

"What do you mean?" Frank demanded.

"I've heard him griping about the discipline and things he had to do. This is a good place to put on the screws."

Frank didn't answer. He'd learned from experience that it was best not to disagree with George too much. If he did, then George only became stubborn.

"Gig them for dusty desks, wrinkled beds, and . . ." George rubbed his finger along the molding, "dusty molding. I'll teach those doolies to look sharp."

As Frank wrote out the demerit slips, he pressed his lips together, determined not to argue with the other cadet.

George turned to go, then stopped, swung on his heel and went to the rifle rack. "I just thought of something," he said slyly. "I wonder if these doolies are smart enough to have found some of our old hiding places."

He lifted up the rifle rack, pulled out the felt from underneath and poked around in the "pit," as the cadets called it. Sure enough, Frank saw him pick out several envelopes.

"Ah-ha!" George gloated. "Success! Look what our little doolie friends have been hiding."

He held several packages of Koolaide in his hands. "Well, he continued, "I suggest we teach them a lesson." With that, he tore the envelopes in two and tossed the grains of Kool-aide all around the room and over the beds.

"Oh, come on," Frank protested, "you don't need to be so hard-nosed!"

"This ought to make them happy," George continued, as he spread a generous pile of grains on Steve's desk. Then he wrote the letters "G.B.S.," in the center. "That's my trademark," he announced smugly. "Maybe, if he's a well-read cadet, he'll think those initials stand for George Bernard Shaw." He laughed triumphantly.

"I still think that's a raunchy trick," Frank said as the two left the room. "If anyone had done that to you when you were a doolie, you'd have wanted to wring his neck."

"Nobody had that much ingenuity," George said cockily. "It takes a smart man to dream up good tricks like that. Anyway, Mr. Lunkhead Clark is a little too big for his britches and needs to be taken down a few pegs."

Frank didn't answer, but later, in his room with Pete, he said, "George is the one who's getting too big for his britches. He really needs somebody to work him over."

"Don't worry," Pete assured him. "The officers aren't so dumb. He's going to be set back on his heels so hard one of these days his teeth will rattle. And it'll serve him right."

"I like that Steve Clark," Frank continued. "I think he has the makings of a good cadet."

"Yeah, he's smart and he's got a lot of gumption. I like to see these young fellows fight back once in a while. It shows they have the right spirit."

"My, my," Frank teased, "listen to Mr. Peter John Day talk. He's the one who knows all about the right spirit."

"Oh, go jump in the lake three times and come up twice," Pete responded. "You know exactly what I mean."

"Well, I'm due at football practice," Frank said as he got

into his clothes. "I'm still plugging away, although some-times I wonder why I'm out there."

"You're doing all right," his roommate told him earnestly. "The team looks a little better this year than last. I still think we're doing pretty good for our third year."

"Sure, sure—so do I," Frank answered impatiently. "But I wonder if I'll ever get a chance to play in one of the big games. I seem to be the perennial bench warmer."

"Somebody has to keep the benches warm." Pete winked. "It might as well be you."

Frank didn't answer. He hurried outside and dog-trotted to the Field House. Sometimes he wondered if he'd made the wrong choice in going out for football again this year. And yet he felt that it was where he belonged. He was do-ing something for his team and his school, if only by being there for regular practice.

At the football field, he was glad to see that Steve was playing on the freshmen team. After practice, the two cadets dog-trotted back to the dorm together.

"That workout was good for me today, sir," Steve said.

"Why?"

"Because I'm so mad at Mr. Shelton I could bust him in the nose."

Frank glanced at the big, broad-shouldered cadet who who was frowning darkly. Finally he asked, "Is Shelton getting your goat, Mister?"

Steve didn't answer immediately. Finally, he said, "That's about it, sir. I had some Koolaide hidden and he found it during inspection. I wouldn't have cared if he'd thrown it out. But he threw is all over our room—whatamess!"

"How did you know he did it?"

"Oh, I recognized his initials, sir. But don't worry. My time is coming and I'll get even, sir."

Frank explained that he had been there too, but Steve

just shook his head and said he knew Shelton was guilty. Frank changed the subject by asking Steve if he'd like to join the Soaring Club.

After asking several questions, the younger cadet said, "It sounds fine, sir. I'd rather join the Aero Club and log some hours in a power plane, but I can't afford to pay for the lessons. My dad's been sick and I don't want to ask for any more money. In fact, I've been saving some of my allowance to send back, sir."

"Well, we'll see you Sunday afternoon, then, at the gliderport," Frank promised.

That week end, when Frank rode out to the soaring field with Pete and several other cadets, he was glad to see that Steve Clark came along. He determined that, between gliding trips, he'd spend some time with the younger cadet and get to know him better.

After they'd helped get the gliders in the air, Frank said to Steve, "Come on, let's sit down over here and watch." He noticed the cadet stood very straight as he replied, "Yes, sir."

"Stand at ease, Mr. Clark." Frank hunkered down on his heels, broke off a long piece of grass and began chewing it. "This is one place we don't have to be too formal."

The other cadet sank down and breathed deeply. "Thank goodness, sir! That is, I'm glad to relax a little. That's one reason why I decided to come out here for gliding—it's a chance to be myself."

Frank glanced at the boy and liked what he saw. He had dark, close-cropped hair and an open countenance and an easy way of moving. "Did you find summer training a little rugged?"

"Rugged, sir?" Steve laughed hollowly. "It was just about

the toughest thing I ever did, sir. I decided, if I ever lived through bivouac, I'd never gripe again."

"Well, you lived through it." Frank changed the subject abruptly. "I'd offer you one of Pete's candy bars, except I know you don't want to break training."

Steve made a wry face. "I wouldn't take it anyway, sir. Right now, I can't bear to look a candy bar in the face."

"Why?"

Steve grinned and replied, "Oh, you know how it is during summer training, sir—no candy, no nothing! Well, my roomie and I persuaded one of the custodians to buy us some candy. We didn't have any small change and had to give him a five-dollar bill."

"So you got your candy?"

"Yes, but he spent the whole five dollars and came back with a huge sack full of candy bars."

"What did you do?"

"First of all, aside from the fact that I couldn't afford to spend that much money on 'luxuries,' we really were in a spot because we had about five minutes to change our clothes, shine our shoes and stash that candy someplace where the ATO's wouldn't find it."

"Did you eat it all?"

"Heaven forbid! We sold some and gave some away to our buddies. We had to be real careful about the wrappers, so the ATO's wouldn't catch on." He stopped and chuckled, then continued. "We'd put the wrappers in used envelopes and tuck them among other pieces of paper in our wastebaskets. It was a real game."

"You weren't caught?"

"No, but I really got my comeuppance. I ate so much candy it made me sick. Now I can't stand the sight of a candy bar. I hope I get over it," he added wistfully. "I really used to like them."

Frank laughed. "Oh, you probably will by the time football season is over. Do you think you will like gliding?"

The other cadet sat up like a shot, his brown eyes glistening. "Like it? That's putting it mildly. I think it's the most wonderful thing that's happened to me at the Academy. That's why I came here—to fly. And what have I done?" He sank back on his elbows. "I've marched, drilled, 'yes-sirred,' and 'no-sirred,' until I'm black in the face, sir. This gliding will save my life."

"Did you fly any before you came to the Academy?"

"Yes, sir. I was a CAP cadet."

"I know what CAP is, but what's a CAP cadet?"

"Well, Civil Air Patrol sponsors high-school people who are interested in flying," Steve explained.

"How long did you belong?"

"You can join the CAP Cadet Program when you're fourteen and one-half years old. Believe me, I joined on that 'half' birthday. I'd been hanging around the hangar since I was about ten years old, in my home town—Bismark, North Dakota. I was known as a hangar rat."

"You must be crazy about flying."

"Crazy—man, that's me! I'd rather fly than eat, sir. I've taken all the courses CAP gave—navigation, flying with instruments. We'd even have flying breakfasts. The CAP officers would ferry a bunch of us cadets to another town, and we'd meet the CAP cadets located there and have a real ball."

"Sounds like fun. So flying isn't exactly new to you."

"No, sir. But I never did get enough."

"And, of course, that's why you came to the Academy."

"Yes, sir. Because I figured this was the place I'd really get to fly." Steve paused and frowned deeply. He lowered his voice as he continued, "But I'm beginning to think I made a mistake, sir."

Frank sensed that the younger cadet had been bottling up some of his problems. A wave of sympathy swept through him as he recalled how he had felt a couple of years ago when he was a doolie. He cleared his throat, then asked, "Why?"

"Because I haven't been up in one single airplane since I arrived in July. Why, that's the longest time since I was a little kid that I haven't ridden in a plane. All they want you to do here is drill, parade, clean up your room and do a lot of crazy things."

"Such as?"

"Learning a lot of tripe that won't ever do you any good, sir. Bracing . . ." he made a sour face, "caging your eyes . . . cleaning up your room when it's already so clean you could eat off the floor . . . shining your shoes when you can see your face in them."

"That's learning discipline, Mister. It's something we all have to go through."

"There ought to be an easier way to learn it, sir—it's really archaic." The cadet's voice was bitter and he slashed at his legs savagely with his cap.

Frank was silent a moment. He recalled how unhappy he'd been with the discipline when he first came to the Academy. Finally he said, "You can take it, Mr. Clark. I know because I lived through it a couple of years ago."

"Sir, I'm not sure I want to take it," Steve answered stubbornly.

"You should have been here the last two years when we had ATO's."

"You mean the Air Training Officers, sir?"

"Yes. They were *our* upper classmen. Have you met Lieutenant Porter over in Phys Ed?"

"Have I? I'll say I have, sir. He's in charge of our boxing class. He really bears down on us."

"Mister, you don't know the half of it. Lieutenant Porter rode me ragged the last two years."

"He did?" Steve's eyes widened. "Sir, I don't know how you kept from punching him in the nose." He balled his right fist and glared at it. "The day I leave, I'm going to belt him a good one." He spoke between clenched teeth, and his dark brows drew together in an angry frown.

"I can sympathize with you, Mister. There were times in the past two years when I would gladly have taken old Hard Nose Porter apart, piece by piece."

Steve's eyebrows raised in surprise. "You mean it, sir?"

"Yes, but you know, now that I look back, I have a different slant on the whole thing—yes, even on Lieutenant Porter."

"In what way?"

"If I could return to my first and second years, I'd certainly be different. As I look back now I realize that too often I was talking when I should have been listening. Every time I opened my mouth, I made a mistake. If I had it to do over, I'd keep still and listen."

Steve looked at him searchingly and Frank continued, "You're rebelling against the strict discipline now—and the methods used to teach you self-discipline. You can't tell me anything about it because I've been through it all. When you first come to this place they take *everything* away from you—all your rights. It seems as though sometimes you're lower than a worm in the dust."

"Yes, sir, and that's what I really resent."

"But did you ever stop to think about it? This matter of Freedom—when you've had everything taken away from you, and then it is returned to you as *privileges*—that's when you really appreciate it. You begin to understand how much *little* things mean. Being able to go off base, even for a few hours. Having a date . . ."

Steve groaned. "Sir, I've almost forgotten what a girl looks like. Do you realize I haven't had a date for over twelve weeks? The first ten weeks we were here, we couldn't have dates—you know that. Then the past two weeks I've been confined to Quarters, working off demerits, sir. I feel like a regular hermit."

Frank put up his hand to hide a smile. He was really sympathetic with Steve, but he also felt so much older and wiser. He finally said, "Well, one thing is sure. When you have your privileges handed back to you, I can promise that you'll appreciate them."

"I probably won't be here then, sir," Steve muttered darkly.

"Of course you will!" Frank glanced around. Gosh, he wished Captain Jenkins were down here on the ground with them, instead of soaring around the air in that glider. He knew the officer would have the right answers for this rebellious cadet.

"The more I think about it, the crazier I think I am," Steve continued. "Why, if I resign here, I can join the Air Force as a flying cadet. I'll get my wings in less than a year and I might eventually be flying that silver-winged dreamboat—the F-104." His eyes lighted up and he sat hugging his knees. "That's for me."

"Oh, no!" Frank put out his hand involuntarily and grasped Steve's shoulder. "You *can't* resign. Don't you remember? You took an oath. Besides, somebody else could have come here if you hadn't accepted the appointment. You've cheated another fellow out of a chance, if you're not going to stay. Don't worry, we'll get to fly one of these days, too."

"Sure, sir," Steve jeered. "You'll get to fly in a thousand years. And I'll be swishing around the wild blue yonder in the 'tiger' or a delta-wing jet."

Frank swallowed painfully. He knew how the kid felt. He could hardly wait to get his hand on the stick and fly a plane himself. But he'd chosen to come to the Air Force Academy to be trained as an officer—as a future commander and leader for world peace. Their professors and officers often reminded them of that great goal.

He glanced up as Steve jumped to his feet. "Here comes a glider," he yelled. "My turn is next. I'm going up."

As the younger cadet ran across the field toward the runway, Frank got to his feet and followed more slowly. He was troubled. Steve was a good guy and fine officer potential—he wanted to help him. He'd just have to get Captain Jenkins or somebody to talk with this discontented fellow. He, Frank, would try to spend some time with the cadet and somehow persuade him he must stay at the Academy.

George Shelton came up beside Steve as the plane hit the runway. Major Foster was instructing and, after he raised the canopy, Pete climbed out.

"Just a minute, Mister," George said to Steve as the latter stopped. "Don't be so gross. Wait for your betters to give you orders."

Frank saw a look of hatred sweep over Steve's face and he thought for a moment the younger cadet was going to hit George. Instead, he turned away abruptly.

Major Foster's clipped voice broke the tension. "Push this plane to take-off position. Mr. Clark, the next turn is yours."

After the glider took off, Captain Jenkins' plane landed. "Let's see," he said, "all of the men who need instruction have had a turn. Now you fellows who have soloed can have your chance. Mr. Shelton, take it up. Then, Mr. Barton and Mr. Day."

Darn, Frank thought. Old George would get the break and soar first this afternoon! But Frank helped Pete wholeheartedly as they did their ground duties and George's glider was launched.

After they had watched the plane soar away, the two roommates sat down and Frank told Pete about his talk with Steve and how he was determined to help the younger cadet in every way.

"Me, too," Pete added. "I like Mr. Clark and I'll do everything I can."

Frank glanced up toward where George was flying. "I don't wish him any bad luck," he said, "but I'd like to see him run out of lift. I want a chance at that glider before we have to go back."

But George hit two or three good thermals and was up for about forty minutes.

"Gosh, I bet we'll never hear the last of this one when he gets down," Frank said.

"Well, I'd brag, too, if I were in his shoes. Wish I was up there."

"Looks as though he finally lost it." Frank got to his feet. "He's flying straight now . . . Yes, he's losing altitude. He's coming in."

George came in on the downwind leg of the pattern. He turned onto base leg south of the field. All afternoon the pilots had been landing toward the south, Frank recalled.

"Well, he had a swell flight," Pete said. "He hasn't anything to gripe about. I hope he lands it short, so we don't have to tow it so far."

Frank saw the cadet turn onto final when the glider began to gain altitude again. "Hey! He got some lift. He'll land long for sure and we'll have a lengthy tow back to take-off position," Frank moaned.

"Pull on those spoilers, boy!" Pete yelled.

The glider continued to rise and George started into a turn.

"No, no . . . you'll never make it, Knucklehead!" Frank was excited now. "Migosh, he's racked it around in a 360." Frank could hear Major Foster saying to them over and over, *never come in on a 360 degree turn on the final approach.*

"Looks like he's going to get away with it—*he* would," Pete muttered disgustedly.

At first the lift seemed to hold, then the glider began to sink rapidly. Major Foster, who had been inspecting an extra tow line beside the pickup, glanced up and saw the glider. He dropped the tow line quickly. "That crazy fool," he said, then he yelled, "Get your nose down or you'll stall it out."

He yanked open the right door of the truck and climbed in beside Sergeant Gary, who was in the driver's seat.

"Let's get going, Sergeant," Frank heard him say. "He's not going to make it. Come on, men. Pile in the back end."

Frank and Pete and several cadets obeyed. As the truck sped north along the runway, Frank saw George straighten out of the turn and disappear behind a row of trees north of the road which bordered the gliderport. The sergeant drove straight to the northern boundary, where they were halted by a fence.

Officers and cadets piled out, climbed the fence and broke into a run across the field. Frank could see the glider which had come to rest with its left wing sticking up in the air. He couldn't see George anywhere.

"Must have hit pretty hard," Frank said to Pete.

"Maybe it knocked him out," Pete said hopefully. "Serve him right."

"At least there's no gasoline in it, so it can't burn."

As they neared the glider, George crawled out from under the wing on the far side, where he apparently had been inspecting the under side of the fuselage.

"Well, he's all in one piece," said Frank as they slowed down.

George, whose face was a sickly greenish-white and streaked with dirt, looked up at Major Foster and said, "I thought I had enough lift to make it around, sir. The vertical speed said—"

"I don't give a hang about the vertical speed," the officer roared. "You've been told *never* to do a 360 on final! There's no room in the military picture for a man who can't take instructions and obey orders. Some day it may not be just your life you're gambling, but the life of your crew as well."

George swallowed painfully and said very low, "Yes, sir."

Frank couldn't help feeling a little sorry for the cadet. He was a sad sight as he turned and looked at the glider he'd almost wrecked.

"That's all the flying for today." Major Foster's voice showed his disgust. "Thanks to Mr. Shelton, we have work to do. . . . Sergeant Gary," he ordered. "Take one of the cadets back to the gliderport with you and hook the trailer on the truck. You can get it in on this side road. Better put the tool box in. We'll push the glider over to the fence and, with everyone working together, we can lift it. But the wings must come off to get it on the trailer. You'll have to use wire cutters on that fence, Sergeant, to get the truck and trailer through. Then the fence will have to be mended before we leave this afternoon."

He turned and they all inspected the glider's damage. Frank noticed that the fabric on the belly was torn and strips of fabric hung from the under side of the elevator.

"Looks as though old Plasterbrain did a good job of keeping us on the ground today," Frank grumbled to Pete.

"Yes, and from the looks of that fabric, this bird'll be out of circulation for a while, too."

"Trust Shelton to hog all the green air and then ground

the rest of us." Frank was really unhappy. "Now we don't get to solo today."

The rest of the afternoon was spent removing the wings and the elevators from the glider. Then the workers lifted it over the fence onto the side road and fastened it on the trailer, where they were careful about padding it to keep it from further damage.

"Mr. Shelton," Major Foster ordered just before he drove away with the smashed glider, "you can mend that fence where we had to cut it." The officer glanced around, then added, "Mr. Day and Mr. Barton, help him."

Pete made a face as the others drove away. "Well, Mr. Hundred Percent, what's your excuse this time?"

"Dry up!" George's face looked like a thunder cloud. "Everybody makes a mistake once in a while."

Pete looked at Frank and winked. "I hope you remember that, Mister, when you're bearing down on the doolies. Or is it just upper classmen who are permitted to make a mistake once in a while?"

George didn't answer. He turned away, took a pair of pliers out of his pocket and started fixing the fence, but Frank noticed that his hands trembled. Suddenly, Frank realized that nobody had said a word to George about whether or not he'd been hurt. Everyone's concern had been for the glider.

"You O.K., Shelton?" Frank asked.

"I'm all right," George muttered.

"Here," Frank directed, "let me fix that fence or we won't get home until morning."

He took the pliers from George and started splicing the wire strands. Pete held the wire taut. Nobody said another word while they finished and walked across the field to the waiting jeep which would take them back to the Academy.

13

Thief! Thief!

"There's something rotten in Denmark around here," Pete said in a puzzled tone.

"Why—what do you mean?" Frank went on writing at his desk, only half paying attention.

"I had sixty dollars in this wallet last night, and there isn't a cent here now."

Frank glanced up quickly. "Are you sure? You know sometimes you forget things and put them other places."

"I'm sure, but I'll dig around and see." Pete looked through his desk drawer and every place the money could have been but couldn't find it. He had a peculiar look on his face when he finally said, "I suppose I was a little careless. I left the wallet here on the bed. You know we're so used to the Honor Code around this place, I never worry about having anything stolen. Probably somebody with sticky fingers couldn't resist the temptation."

"But who could it be?" Frank looked puzzled. "Nobody gets in these dorms except the cadets and the janitors."

149

"And you know Jake Cline, our janitor, wouldn't take anything—why, the guy's been around Lowry for fifteen years or more."

"I know it. Well, I suppose I'll have to report the loss."

Pete left the room. Then minutes later, he came back with Captain Jenkins.

Frank stood up. The officer said, "At ease, Mr. Barton. I came over to take a look around here. I'm sorry to say there have been several petty thefts—and some not so petty—reported in this dorm and the one next door. We've purposely not said too much about it, thinking that the culprit would be caught. But finally we've had to notify the OSI,* and they're going to look into it."

That evening, one of the OSI officers knocked and came into their room. After making a thorough search he asked, "Who has been in your room during the past twenty-four hours?"

Pete thought hard for a minute, then said, "Well, Bob Elspy was here, Tom Lansing and George Shelton. We had a bull session in here last night."

Frank added, "Yes, and Steven Clark and Andy Jones were here just before dinner."

"What about your janitor? Does he ever come in the room?"

"Sure—he can come in," Pete answered. "But Jake Cline wouldn't take anything. He's a swell guy."

"How about the other janitors? I mean, the ones in the other buildings. Do they come in?"

"Not very often," Frank answered. "Once in a while we'll see one. But we figure they've been cleared by the Head Shed."

The officer looked thoughtful, then said, "We're going to

---
* OSI—military version of FBI.

have to do something drastic about this pilfering before it gets out of hand."

"Yes, sir," Frank answered, glancing at Pete, whose freckles were beginning to stand out. His ears wiggled slightly, too.

"I'm going to let you two men in on our plan. We're going to plant a wallet containing some money in one of the rooms. But this time the wallet will be sprinkled with some spotting powder."

"Spotting powder, sir?" Pete's eyes bugged a little in surprise.

"Yes. This powder can't be seen, but anyone handling an object covered with it gets it on his hands and usually his clothes. When these are put under an ultra-violet ray, the powder shows up. It's a dead giveaway."

"Gosh, this sounds like something out of *Dragnet*, sir!" Frank said. "I've never been in on anything like this."

"Just don't mention it to any of the cadets—or in fact, to *anybody*," the officer ordered. "We'll see if this plan will work."

The next day, Dave Henderson reported to Security Flight that a wallet with forty dollars in it had been stolen from his room. Later, Captain Jenkins told Frank that the wallet and money had been sprinkled with the powder and now it was just a question of running the cadets and other personnel under the ultra-violet lamp.

Just before Frank was ready to leave for football practice, George Shelton burst into his room and said, "Barton, I have news for you, and it's not good."

"What's up?"

"I was down at the cadet store just now and heard Mr. Clark get a money order for forty dollars."

"So what? There's no law against that, is there?"

"Doesn't it strike you as a little peculiar that Mr. Clark

would be sending the exact amount of money that has just been stolen?"

"I don't know why. Lots of men have had forty dollars during their lives." Frank felt a slow burn working up inside him.

"But the peculiar thing about Mr. Clark is that yesterday he told me that he didn't have any money to take flying lessons; then today he comes up with forty dollars."

"Maybe he didn't want to spend it on flying lessons."

"Not that guy—he'd do anything to get in the air."

"Well, what am I supposed to do?"

"You're an Honor Rep, aren't you? Well, I'm reporting an apparent breach of the Honor Code to you. *I* think this case warrants an investigation."

Frank felt his face flush. He was so angry he couldn't speak for a moment. He kept repeating to himself, *A cadet shows no emotion.* But this was a tough spot to be in.

"Thank you, Mr. Shelton," he said in a tight voice. "I'll report your charges."

When George left, Frank went slowly to his locker and got his cap. This was one of the toughest spots he'd ever been in. It was as bad as the time, a couple of years ago, when he'd had to report Pete, thinking that his roommate had cheated in a test. Luckily for both of them, Pete was innocent. And now here was Steve, the young cadet he'd been trying so hard to help, up against a charge like this.

Of course, if Steve were found guilty, he'd have to leave the Academy. *We will not lie, steal, cheat, or tolerate those among us who do,* Frank thought. That was their code and he, as an elected Honor Representative, would have to do his duty. He took a deep breath before he went into Major Danforth's office.

After his report, Frank hurried over to football practice, but he had a hard time keeping his mind on the game.

"What's the matter with you, Barton?" Lieutenant Porter asked after he had fumbled the ball several times. "You certainly have butter fingers today. You couldn't carry that ball in a basket."

But Frank didn't pay much attention. He was too disturbed by the suspicion gathering around Steve's head.

Immediately after dinner, the squawk box announced that all the cadets in the dorm were to report to the Security Fight room. When they had assembled there, Captain Jenkins took charge and said that they were having a testing program and that each cadet was to hold his hands under the ultra-violet ray lamp.

Frank swallowed convulsively a couple of times and drew a deep breath to steady himself. *Don't let anything show up on Steve's hands,* he prayed silently.

Each cadet was cleared until there were only two left, Steve and Tom Lansing. Frank watched anxiously as Steve put his hands under the light. They brightened up immediately, showing the tell-tale marks of the powder.

Frank caught his breath sharply and held it for a moment, then let it out slowly as Captain Jenkins said sternly, "Step over here, Mister."

They tested Tom Lansing, too, and he was cleared. "You men go back to your rooms," Captain Jenkins ordered. "Mr. Clark, you'll stay here."

Frank and Pete walked out together, silently. What could he say, Frank thought. Surely there was some mistake.

George Shelton caught up with them and, for once, he seemed subdued, too. "I'm sorry, Barton," he said. "I was hoping the kid hadn't stolen the money. I hope you won't hold it against me that I turned him in."

"No," Frank said mechanically, "you only did what you were supposed to do."

"But don't forget," Pete said impulsively, "he's not really guilty until he's proved guilty."

That was small satisfaction, Frank thought dismally. Everything pointed to Steve's guilt.

An unnatural silence settled over the dorm as the cadets went back to their rooms. In a few moments, Frank heard footsteps and he glanced toward Pete.

"I suppose they're going to search his room," Pete whispered.

Frank stood up quickly. "I know I'll be gigged if they catch me, but I'm going to watch, if I can. I just can't believe Steve would do such a thing."

"Me, too," Pete answered. "Come on."

The two boys opened their door softly, then eased along the wall until they could see into Steve's room through the door crack.

Captain Jenkins and another officer were taking items of clothing and other articles and putting them under the lamp.

"It's funny," the two cadets heard Captain Jenkins say, "but none of these things show any traces of the powder. You'd think, with the quantity that was sprinkled on that wallet, that it would have rubbed off on some other things."

Frank could see Steve standing against the wall. His face was still pale and his fists were clenched until the knuckles showed white.

Captain Jenkins picked up a science magazine and what he saw made him exclaim, "Major! Look here! This really puzzles me."

The other officer stepped over and examined the magazine. "That's strange," he said. "This printing shows faint traces of that powder—look, every letter stands out."

"What do you suppose . . . ?" Captain Jenkins muttered.

"I know!" The major slapped his thigh. "I remember now

when we were studying these procedures in school. We were told then that some printers use this powder in their ink. And, of course, it would show up under the lamp."

"Do you think . . . ?" Captain Jenkins looked toward Steve. "Where did you get this magazine, Mr. Clark?"

"From—from the library, sir," Steve's voice shook slightly. "I got it right after dinner, sir."

"That would account for the fact that his roommate's hands didn't show any traces. He probably hadn't touched the magazine."

Frank saw Captain Jenkins look at Steve again and say, "All right, Mister. It looks as though this may exonerate you. I want you to know, Mr. Clark, that I didn't think you were guilty. But you realize the evidence was against you."

"Yes, sir, thank you, sir." Frank could scarcely hear what Steve said, but he could see the cadet's stiff lips move slightly. He looked as though he would burst into tears any moment.

Frank's chest felt as though a tight band encased it and he found it hard to swallow past the lump in his throat.

"Come on," Pete whispered, tugging at his elbow. "We don't want to get caught."

The pair eased back into their room and closed the door softly.

"Whew!" Pete let out a long breath. "Wasn't that something? And, man, good old Steve isn't guilty!"

"I knew he didn't do it," Frank said firmly. "He just isn't the type."

They heard heavy footsteps in the hall and Pete said, "There go the officers."

Frank went over to the door and opened it a crack, "There —I heard the outside door slam. Come on—let's see Mr. Clark."

The two cadets hurried over and knocked on the door,

then walked in. Steve sat at his desk, his head buried in his arms. He looked up slowly as Frank and Pete came in. When he saw the upper classmen, he stood up and called the room to attention. Frank saw him wipe his eyes surreptitiously and swallow convulsively.

Frank gave him, "At ease, Mister Clark."

"Man, are we glad!" Pete's enthusiasm seemed to clear the air of gloom. "We knew you didn't take the money, Mister."

"We certainly believed you," Frank added. "Boy, that was rugged! Now I know what they mean by circumstantial evidence."

Other cadets crowded into the room now, each congratulating Steve on being proven innocent. Then, at a sudden silence, Frank looked up to see George standing in the doorway. He took a step toward the desk and said, "I'm quite happy, Mr. Clark, that they proved you didn't do it."

"Thank you, sir." Steve looked him straight in the eye, his face stiffening.

"You know, I was the one who turned you in," George said loudly. "I hope you understand. I felt it was my duty." He held out his hand. "Shall we forget about the whole thing?"

Frank held his breath as he watched the big cadet's face. At first it looked like a thundercloud, then, suddenly, he smiled shakily and answered, "All right, sir. I understand. After all, we took the pledge that we wouldn't tolerate anyone among us who stole. And you thought I took the money."

"I'm sorry." George's voice sounded contrite. "I think I've learned a pretty good lesson—not to jump to conclusions so fast. And I've learned something about circumstantial evidence, too. I hope I remember it if I'm ever in charge of men after I graduate." He turned abruptly and left the room.

"Well, that I should live long enough to hear Mr. Shelton apologize!" Pete murmured to Frank.

"Shut up," Frank said, his voice trembling slightly. "I think we all learned a good lesson tonight—including me. I've jumped to plenty of conclusions, too. And I'll have to admit that it took a lot of guts for George to come in here and apologize in front of all of us. Come on, I have some boning to do on history."

A few days later, in one of their meetings, Captain Jenkins said to the cadets, "I just want you men to know that we caught the fellow who was stealing in the two dorms. It was a custodian clear down in the last dorm at the other end. He's confessed. He thought if he confined his stealing to a dorm where he didn't work, he wouldn't get caught. You'll be glad to know he isn't one of our regular custodians —we know they're all good men. This chap is a substitute. The OSI has found his papers were forged and he has a pretty unsavory reputation."

"Well, that's that," Frank said to Pete later. "I'm glad they found the guilty guy. Now we'd better knuckle down and study."

About a week later, George Shelton stopped in to see Pete and Frank one evening. "You know I have my student pilot's license now," he reminded them. "Well, I've been invited to spend the week end in Kansas City and I'm looking for somebody who will take a leave and go along with me, sharing expenses."

Frank looked at Pete, then at George and exclaimed, "Gosh, I'd love to go as far as Prairie View and see my family!"

"Why don't you?" George asked. "It won't cost much. You only need share the gas expense. I'll pay for renting the airplane. Think it over."

When he had left, Frank asked, "Why don't you come too,

Pete? We could have a ball. And besides, we'd split the gas three ways—you know Scotch me. Mom would be tickled pink to have you."

Pete's eyes lighted up. "I'd love it!" he exclaimed. "I'm going to start packing right now."

As Frank got his books together for class, he had a few feelings of doubt. George hadn't had too much experience as a pilot, and he *was* impulsive sometimes.

"I hope we aren't making a mistake, going with Shelton," he said to Pete later. "He's pretty set in his ways and if he makes a mistake, he sure hates to admit it."

"Well, we know a little bit about flying ourselves. Among the three of us, we ought to be able to get there and back."

"I hope so." Frank frowned, then brightened. "Gosh, just think of it, Pete—to fly home for the week end!"

14

~~~~~

On the Hairy Edge

A couple of nights later, Bob dropped in on Frank and Pete in their room, when they were talking over plans for the week end with George. "Gosh, you guys really are lucky! I wish I could go with you," he said enviously, his eyes shining. "What are you going to fly?"

"I've rented a Cessna 170 from the Sky High Airport. It's a little honey," George told him.

"But what will you do if the weather socks in? You guys *have* to get back or you'll really be pounding the ramp."

"Well, unless it gets too bad, *I'll* fly it," George said confidently. "That 170 has a turn and bank and sensitive altimeter. Don't worry," he continued, as Bob frowned, "I've been boning up on things. Got a swell book on instrument flying at the library."

"It takes more than just reading about it in a book." Bob looked questioningly at Frank.

"Well, I had two hours in the Link trainer last year, besides," George went on. "I know I could fly the stuff if I

159

had to. At least, I know enough to climb up on top and let down through at destination!"

"Yes," Frank said uncertainly. "George has logged quite a few hours. I *know* we'll be all right." He wasn't so sure, though. Once again, he began to wonder if he'd done right in planning this trip. But he couldn't back out now!

"I don't know," Bob went on dubiously. "You've never done any flying in the soup. Remember that flying safety lecture we had? They say you can't do it without practice."

"Don't let them kid you," the big cadet swaggered to the door. "There's a man in my home town who owns a Bonanza. Does it all the time. Climbs up on top of the stuff, flies in the clear, then lets down through it when he figures he's about reached destination. He says it's easy. You just have to get things trimmed up right. But don't worry. I've arranged with the U. S. Weather Bureau to give me CAVU.* "

When George had left, Frank looked at Bob and then Pete uncertainly. "I hope we haven't made a mistake in going on this trip," he said. "Shelton has been a pretty good guy lately. But whenever he gets a little authority or is in charge of something, he really pulls brass."

Pete was silent, but he looked rather worried.

Bob said, "I don't know about that guy—I just hope he knows what he's talking about."

"Well, Pete, what do you think?" Frank asked his roommate. "Shall we tell him we've changed our minds?"

Pete hesitated, then shook his head. "No, I'm willing to take a chance, if you are. Among the three of us, we ought to be able to get a little old Cessna back here without any trouble."

"That settles it." Frank turned to Bob. "We'll probably have a lot to tell you when we get back."

---

* CAVU—Ceiling and Visibility Unlimited.

Bob brightened. "I hope so. Anyway, I still envy you two. It would be wonderful to fly that bird on your own."

That week end as the three cadets took off in the bright Colorado sunshine Frank thought how silly he would be to hesitate, even for a minute, to take advantage of this chance.

The Cessna was equipped with dual controls and the trio took turns flying it and navigating.

"Here's where our hours on navigating missions pay off," Pete shouted happily. He looked at his map. "We're right on schedule. There's Hays, Kansas down there now."

In almost no time, they were coming in for a landing at Prairie View airport. It looked much smaller from the air than it did when you were below, Frank realized. He glanced at George nervously and hoped the inexperienced pilot wouldn't overshoot it.

However, George set the Cessna down like an old pro.

"Good work, man!" Frank congratulated George. "You did a swell job. I wish I had enough hours to solo and land."

"That was great," Pete added. "I'll raise your wages next Saturday," he continued as he climbed out of the aircraft.

After taking on more gasoline, George flew off after making arrangements to pick his flying companions up on Sunday afternoon.

It had been a wonderful week end, Frank thought, after his parents had driven him and Pete back to the airport on Sunday. He and his roommate had slept late, had gone to church, had eaten a hundred or more cookies and all the good food his mother had cooked for them. And his friends had liked Pete immediately and included him in their good-time plans. But best of all was the fact that his father seemed so much better.

Frank was a little worried now, though. He'd listened to some weather reports over the radio and it sounded as though they might run into some trouble as they flew toward Denver. He noticed a little haze when he looked at trees in the distance. The sky was overcast.

George came in on schedule. He immediately called the weather bureau from the airport and asked, "Can you tell me what the flying weather will be between Prairie View and Denver, taking off about two o'clock?"

Frank could hear the weatherman's voice saying, "We're estimating 3000 feet and four miles at Prairie View at two o'clock, lowering to 1000 and two miles between Prairie View and Goodland by four o'clock. Tops at 6000. From Goodland on there should be gradual improvement west with 10,000 foot broken, 13,000 overcast and ten miles by five o'clock. The winds at 5000 estimated 20 to 30 knots from 290 degrees."

"Thanks," said George as he hung up the receiver.

"Well, the weather's not too hot," George said to Mr. Watkins, the airport manager, and a good friend of Frank's parents. "We've got some marginal stuff between here and Goodland. But I know I can make it. The lowest forecast was 1000 feet."

"That's cutting it a little thin." Mr. Watkins shook his head. "The way things work out around here, they can miss that by 500 feet or so. Then you'll be right on the deck to keep under the stuff. Visibility doesn't look so hot, either."

"I'm not worried," George assured him.

Pete muttered in Frank's ear as the two followed George out to the runway, "I don't know—I think he's getting a little cocky and I don't like it. We ought to file a flight plan.

Then if anything happens, they'd at least know where to start looking."

"I know—but we just came along for the ride, remember? I don't think George is in any mood to argue," Frank replied, reluctant to start any unpleasantness.

The three cadets climbed in the airplane and in a few minutes, they were airborne, winging westward. A short while later, George yelled over the engine noise, "Those weather birds surely can miss it! This ceiling's a lot more like 2000 than 3000 feet. Getting hazy, too. Guess I'd better drop down a bit."

He flew lower and, for a while, all went well. But Frank kept looking apprehensively at the clouds, which were getting lower and lower. George was forced down again.

"We're only about 500 feet above the ground," Pete shouted. "I don't like it."

"Where do you think we are?" George asked. "Seems to me there ought to be a town over to the left somewhere."

Pete consulted the map and made some rapid calculations with his computer while Frank peered out the window. "I can't see far in this darn haze," the latter announced after a while.

"We ought to be coming to a railroad in about five minutes. We can follow that to the north of Hill City and on into Goodland," George said.

They continued flying for what seemed ages to Frank, but they didn't see any railroad. Finally, Pete grabbed George's shoulder and yelled, "There's the railroad—see—off to the right."

George looked at it and made a wry face. "It's going in the wrong direction." He was silent for a moment, before admitting, "I'm really confused now. What did the weather man say was tops."

Frank answered, "6000 feet—why?"

"That's not so high. I'm going upstairs. If we can fly on top, we'll pick up Goodland Omni.* Then we can drop down through the stuff west of Goodland."

Frank saw the pilot take a deep breath, trim the stabilizer for climb and apply more power. The haziness increased. Frank glanced below and saw the ground grow dim and finally disappear from view. They were entirely surrounded by a heavy white mist. For a minute, he felt a certain giddiness, then he pulled himself together and glanced back over his shoulder at Pete.

The cadet was braced back in his seat, staring out the window. His lips were pressed tightly in a firm line, but both his ears and his freckles stuck out prominently, as they always did when he was excited or scared or worried.

Frank turned toward George. The pilot's forehead glistened with perspiration and his lips moved. Frank could almost read what he was saying aloud, "Needle, ball and airspeed." He knew now that George was plenty worried and was trying to concentrate on the instruments. How he wished they had a directional gyro and artificial horizon!

Frank saw the ball in the turn-and-bank indicator slide go a little to the left, but George corrected quickly with the left rudder. Good! Frank breathed a sigh of relief. Now the ball was slightly to the right of center, but not far enough to make any difference. The needle was to the left, though. These readings indicated crossed controls and hence they might not be turning, even though in a bank.

He saw George give the plane the right rudder and aileron. Frank realized that the pilot had been concentrating on the turn and bank so much he'd forgotten the airspeed. It had fallen off quite a bit.

"Get the nose down before you stall," Frank shouted.

---

* Omni—a radio navigation station.

George put forward pressure on the wheel. The air speed increased. Frank glanced at the air-speed indicator. They were doing 100, then 110, 120. He realized that George had overcorrected and now their nose was too low. The pilot must have realized it too, because he pulled back on the stick.

Frank glanced at the turn indicator as they banked. The plane was in left turn again, and again George gave it the right rudder and right aileron. Frank looked at the compass —maybe that could help them. But it was swinging, and he couldn't read it. Was that 45 degrees or 55 degrees?

"I think we're heading northeast," Frank called. "We want to go west."

He could see George feed in left rudder and aileron cautiously. That did it. They made a nice coordinated turn to the left, then Frank realized that the cadet pilot probably didn't know how far to turn. He'd heard that the compass had a lead effect—or was it a lag—to the north. Anyway, he recalled some officer saying that you couldn't trust a magnetic compass in a turn.

He pressed George's shoulder and ordered, bending over close to his ear, "Level out now so we can read the compass."

George nodded. He used the right rudder, right aileron and brought the nose down. Frank sighed with relief as the needle centered, and the ball centered. The compass read 340 degrees.

Then he tensed again. Something was wrong. They were in a right turn. He knew it. He could feel it. He stared at the compass. Why should the needle be centered when they were turning right? The instrument must have gone bad. What a time to have it fail! He could feel the airplane turning positively, relentlessly in a right direction. The engine was revving up badly, too.

Frank didn't realize that he was gripped by vertigo—that

like most uninitiated pilots, he had made the common mistake of losing confidence in his instruments and believing his confused senses, which, after all, were designed for walking on the ground, instead of flying through clouds.

He felt Pete grab his shoulder and saw him point to the altimeter. To his horror, he saw it was unwinding swiftly.

"We're dropping fast!" he yelled at George. "Give it the left rudder and left aileron." Maybe that would get it out of the right turn and then come back on the wheel to check the airspeed.

Perspiration ran down George's face and he clutched the wheel convulsively. *You can't do it without practice,* Frank remembered the officers saying that over and over.

"I'm going up—up on top," George yelled. "Don't worry, we'll be all right." He gave the airplane more left rudder and pulled back on the wheel.

Frank thought the airspeed seemed to be building up as George pulled back on the wheel. He felt himself pressing into his seat. Why didn't the elevator respond? He could see that the wheel was almost all the way back now. He glanced at the needle and it was far to the left.

Suddenly, with a cold chill, he remembered something he'd read about the tight spiral—the deadly maneuver that sometimes yanked the wings off an airplane in the clouds. They were probably in a tight turn, and, when George pulled back on the wheel, he was simply tightening up on the turn. He didn't dare put forward pressure on the wheel —that would only result in a faster dive.

Frank saw with dismay that the airspeed needle was hovering around the readline. Structural damage could occur at any time. "Pull the throttle all the way back," he yelled. How he longed for those comforting chutes they had on navigation missions. Now was when they really needed them.

Frank could see George staring at the altimeter, which was unwinding fast. He knew the pilot dared not pull back nor push forward on the wheel. Had the trap closed around them? Would they hit the ground before they pulled the wings off? What difference did it make which came first?

Suddenly, Frank remembered something he'd read somewhere. Level the wing! That was it! "Get the left wing up. Right rudder, right aileron and get the nose down." He sank his fingers into George's shoulder as he yelled the instructions.

That did it. The needle and ball were centered. George eased up a bit on his backward pressure on the wheel but must have overcorrected and dropped the nose far below the horizon, he realized. He could see the airspeed was slightly over the warning red line on the dial. Would George be able to pull out in time?

Frank watched him slowly and gingerly apply back pressure on the wheel. His body pressed downward in the seat. Would the airplane hang together? He knew the stresses were terrific and he was afraid to look at the altimeter. They surely must be near the ground now!

Frank glanced out the window and, suddenly, there were dark patches in the mist. The whiteness seemed to be breaking up as they dived through it. The air speed needle backed off from the ominous red mark on the dial. How long had it been? It could have been hours—or only a minute. Time had no meaning. He was limp as a rag doll and numb all over.

Now they seemed to be flying level with the top of a tree off their left wing. They were out of the overcast, though it was still close above. A wave of relief swept over Frank as George jammed the throttle forward. He could hardly believe in their luck!

Then the engine coughed and spit. There was silence as

Frank stared unbelievingly at the prop, stopped in horizontal position.

"Of course," George said hoarsely, through stiff lips, "the carburetor heat. When we took that dive through the clouds with the engine throttled, there was no carb heat. Our carburetor has iced up. What could I expect?"

Frank strained frantically toward the windows, looking for a place to land—a field—*any field*, he prayed, that's halfway level. "There—" He grabbed George's arm. "That field looks pretty good. At least there aren't any trees." He could feel George shaking as he clung to his arm. The pilot was in no shape to have good judgment on a landing. Well, Frank thought hopelessly, this one didn't need any judgment. There was only one place to go—straight ahead.

George's face was strained and his eyes bugged out with effort as he tried to steer the plane. Frank glanced quickly over his shoulder at Pete. He was chalk white, his eyes were screwed tight shut and his mouth worked, but no words came.

Frank turned back to the air speed indicator. The airspeed dropped to 70 then 65. They were settling fast. He hoped they wouldn't stall now. He saw George ease forward a little.

"Watch that fence!" Frank yelled. "We're going to hit it!" But they didn't. Some miracle took them over the top with only inches to spare. Frank caught his breath sharply. Now he noticed that the field was shorter than he had first thought. "Pull back on the wheel," he ordered loudly. "We'll have to get it on the ground fast."

Then the bottom seemed to drop out of things, as the airplane stalled and hit the ground with a jarring thud. Too late, Frank and George saw the ditch ahead. If George applied the brakes too soon, he'd nose over. But if he hit the ditch with any speed, he'd wreck the plane for sure.

Frank could feel him applying the brakes gingerly. The tail came up. "Not yet," he said. The plane slowed down. "Brake it again, a little."

George was obeying Frank's orders automatically now, apparently with no thought of his own. The airplane slowed to a halt on the edge of the ditch, seemed to perch uncertainly on the edge, then very slowly slid down the incline and came to rest, tail in the air and prop spinner touching the ground.

For a minute, there was no sound in the aircraft as the three cadets sat in stunned silence. Then George dropped his head forward on the wheel and shuddering sobs came from him. Frank took a deep breath and exhaled slowly, as if testing his lungs. He turned and looked at Pete, who sat perfectly still, staring straight ahead.

Frank braced his hand against the instrument panel, to keep himself from sliding forward as he unfastened his seat belt. He tried the door, but it was jammed. He struggled to get it open for some time. Finally he raised the handle, gave the door a desperate blow with his fist and—it opened. He climbed out, still shaking. When his feet touched the ground, he had a wild impulse to kneel down and kiss the earth.

George followed him slowly, trying to control himself, still not saying a word. Frank went back to the door and leaned inside. "Come on, Pete," he urged. "We're on terra firma." He tried the feeble joke, hoping it would help the other cadet.

Pete unfastened his belt and climbed out. He stood for a moment, looking around as if he couldn't believe his eyes. Then he walked over to George, put his face close to the other cadet's and said, "You rat!" His voice rose in a high squeak, as it always did when he was upset or excited. "If

I didn't have the energy drained out of me, I'd knock the stuffing out of you."

Frank grabbed his shoulder and pulled him back. "Lay off," he ordered sharply. "He did all right. We're alive, aren't we?"

"If I had the strength, I'd take him apart, piece by piece," Pete muttered, some of the color coming back into his face.

"I don't blame you," George said, his voice so low Frank had to strain forward to hear him. "I deserve anything you want to do to me."

"Aw, cut it out." Frank felt his ability to act coming back to him. After all, they'd had a close call, but they were alive and that was all that mattered right now. "We had a narrow squeak. But *we're all right*. That's what counts," he told the others.

George leaned against the airplane as if he were too tired to move.

"I'll look it over," Frank offered. "Come on, Pete, let's see how much damage was done."

Pete followed him around the plane, still muttering to himself as he wiped the perspiration off his face with his sleeve. They were happy to find little damage—just a dent in the right wing tip, where it had come to rest against the opposite side of the shallow ditch.

Frank walked around to the left wing tip. Then a cold shiver ran through him as his eye caught sight of something green. There was a piece of reflecting plastic outboard of the wing light. Caught in the crevice between the plastic and the wing was a piece of leaf.

They must have snagged it from that tree with their left wing when they pulled out of the overcast. Frank gazed silently at the bit of leaf. That close! It had been that close! What a small margin between life and death, he thought. Gingerly, he took the scrap of leaf from the wing tip and put it in his wallet. They'd have enough explaining to do without letting the authorities see *that*.

Then he recalled what Major Foster had said to the trainees, that first day they'd been soaring in the gliders. *Aviation in itself is not inherently dangerous. But, like the sea, it is terribly unforgiving of any carelessness, incapacity, or neglect.* How true, Frank thought. They'd been lucky this time, although they didn't deserve it, he knew. They had broken too many flying rules. The principal one they'd disobeyed was flying through an overcast.

He, Frank, should have insisted on landing someplace as soon as the ceiling came down. He knew they shouldn't try to fly through clouds without the correct instruments. But he had allowed George to make all the decisions, so he, Frank, was equally to blame. One thing was sure—he'd learned a very dear lesson which he'd never forget.

"Come on," he said. "I saw a farm house about a mile from here. We'd better walk over there and start telephoning."

As the three cadets started across the field, George said, "Thanks, Barton, for helping me. I never would have made it if you hadn't taken over the way you did."

"I didn't do much. I just remembered a few things as we went along."

"I'll never forget it," George said earnestly. "And I've learned a good lesson. I hope it sticks with me the rest of my life."

"Well," Pete said, trailing behind, "I might be able to overlook some of this later, but I'll have to wait until I recover my breath."

Frank grinned back at him. Pete was returning to normal. He wasn't the kind to hold a grudge for long. Some day they'd probably look back on this experience and maybe even be able to laugh about it—at least a little. But right now he was too shaken. He alone knew how close they had come to disaster.

They didn't have to walk far, because the farmer had seen them land and came out to meet them in his car. He took them back to the farmhouse, where they telephoned the airport in Denver and reported the accident. "Sky Port Rental Service will send somebody out to repair and pick up the Cessna," George said as he hung up the receiver. Then he sighed with relief. "Thank goodness they carry insurance to cover accidents like this, or we'd probably be in hock for years."

Then the farmer drove them to the nearest town, where they caught a bus. From the bus station, they took a cab. As they drove into the Academy grounds, Frank looked at his watch and said, "Well, we're five minutes late. That means some demerits."

Pete answered, "I don't even care if we are late. Good old Air Force Academy, here we come! You don't know how near we were to not getting back." His voice shook slightly.

Next day, George came into the room where Frank and Pete were studying and said, "Well, I had my pilot license suspended for six months by the CAA.* It serves me right. And I hate to tell you men, but we all got '6 and 6' ** for being five minutes late."

Pete responded quietly, "For the first time since I've been at the Academy, I don't mind walking that ramp out there. I'm just glad for one thing—I'm all in one piece to walk it!"

---

* CAA—Civil Aeronautics Association.
** "6 and 6"—six demerits and six walking tours.

15

Problems, Always Problems

It was a busy, jampacked fall, with activities piling up one after another. "Sometimes I meet myself coming and going out of this dorm," Pete complained. "I don't know where the time goes—time off is my rarest commodity."

"I know what you mean," Frank answered. "Last year I didn't think we could possibly have any more pressure put on us. This year it seems worse than ever."

"I suppose I was crazy to take on more assignments by working on the *Talon*," Pete observed. "Being photography editor this year is fun though. I'm hoping I'll get to be sports editor next year, when we're first classmen."

George Shelton knocked on their door and came in with a wise look on his face. Unexpectedly since their harrowing experience together in the airplane, the three cadets had been on quite friendly terms.

"Listen, you two," George said, "I'm getting awfully fed up on nothing but routine around here."

"We were just saying the same thing," Frank answered.

173

"Any suggestion from you? After all, you're considered the Brain in these parts."

"Thanks, pal. Yes, I've got a good suggestion. Let's get some of the men together, sneak out after hours tonight and bring one of those older airplanes over here from Lowry Field. We could plant it right in front of the Com Shack." *

Pete's face lit up, then he sobered. "It's a swell idea, but I don't want to get any demerits. I have a pretty good record this fall and I want to keep it that way."

"It's all right with me," Frank said. "You name the time."

"Make it 0130 hours, and I'll round up some other men to help."

At that, Pete changed his mind and said he would go along.

The two roommates set their alarm clock and when it went off under his pillow, Frank was awfully tempted to just forget the whole deal. But he didn't. Pete complained when Frank dragged him out of bed, but soon the pair crept out of the dorm and joined the other fellows who were in on the stunt.

They had started across the area, keeping well in the shade of the buildings, when, suddenly, an officer came around the corner. It was Lieutenant Porter. He stopped short when he saw the huddled group of cadets.

Frank groaned. "This is it!" he whispered to Pete. "Now we'll get gigged and won't have our fun, either."

But this time he was wrong about the young officer. After George had told him what they planned to do, Lieutenant Porter said, "You'll probably need some help. I'll get a jeep and take you over to Lowry No. 1."

"Blow me down!" Pete muttered. "Will wonders never cease?"

---

* Com Shack—Commandant's headquarters. Also known as "Head Shed."

The officer took the cadets over to the hangar and helped them select an old plane. Because they had no tow bar, they had to attach the aircraft to the jeep by a rope. The lieutenant called the Control Tower and requested permission to tow the plane across the active runway to the Academy.

The request was granted and the group waited at the runway until the tower flashed the green light. Then they towed the aircraft across and finally managed to get it onto the Academy grounds, where they placed it right in front of the Com Shack door. All went well until they were ready to tie it into position.

Suddenly, they all heard an automobile coming down the road. The cadets dropped the rope and scrambled into the jeep—all except Pete, who got tangled in the rope and fell sprawling.

Lieutenant Porter called urgently, "Come on—we've got to get out of here!"

Frank ran back and grabbed Pete, pulling him to his feet. They galloped in pursuit of the jeep until the other cadets managed to haul them in.

They saw the AOC jump out of his car and run up to the airplane. By that time, the jeep had turned the corner. Lieutenant Porter drove the cadets up to their dorms, where they spilled out and ran for their rooms.

"That was a close call," Pete said as he and Frank crawled back in bed.

"Man, were *we* lucky?" Frank pulled the covers up and turned over.

But they didn't think they were quite so lucky the next day when they stopped in front of the bulletin board and saw their names posted.

"Well, I'll be . . . ," Pete stared stupidly at the notice. "How did Major Sellers know we were the guilty ones last night?"

At that moment, George walked up. Without looking at the notice, he remarked, "Well, we got gigged, didn't we? I just saw Major Sellers down on the area and he said for me to tell all those smart guys who pushed that aircraft up in front of Head Shed to report at 1630 hours and push it back where it belongs."

"How did he know we did it?" Frank demanded.

"He'd inspected our rooms and found us absent." George shook his head. "He's too observing!"

Lieutenant Porter joined the trio at the bulletin board and looked at the list. "Well, men, if you must play these little tricks to let off steam, and get caught, you have to pay for it," was his only comment.

As Frank watched him walk away he said, "You know, Old Porter isn't too bad at times. I think if I stay around here long enough, I might even get to like him."

Frank was enjoying his football experience more this fall. He'd had a chance to play for a few minutes in every game early in the season, and it gave him more confidence in himself.

"I think it's great that you've been in action during the games this year," Pete complimented him. "You're doing all right."

"Well, I'll admit it's a little more fun than sitting on the bench through every game. But I have no illusions about myself. I'll never be a big player. I'll probably always be one of the substitutes."

"They're important, too," Pete reminded him. "If you can help build our team, you should be proud."

"I am," Frank said sincerely. "And I'll be there every game, whether I get to play or not."

A few nights before the University of Denver game, somebody painted the letters "AFA" over the DU stadium. There was a great deal of hub-bub over the trick and DU threatened to retaliate.

"It would be just like them to steal one of our static aircraft * out in the area," Pete said. "I think I'll get a bunch of the men together and we'll watch tonight."

"Say—," Frank stood up so fast he knocked his chair over. "That reminds me. I have to see Captain Linstrom about something."

"How about it? Can you stay up tonight and help guard?"

"No," Frank answered firmly, "I have to keep hours—you know I'm in training."

The next morning, just before the buzzer sounded for the cadets to get up, a very sleepy Pete stumbled into their room. "Man, am I bushed! I'm going to sack out," he murmured as he undressed.

"You can't miss chow," Frank protested.

"Yes, I can. I have permission."

"First tell me what happened last night," Frank demanded.

Pete yawned loudly. "We got permission from the Head Shed to keep watch all night, so that none of those guys from DU could sneak in and do any damage. The brass even gave us walkie talkies and we stationed men at intervals all along the fence. We had a system all worked out. Different dorms supplied men throughout the night."

"Did you have any trouble?"

"Not too much," Pete answered as he crawled into bed. "Several carloads of guys came around different times in the night." Then, suddenly, he sat up in bed, his eyes open wide. "Gosh, I'm so bushed, I forgot to tell you! One thing

---

* static aircraft—obsolete planes placed on the area for "atmosphere."

did happen. A couple of fellows crawled over the fence and sneaked up to the falconry. They swiped Mach One."

Frank threw back his head and laughed loudly.

Pete looked at him in astonishment. "Did you hear what I said? They stole our mascot. I don't think it's a laughing matter. They got away before we could catch them."

"Well, those fellows got the surprise of their lives," Frank said, still chuckling. "I told Captain Linstrom yesterday afternoon that they might try to steal our falcons, so we put some chickens in the falconry instead and that's what your DU friends swiped."

Pete hooted with joy. "Wait till the men hear this!" he cried. "Be sure and announce it at breakfast." He turned over and closed his eyes, then murmured, "Maybe you didn't get to take part in the night's activities, but you ought to be decorated for responding to the threat beyond and above the call of duty."

From time to time during the fall, Frank tried to find chances to talk with Steve Clark. "I don't know why it is, but I feel kind of responsible for him," he confided to Pete. "I think he's a good man and I worry that he might get turned out or just quit."

"Are you sure you aren't just wasting your time? If a man isn't sold on this place, should he be encouraged to stay?"

"If he's a good man like Steve, yes—at least, that's the way I feel about it. And I'm going to keep trying in every way to encourage him."

Fortunately, Steve was in his Flight, so Frank worked with him and had a chance to discuss things with him from time to time. In addition, whenever Frank saw the young cadet in the library or any other place in the area, he would stop and talk with him.

There were the afternoons when they went soaring, too.

Steve was always at his best then. Anything having to do directly with aircraft seemed to bring out his enthusiasm.

He seemed to like Frank and he loved to discuss flying in general and his experiences as a CAP cadet in particular with him.

"Gosh, that was wonderful, sir," he said one day. "Those men in the Civil Air Patrol spent a lot of time with us kids. I'm even thankful for the drilling they gave us. It helped me here, sir."

"You're really sold on the program, aren't you?" Frank asked.

"To the hilt—I think it's great for boys in high school and I'll always be grateful for my training. It's good for men— and girls, too. It's one way of getting into the blue."

But Steve had his problem days, too, and that was when Frank noticed that his work in the Flight suffered. One day Frank took the younger cadet aside and told him that he'd like to help him.

"What's the matter, Mister?" Frank asked.

Steve's dark brows drew together in a frown. "Sir—it's just that—well, I guess I'm pretty mixed up."

"Would you like to talk it over?"

"Yes, sir. Thank you, sir. You see—it's my dad. He's been sick—had a serious operation, and well, sir," the cadet stopped and swallowed, then continued, "the doctors aren't really sure he's going to make it."

Pity swept through Frank. He felt a close sense of sympathy with the other cadet. "I'm sorry, Mister. I know how rugged this is. My dad's been sick, too. He has a bad heart —although he has improved a lot. It's tough to stick enthusiastically by a job when you feel maybe you ought to go home and help instead."

Steve nodded in agreement. "I'm afraid, sir, it hasn't improved my attitude here. Besides, sometimes I feel that the stuff they make us do is so silly when there are more important things happening in the world, sir."

"Discipline really racks you, doesn't it, Mister Clark? But I think some of the rough edges are wearing off a little. You don't bristle quite as much as you did at first."

"Sir, I try. But sometimes, when I have to quote a lot of stuff and nonsense, it almost chokes me. And that ramrod stuff—'eyes caged' and 'chin in' and all that kind of junk—makes me sick, sir."

"I think you're missing the point, Mister Clark. This 'junk' that you're talking about is just a means to an end. I don't mind telling you that I felt the same way about a lot of the discipline when I first came. But now I can see some of the other sides, too. I guess being a second classman helps."

"Yes, sir."

"One of the first things you have to learn at this Academy is that the officers make everything as tough as they can to see if the cadet has the staying quality the Academy wants in its men. That's part of the reason behind some of these things we have to do. But all of this does have its compensations, too."

"Compensations, sir? What compensations?" Steve asked bitterly.

"One of the chief compensations is gaining the ability to discipline yourself. That's the hardest job of all. I don't mean that I've surmounted the job yet—I'm still working on it—and plenty. But let me tell you, Mister, I'm a lot better at it than I was two years ago, when I was a doolie."

Steve looked at him soberly. "Yes, sir. Thank you, sir. I'll remember what you've told me, sir."

"Why don't you talk it over with Colonel Oberg, Mister? You know, he's in the counselling department. He's a terrific officer and very understanding. I always talk to him when I'm down in the dumps."

Steve swallowed, then said, "I will, sir. Thank you again, sir."

A couple of weeks before Christmas, Pete burst into his room, brimming with news. "Guess what? I've just been talking with some other fellows and we've planned a big surprise for the doolies for Christmas."

"What is it?"

"There's a meeting in Bob's room tonight, just before taps. We'll talk it over then." Pete smiled mysteriously.

16

Surprise for Christmas

Two weeks later, Frank asked, "Can you possibly give me a scientific explanation about time and the way it gallops just before Christmas leave?" He was frantically pushing things into his B-4 bag.

"There isn't any answer, pal." Pete's voice was muffled by the pile of clothes he was carrying from locker to bed. "Of course, I imagine that time's dragging for those poor old doolies because they think there ain't no Santa Claus."

"Yep, it's tough for the fourth classmen. I remember what sad sacks we were two years ago tonight. And I don't particularly recall getting any sympathy from the ATO's. I think our plan is better." He glanced at his watch. "We'd better post down to Arnold Hall right now for that planned celebration."

It seemed everybody was converging on their social center. And anyone could tell the difference between the fourth classmen and the upper classmen by the anticipatory smiles on the latters' faces, Frank thought.

Inside, the Hall was gaily decorated with Christmas greens, and an air of festivity seemed to hang over the place.

Several cadets lined up the fourth classmen, then Frank stepped in front of them and said, "All right, men, double time back to your dorms. Take a shower, military style, immediately. Dress and return to this hall in one-half hour. You will be supervised by members of the second class."

Frank could sense the feeling of rebellion going through the younger cadets. He knew just how they felt—like taking all the upper classmen apart, piece by piece. He held back a grin because he knew they'd change their tunes before the evening was over.

As the younger cadets ran out, Pete came over and said, "That was the dirtiest order I've ever heard given. I'll bet you are Public Enemy No. 1 to that bunch right about now. I imagine they're a little shook about having to take another shower, since they all took one just before they came over."

Bob came up and said, "Man, oh, man! We used to complain about Hard Nose Porter. He never did anything like this to us. Those poor doolies—all dressed up, plenty of spit and polish and razor-sharp creases in their trousers."

"Don't blame me," Frank protested. "I'm just following the committee's orders."

Twenty-nine minutes after the dismissal, the fourth classmen were all back, standing straight as statues.

Frank stood before them again, his sternest look on his face. "Men, as you know, the upper classmen are going on Christmas leave. We're awfully sorry to tell you we can't take care of all those 10-A's you've miraculously acquired during these past few weeks." He had a hard time keeping his face straight.

The poor doolies stood there like a group of wooden Indians. Frank knew some of them were fighting hard not to look bitter or mad. Some of them might even be holding back tears, he thought. He looked at Steve, whose face had grown dangerously red.

"All right, men," he continued. "Let's break it up. At ease! Relax. Merry Christmas from all of us to all of you!"

Slowly at first, then quickly, something like an electric current rippled through the room. The fourth classmen relaxed their stiff positions. The older cadets started to laugh, then they burst into a song.

Merry Christmas to you! Merry Christmas to you!
Merry Christmas, fourth classmen, Merry Christmas to you!

Frank held up his hand for silence and, when the cadets had quieted down some, he said very seriously "We really want you to have a good holiday. Don't think we don't realize how tough it is not to go home at Christmas. We've been through that and we know. You probably forget that we were fourth classmen once. But we've not forgotten and we want to make a joint Christmas gift to all of you."

Two cadets came from another room, carrying a huge box, gaily wrapped in silver and green paper and decorated with silver and gold stars and tied with red and green satin ribbons. They placed it carefully on a table which had been set up in the middle of the floor.

Frank read from the tag attached to the box, "This says 'To the Fourth Classmen from the Second Class.' Will some fourth classman accept this for all of you?"

Several men pushed Cadet John Stewart forward. He and two others, urged by the rest of the class, unwrapped the handsome package. Inside the first box was another box, also gaily wrapped. And so it continued through several boxes, each getting a little smaller.

The cadets laughed and joined in the fun, leaning forward excitedly, hoping that each box would contain the gift. Finally they reached the last box and inside was a wastebasket filled with dozens of 10-A forms. On top of the pile was a scroll and Cadet Stewart read what was written on it: "Merry Christmas, Fourth Classmen, and we hope you will enjoy making a bonfire of all the 10-A's you've earned through your misbehavior. Here they are. They're cancelled AS OF NOW."

Everything was quiet for a second, then the fourth classmen burst into yells and cheers.

"I hope they don't blow the roof off," Pete shouted at Frank. "Did you ever hear such yelling and laughing?"

Frank felt a warm glow surge through him as he thought of what this fun and fellowship between the upperclassmen and the fourth classmen stood for. But there was one more thing he had to do. He must see Steve Clark before he, Frank, took off. He wandered around through groups of cadets, all laughing and visiting informally, until he saw Steve standing over by a door. He hurried over to him.

"Hello, Mister," he said. "I'd like a few words with you."

"Yes, sir," Steve replied.

Frank found a couple of chairs over in a corner, away from some of the confusion. "Mister," he said, "I was talking with Colonel Oberg this morning. He told me he was pretty sure you'd be granted special dispensation to go home for Christmas because of your dad's illness."

There was a long pause. Frank could see that the other cadet was struggling to control his feelings. Finally he spoke. "Thank you, sir. But it didn't go through."

"Didn't go through?" Frank repeated unbelievingly. "I'm sorry to hear that."

"No, sir. I understand it was approved all the way up to the Superintendent himself. He canceled the leave. So—I stay here. That is, unless I just decide to hand in my resignation." Steve looked away as though he didn't want to meet the older cadet's concerned gaze.

Frank's heart sank. This was a real blow to Steve. He drew a deep breath. "I don't know exactly what to say, Mister. First of all, I want you to know I'm sorry. I'd hoped they'd let you go, that it would help your family. But, most of all, I thought it might help you—boost your morale. As Bob Elspy would say, though, it's just the way the ball bounces."

There was another long pause. Frank recalled his fourth class training: a cadet shows no emotion. This was a pretty tough spot to be in—for both of them.

"Sir," Steve broke the silence, "after Colonel Oberg told me I couldn't go home, I was pretty shook. And I'll admit I went back to my room with the full intention of writing out my resignation.

"When I got there, I found a letter from my pal back in high school. He and I both tried out for the Academy appointment and I won. His folks couldn't afford to send him to college, so he went into the regular Air Force. When I saw his letter, sir, the whole thing swept over me. Why, I'd accepted the appointment instead of letting him take it. If I washed out, I'd not only be cheating myself, but I'd be cheating him. I felt lower than a worm. I recalled you told me the same thing last fall and it helped me make my decision. Sir," Steve stood up and held out his hand, "will you please shake hands with me? I've made my New Year's resolution early. I'm going to try to be the best cadet who ever attended this Academy."

Frank jumped to his feet and grasped Steve's hand. "I know you will, Mister. And I'll do everything I can to help you."

"Sir, I'm not kidding myself, though. It's still going to be a tough pull. I'm stubborn and hot-headed and I know the discipline will still get under my skin, but I'll try."

They were interrupted by Pete who came dashing up and

exclaimed, "Mister Barton, if we don't post over and pick up our B-4 bags, we're going to be spending Christmas right here with the doolies."

"I can think of worse things to do," Frank answered as he waved good-by to Steve.

Christmas at home was pleasant for Frank. There was the usual round of skating parties, dances, with lots of good food to consume—and again his father's health seemed to have improved. Throughout the holidays, Frank felt an extra special glow whenever he thought about Steve and the victory the young cadet had won.

Then the cadets were back in school and the well-known Gloom Period engulfed them. "I guess it's just automatic to have a Gloom Period," Pete said one evening. "After all the fun of Christmas at home, things are a little routine and dull around here."

But things weren't quiet. There was always plenty to keep the cadets busy. Academics kept most of them well occupied. Then the extra-curricular activities of all kinds ate up their spare time.

Frank and Pete went skiing several Sundays. They had both learned how to handle themselves well in the famous powder snow of the Rockies.

From time to time, Frank would think about Ann and wonder if he'd ever see or hear from her again. Those were the times when he'd become moody and touchy.

"What's eating on you?" Pete asked sharply one evening, after Frank had snapped him off a couple of times. "You're about as pleasant to have around as a hornet."

"I'm sorry, Pete," Frank said, feeling ashamed of himself. "I was thinking about Ann and wondering what excuse I could make to get to see her."

"She certainly wouldn't want to see you in your present mood. You'd probably bite her head right off."

"I think I'll call her just after study hour tonight. I might as well try again."

"Good for you, roomie! Never say die."

Later that evening, Frank went to the phone booth, where he had to wait for two other cadets to finish their conversations before he got his turn. Then he had trouble getting the long distance operator. Finally, after giving her Ann's number, he heard the busy signal. He let it buzz for about five minutes while two other cadets made caustic remarks about people who tied up the telephone.

Then he gave up in despair as the warning buzzer sounded for lights out. He hung up and ran to his room, slamming the door.

"Any luck?" Pete asked.

"Luck? What's that? I never heard of such a thing in connection with Frank Barton. Just call me 'Hard-luck Barton,' " he retorted. Grabbing up his towel, he started for the shower room.

17

Ann Speaks

Frank was really racking it up in the library one afternoon when Pete came in like a small whirlwind. Frank glanced apprehensively toward the librarian's desk, then breathed a sigh of relief to see he was away.

Pete looked around frantically, finally spotted Frank and came over, saying breathlessly, "Come with me, immediately. It's about Ann." He turned and hurried out.

Frank jumped up, grabbed up his books and cap and followed his roommate into the hall. There he seized the cadet's shoulder and demanded, "What's the matter? Did Ann get hurt?"

Pete looked at him in surprise, then answered, "No, of course not—it's good news." Frank breathed a sigh of relief as Pete continued, "I just saw an announcement in the paper. Ann won the first prize in a national all-collegiate contest for her essay on Peace. She's appearing as a member of a discussion panel on TV in a few minutes. We're headed for Arnold Hall to see it."

Frank walked as if in a daze. Conflicting thoughts crowded through his mind. This was really wonderful for Ann, even though the two of them had been quits for a long time now. An essay on Peace! How ironical, he thought. After all, it had been the whole subject of the best method of attaining peace which had come between them.

He frowned and tightened his lips as he realized this might mean an even closer friendship between her and that —that Craig Brown. He doubled up his fists unconsciously at the idea of the other fellow. That Brown guy certainly thought he was the great crusader for peace! He probably considered himself the prosecuting attorney against the Air Force Academy and all the cadets—especially one.

"Man, it's a great occasion, from the little I had time to read in the paper."

The two friends ran up the steps of Arnold Hall and into the lounge. Several cadets were watching a sports program on the TV set.

"Excuse me, gentlemen," Pete said as he walked up to them. "We have to watch the next program. It's a matter of life and death."

"O.K., O.K.," Tom Henderson said. "Do you mind if we stick around and see what all the excitement's about?"

As he twisted the dial Pete said, "Sure—stay if you want to." Then he glanced at Frank. "I don't think Mr. Barton will mind, even if it is his ex-girl friend on the program."

Frank found his face getting red, but he tried to act nonchalant. He really *did* mind, but he wasn't going to say so. "Stay if you want to," he said shortly. Then he forgot all about the other cadets as Pete tuned in the right station.

The program was already under way. A young man had just finished speaking. He sat down. "Thank you, Mr. Brown," the moderator said. "That was Mr. Craig Brown who just gave his views on 'Why I Believe in Pacifism.'"

Frank started as he recognized the name. Then he gained control of himself, but his heart began to pound and his breathing came fast and shallow.

"Well, if it isn't the creep himself—your rival, old Knothead Brown," Pete said sarcastically. "I'd like to muss up those curly locks for him. We really ought to go down some day and choose that guy. I'd like to work him over."

"Pipe down!" Bill Samanski exclaimed. "This sounds interesting."

The moderator was saying, "We're especially proud of our next speaker, Miss Ann Williams, of Colorado College, who is the national collegiate winner of the Willston Peace Fellowship because of her essay, 'Wings for Peace.'"

Frank sat forward, gripping the arms of his chair. The camera focused on Ann, who stood up while the other panel members clapped. Gosh, Frank thought, she's as pretty as ever! His mind flashed back to the first time he'd seen her, wearing her pretty green formal at a dance right here in Arnold Hall.

His thoughts were pulled back by the moderator's voice. "This honor means that Ann will spend next summer at the University of Geneva, attending an International Workshop for Peace." He turned to her and repeated, "Miss Ann Williams."

"Thank you, Mr. Chairman." Ann's soft voice sounded natural in Frank's ears. He held his breath so he wouldn't miss a word.

She continued, "I will only have time here for a summary of my essay, 'Wings for Peace.' I'd like to say that we must use many approaches for peace. And this doesn't mean just the military man. It means the butcher, the baker, the jurist, the housewife—yes, even the student, as he puts into his thinking and conduct the real meaning of democracy and as he cultivates an understanding of what makes a peace-loving world and as he takes on an individual assignment of interpreting a peaceful world community."

The moderator asked, "What about the students' parents—the adults? Does your essay mention them?"

Ann's answer was quick. "Yes, indeed! The businessman as he deals with his trade, both local and foreign; the diplomat as he sits in high places in other lands; the tourist as he travels around the world. Each and all reflect *America*—its best and its worst and all the degrees between.

"It's important for us to be good representatives of the best our country has to offer, educationally, morally and spiritually. If we worked as hard at peace and democracy as the Soviet Union and other world powers work for their beliefs, in a measure we might deserve the freedom on which our country was founded."

Frank saw her eyes sparkle and her voice took on greater animation as she continued, "If we love our country, we must keep it safe. Study, perfection of skills in human relations, understanding of the peoples of the world—each of these are important ingredients for building peace.

"Our hope, of course, is that all the countries in the world want peace as we do. *But*, if we love our country, the rest of the world must know that *if* they won't respect our ideals and our country, and *if* they would damage our country, we will protect these things we love by strength."

Frank sat up straighter and his eyes widened. The moderator interrupted Ann by asking, "Miss Williams, might that interpretation include military preparedness?"

Ann answered quickly, "If necessary, yes. It certainly does not mean turning the other cheek to people who will take advantage. If we would keep the peace, we must become strong and let the world know we have strength. This doesn't preclude our working for world-wide peace. It seems to me the Air Force Academy in our state is training its cadets to be ambassadors of peace. When those men finally fly, it will be with *wings for peace!*"

Several of the cadets applauded and Art Grigsby exclaimed, "Good for her! That's the old spirit!"

Don Burke turned to Frank and asked, "What's the matter with you, Mister Barton? How come you let a real hep gal like that slip through your fingers?"

Frank shook his head as he reached down to pick up his books which he'd tossed on the floor when he'd hurried in to watch the TV program. Then he straightened suddenly. He had an idea!

He jumped up and grabbed Pete's arm. "Pete! I have a brain wave!"

"Well, don't yank my arm off after I've just done you a favor," Pete complained. "Besides, I doubt you could."

"Come along—I hope I find the phone free."

"What's up? What are you going to do?"

"I'm calling that TV station. Maybe I can talk to Ann while she's still there."

"Good idea!" Pete clapped him on the shoulder. "I'll stand by and hold you up. Here," Pete reached in his pocket and brought out some change, "I'll even donate a dime to the cause."

For once, the phone booth was empty. Frank's hand shook as he leafed through the telephone directory. Finally, he found the number and dialed. When the operator answered he asked breathlessly, "If Miss Ann Williams is still in the studio, may I speak with her?"

There was a pause, then Ann's voice said, "Hello? This is Ann Williams speaking."

Frank gulped. . . . "Ann! It's me—I mean, it's I—it's Frank." His voice sounded strange in his ears.

"Why, Frank, how nice to hear from you!"

"I—that is, some of us heard your panel on TV. Gosh, Ann, it was wonderful!"

"Thank you, Frank. I'm glad you heard the speech—it will save me writing you."

"Did you mean it, Ann? Did you mean all that about peace—about being prepared—about strength in the military?"

Ann laughed softly. "Of course I meant it. You know I wouldn't write an essay like that if I didn't believe in what I was writing."

Frank took a deep breath. "Gosh, Ann, that was wonderful, you know, what you said about the Air Force Academy—about our flying with *wings for peace.*"

"That's what you'll be doing, so why shouldn't I say it," the girl answered. There was a short pause, then she asked impulsively, "Frank, do you still have those silver wings I used to wear? Or have you given them to someone else? I know I was silly and—and stupid ever to question you—"

Frank heard her voice quaver and he answered hurriedly, "I still have them in my desk drawer, Ann. Would you—"

But she interrupted him, "Will you send them back, Frank? Nothing would make me happier or prouder than to wear them again."

"I won't send them—I'll bring them in person," Frank almost shouted into the phone. "I have an open post this week end, and I hope you haven't planned to do anything except see me."

"I'll—I'll clear the ramp," she promised. "Now, I must hang up. The rest of the panel is yelling at me—we'll be late."

"Oh, gosh, Ann, wait a minute!" Frank begged desperately. "I forgot to congratulate you on winning that prize."

"Thanks, Frank—darling." She hung up.

He put the receiver back on the hook slowly and drew

a deep breath. Then he turned and looked dazedly at Pete, who was grinning widely.

Frank tried to cover his emotion by saying, "You look exactly like a Cheshire cat. What's so funny?"

Pete chuckled. "I suppose I'll have to listen to 'Love's Old Sweet Song' from now on. Ho, hum! Well, I guess I can stand it—but it will be hard."

The next Saturday, after parade, Frank caught a bus for Colorado Springs. He'd written Ann a short note, asking her if she could pack a picnic lunch—he had someplace he wanted to show her and they'd need something to eat before they returned.

When Frank arrived at Ann's dorm he found that she had borrowed her roommate's car, and now they swung north on the highway. "Where are we going?" Ann asked.

"I thought we'd drive up to the new site where the Academy is being built. Then I have other plans."

Ann laughed happily. "You sound so mysterious. I won't ask you any more questions."

They spent some time driving and walking among the Academy buildings which were rising rapidly on every side. Frank explained what each one would be—the dorm, the academic building, the dining hall, the administration building.

"Here's where the chapel will be," he indicated an empty area across the way. "But it will probably be the last built because there has been quite a controversy over the design."

"I know—I've read everything I could about this new site."

Finally, they got back in the car and followed a winding dirt road to the northwest. When it ended, Frank turned off the engine and said, "Come on. We hike from here. And let's not forget the lunch. We'll probably need it before we're through."

"You sound like Pete." Ann smiled at him. "Does Pete still eat as much as ever?"

"More—if that's possible." Then Frank fell silent and they walked hand in hand for some time toward a large white rock.

Ann broke the silence by saying, "That's Cathedral Rock, isn't it? I think it's wonderful that they built the Academy so close to it." She paused to get her breath. "It does look like a cathedral, doesn't it? See—there are the towers and even some windows. Do you see that spiral staircase twisting around one of the towers?"

Frank laughed. "Yes, if I use my imagination real hard. Right now, though, I'm interested in something very real. Oh, it includes Cathedral Rock, don't worry. In fact, I hope to start a tradition here for the Academy."

"What do you mean?"

"You've probably read about Flirtation Walk at West Point and the famous Kissing Rock. Tradition there says that, if a girl refuses to kiss the cadet who walks underneath it with her, the Rock will fall." Frank paused, then rushed on, "We need something like that here and I propose to make it Cathedral Rock."

He put his arm around Ann and drew her toward him. "You wouldn't want Cathedral Rock to crumble into a thousand pieces, would you? Well, that's what's going to happen if you don't kiss me *right now.*"

Several minutes later, Ann said, "You've forgotten something, Frank."

The cadet looked at her blankly. "What?"

"You told me on the phone last week that you were going to deliver something in person."

Frank grinned and reached in his pocket. "The wings," he said, bringing them out and pinning them on her dress. "Now they're back where they belong."

Ann put her hand up and touched them lightly. "I'll never give them up again, Frank. That is a promise."

Later, they found a spot under some pine trees where they spread out the lunch. Not far away was a barbed wire fence, marking the boundary of the Academy grounds. Just as they finished eating and Ann had put the scraps back into the box, an old man and a sheep dog came along the fence.

Ann jumped to her feet. "Let's go talk with him," she suggested. "I'll bet he could tell us some interesting tales about this part of the country."

Frank introduced himself and Ann to the old fellow, who said his name was Lon Catlett. "I'm what you might call a handy man around here," he explained. "This is the old Pring Ranch—belongs to Mr. Walker now. My duty is to mend the fences and do odd jobs." He patted the big dog's head. "This here is Shep."

"Have you lived here long, Mr. Catlett?" Ann asked.

"Nigh onto forty year," the old man answered. "That is, around these parts. But I've lived in Colorado all my life— I'll be eighty years old next month," he said proudly.

"Do you know anything about the history of this part of the country, or where you've worked?" Ann asked eagerly. "Were you ever a miner?"

The old man's leathery face lighted up and his faded blue eyes twinkled. "I don't know if it's history, or not. You don't call it that when you're living it. But yes, I've been a miner—both kinds."

"What do you mean—both kinds?" Frank asked.

"Well, now, young man, I've panned for gold and I've done hard rock mining—that is, where you go down in the earth and dig for gold. My folks were living in Como, up in the mountains, when that cowboy struck gold in Cripple Creek, back of Pikes Peak. We moved down there and I worked in the mines there. In fact, me and my father have worked in almost all the big gold and silver camps in the state at one time or another."

"You mean in Central City and Georgetown?" Ann asked.

"Yep, and Silver Plume, Nevadaville, Leadville, Aspen— even down in the San Juans, at Creede and Ouray and Silverton."

"Did you ever see Baby Doe Tabor?" Ann's eyes were wide now.

"Sure thing. I was just a young feller, but I remember when her and old man Tabor got married at the White House in Washington. Then he lost all his money and died a pauper. So did Baby Doe, you remember?"

Ann nodded, then asked, "Did you ever see Silverheels up in Fairplay?"

The old man chuckled. "I'm not quite that old, young lady! That was afore my time. But I remember seeing the saloon up near Alma which Buckskin Joe, her lover, owned and where she danced. I always felt sorry for that poor gal. First the nice ladies of the town wouldn't have anything to do with her. Then, when they had the big smallpox epidemic and Silverheels nursed so many and saved them, she died herself." He shook his gray head sorrowfully.

"What about Indians—do you remember them?" Frank asked, his interest thoroughly aroused.

"Not too many—they was pretty well cleaned out by the time I was born. Oh, we'd see some once in a while, but it wasn't like in the old days, when they'd ride down out of the hills and attack the wagon trains."

"Were there any Indians around here?" Ann asked.

"Yup, this was Ute and Arapahoe country. They used to fight a lot between themselves. Up there at Manitou Springs is where they'd come to get rid of their rheumatiz and other ailments. Back of this here Rampart Range," he jerked a gnarled finger toward the front range of the Rockies which they faced, "is the old Ute trail. Them Injuns used to ride and walk that trail from South Park to the buffalo country up north."

"Did you know any of the men who built the railroads?" Frank asked. "I've read a little about them and they certainly led interesting and exciting lives."

"Sure thing. There was a parcel of 'em—Dave Moffat, John Evans—but the one I liked the best was General Palmer—you've seen his statue down there in Colorado Springs." The two young people nodded. "He was a humdinger, that Palmer. He built all the narrow-gauge railroads all around this part of the country. He even had a war with the Santy Fe Railroad, down there near Canon City in the Royal Gorge."

"Who won?"

"Palmer, of course, although a lot of folks thought it was a draw." He looked at them closely for a moment, then asked, "You got anything to do with that 'Cademy over there?"

"Yes, sir," Frank answered proudly. "I'm a cadet—second classman. And I'm very proud of our new Academy."

Mr. Catlett squinted toward the site, then said, "Looks like it cost a lot of money. I hope you fellows appreciate it."

"Oh, they do, Mr. Catlett," Ann told him earnestly. "The cadets really study and work hard."

"You heerd anything about a Centennial Celebration next year, young lady?"

Ann nodded. "Yes, we're making plans to help celebrate at Colorado College, where I go to school."

"The Academy is making plans, too, sir," Frank added. "We're planning a museum to hold all kinds of aircraft from all over the world. And we're hoping that the President of the United States will attend our first graduation exercises," Frank said proudly.

"Now that will be real fine," Mr. Catlett approved. "I'll see if I can hustle me a seat. But if I can't, I know some pretty good lookouts back up here in them hills. I'll just get me a place there and watch everything."

Frank smiled. "I hope you can get a seat, sir."

"Seems like I heerded the falcon is your mascot. That true?" When Frank nodded, he continued, "They're good birds—fearless, fast and wise. I don't hold no truck with guys that say they kill chickens. Falcons keep down rodents in the fields—they're good birds—you ought to be proud. There's a Mount Falcon up northwest o' here, in Indian Hills. It's quite a landmark." He paused, then said, "Well, this ain't gettin' my work done. I'd better get busy before Mr. Walker up and fires me. Come on, Shep. It was right nice talkin' to you two."

"Thank you, Mr. Catlett," Ann said. "We enjoyed it so much. You made history come to life."

"That's right," Frank added.

"See that you add to that history, young feller." The old man winked at them as he walked away along the fence, the shaggy dog at his heels.

"That was really an experience," Ann said as she and Frank turned away. "This has been a wonderful afternoon— I'll never forget it."

"Well, I should hope not." Frank smiled and took her hand in his. "Come on, I'll race you to the car."

18

Ring Dance

The following days flew by on jet-powered wings. April rolled into May, with finals and the end of the academic year just around the corner. Frank had been able to get in a few dates with Ann, but toward the end of the month, there just wasn't any time to see her until the Ring Dance.

He wrote her saying,

> Dear Ann,
>
> This is just a reminder that our Ring Dance is next Saturday evening. Our class rings will be presented in the afternoon. Then we're having a class banquet at the Town House. They're both stag affairs, but the dance starts at eight o'clock. I'll see you there. Wear your prettiest dress!
>
> > Love,
> >
> > Frank

And now it was Saturday and Frank and Pete went to the auditorium, where they joined their classmates. After a brief introduction, General Saunders said, "One of the things that a graduate of a military academy cherishes long-

est as a symbol of his school and his military way of life is
his Class Ring. It becomes the physical embodiment of the
loyalty and memories that the graduate has of the Academy
and his class."

The speaker held a ring in his hand, and every eye was
turned to it.

"The Ring Committee of the Class of '59 is to be congratulated," General Saunders continued, "on its hard work.
For two years they've striven to choose and design a ring
that would reflect the spirit and pride of the first graduating
class. This, I believe, they have accomplished. The white-
gold chosen differs from those of West Point and Annapolis,
whose rings are of yellow gold. This distinguishes the Air
Force Academy ring at first glance from all others."

He held up the heavy ring. "On one side is the Academy
crest, balancing the class crest on the other. Your crest—
a four-pointed star, symbolizing Polaris, the North Star, is
appropriate. The eagle and clusters of laurel, the bolts of
lightning are all right there, standing for the fliers you men
will become."

Frank felt his heart beginning to pound and he wondered
if the other men felt the way he did.

The general continued, "Perhaps the thing that really
makes your ring unique is the number one, which signifies
that you are the first class of graduates from the Air Force
Academy. This numeral one and the official sword pommel
and the large numbers '59' and, of course, our treasured
mascot, the falcon, all combine to give you a ring of which
to be proud."

Loud applause followed. . . . Then each AOC handed
the rings to the men in his squadron. As Frank walked up
to receive his, he hoped his hand wouldn't tremble. This
was a memorable moment—and a very proud one.

As he slipped the ring on his finger, he looked down at

it, allowing his thumb to trace the heavy white-gold band, etched with bolts of lightning and engraved with the four-pointed star, Polaris.

The beautiful star sapphire with which it was set reflected the overhead light. It reminded Frank of the clear blue Colorado sky through which he had flown so many times during the past three years.

After the ceremonies, the cadets went to the Town House, where they celebrated a "dining in" party. It was was patterned after a similar party, where the cadets at Cranwell in England had entertained them.

Then they hurried back to the Academy, to Arnold Hall, where their dates had gathered for the Ring Dance. The recreation hall was soon a sea of gay dresses and blue uniforms.

Frank spotted Ann over to one side of the room and, as he walked toward her, he decided that her blue gown was just right for her. It brought out the copper glints in her hair. The yards and yards of billowing chiffon made her seem smaller than ever. Suddenly he realized that the dress was the same color—sapphire—as the stone in his ring and the stone in the smaller replica which he planned to give her later in the evening.

"Ann's a real slick chick," Pete said approvingly. "Gosh, she looks pretty tonight!"

After greeting the two cadets, she said, "This is all so thrilling. I don't see how you two can look so calm."

"We're not calm inside," Pete told her with a wink. "But we're cadets and a cadet shows no emotion."

"Let's see your rings," Ann demanded. "I've been dying to look at them."

Frank and Pete held out their hands while Ann admired each ring separately. Then Pete said, "Well, happy landings, my friends. I'm going to see if I can scare up some other stags. Maybe we can sympathize with each other."

The band struck up a dance tune and the Ring Dance began.

"Come on," Frank said, putting his arm around Ann. "I've been waiting a long time for this evening."

As they swung out on the floor, the girl smiled and began to hum to the band's tune, " 'Some Enchanted Evening . . . Once you have met her,' "

" 'Never let her go . . .' " Frank whispered in her ear.

At the end of the dance, Frank suggested, "Let's go out on the patio. I have something to show you."

Several other couples had the same idea of finding privacy on the patio which the cadets had built two years ago. Frank finally found a dark corner and said, "I had this place reserved just special for us."

"Seems to me I remember this place." Ann smiled reminiscently. "Didn't Pete turn the bright lights on us out here one time?"

"Sure, leave it to Pete to pull some kind of gag." Frank looked around. He hoped that Pete wasn't up to any tricks now. What he had to do was serious business and he didn't want any flashy interruptions.

He reached in his pocket and brought out a little leather case which he opened and took out a ring—a smaller edition of the one he had just received. He took her left hand and slipped the ring on her finger, saying, "This is yours, Ann. It's a miniature—matches mine. Shall we wear them—always —for keeps? This probably isn't the most romantic place to tell you I love you, but I do."

"Oh, Frank—" He heard her voice catch in her throat. "I—I—well, the answer is, 'Yes, I'll wear it for keeps.' " She put her hands on his shoulders, stood on tiptoe and kissed him on the lips.

A moment later, Frank glanced over his shoulder guiltily.

Gosh, he hoped no officer had seen them! Then he grinned and said, "I just happened to think, Ann. If any officer had seen us just now, I'd be gigged for PDA.* But it would be worth a few walking tours, even at that."

He put his arm around her waist and they danced across the patio toward the Hall.

Monday was Recognition Day, that very special day in the Academy's calendar when the doolies became third classmen. As Frank and Pete hurried over to take their place in the parade formation, Frank said, "I suppose I'm just an old softie, but I'm almost as glad for the fourth classmen today as if it were my own Recognition Day."

Pete agreed. "I feel the same way. Remember two years ago at lunch time—the last time we had to run our chins in?"

"Do I remember? Old Hard Nose Porter was still pouring it on. I had to repeat one of General MacArthur's speeches ten times."

"Look over there," Pete nodded his head. "There's Mutton-head Shelton getting his last dibs in on Mr. Clark. That poor doolie has lost pounds this past year because of Mr. Shelton breathing down his neck."

"That's another reason I'm glad Recognition Day is here. Mr. Clark has made a good record. I'm really awfully proud of him. He's going to be all right."

After the parade, the upper classmen walked down the line of younger cadets and congratulated them on their first year's achievement. Frank held back after his squadron was dismissed, then fell into step with Steve Clark.

"Well, Steve, you've made a good comeback and I'm glad for you."

_____
* PDA—Public display of affection not permitted.

"Thank you, sir. You've helped me this year and I appreciate it. Do you have a split second, sir? I'd like to show you something."

Steve pulled a paper from inside his blouse and unfolded it. "I'd appreciate your reading this, sir. I've always been interested in writing. And these things have been on my mind as you know. I finally got them written down."

Frank took the paper and read:

Years ago, an Indian youth left his village, carrying only his bow and a small amount of dried meat called jerky. During his early life, he had played with other boys and learned the skills that would be required of him to become a man. But he was not allowed to associate with the men of the tribe, nor to participate in any of their activities.

Finally, when he had thoroughly prepared himself, he left to spend several days in a battle with the elements. If he was successful, he could return to the village victorious. After much hardship, he won the battle. Then he returned as a man to the village he had left a short time before as a boy. For a reward, he received from the older men that one thing that nothing but a true test can win: Recognition!

Just as this young Indian proved himself, we, too, of the Fourth Class and those before and after us have, are, or will have to prove ourselves. In many ways, our test is not as hard; in others, it is even more trying.

For a full year, we have known the punishment, both physical and mental, that befalls each entrant to any military academy. This punishment has been dealt out unmercifully, until at times it seemed that we were being forced toward resigning. Some do. Those who stay bolster their courage, display their stubbornness, draw on their strength of character. Where they find this strength varies from cadet to cadet, but when they find it, they stay.

They stay, in the hope that one day they, too, may "return victorious to the village." They stay because they want to stay; they want to face the test. Often everything, including their own minds, works against their staying. They begin rationalizing, telling themselves that they really don't want to stay, that they just don't care, that the only smart thing to do is to resign.

But they don't! They can't, because something molded deep within them keeps driving them on. Perhaps it is the love of the very freedom that they are temporarily sacrificing. Perhaps it is the hope that they may find themselves fit to defend that freedom for others. Whatever it is, it keeps them here, as the days become weeks, then months.

After many months, they have finished at least the first part of the test. I say the first part because that is not the end by any means, but rather the beginning of the greater test that is to come. Only now the challenge is different. They will be meeting this newer and even longer test alongside the very men who imposed the initial hardships upon them.

What of the upper classmen who dispensed this test with apparent reckless abandon? Was their only purpose in making the fourth classmen's life miserable—a kind of morbid pleasure? Perhaps, but probably not. True, there were those who did, but they were few in number. The vast majority dispensed it for the same reason that the fourth classmen accepted it. That reason? That intangible known as duty. The thing which causes men to take the hard way, the right way, rather than the easy way. It was their job to test our ability to achieve the standards necessary in this day of temptation and trial, just as it was and is now their job to prove their merit.

What does all this have to do with Recognition or Breaking Out? Simply, or maybe not so simply, this is the day the Indian boy becomes a man. This is the day the fourth classmen receive the recognition of their tormentors of the past year. This is the day when the upper and lower classes start to weld the bond that will stand throughout time.

Frank tried to conceal his feelings, but he found it hard to keep his voice from shaking as he exclaimed, "This is great, Mister! I hope you'll let me give it to Pete and ask him if they'll print it in the *Talon*. I think every cadet here should read it." Thrusting out his hand, he said warmly, "Welcome to the village, Mr. Clark."

A couple of days later, the cadets had packed their bags and the classes were ready for summer tours. Before they left, they were given briefings by various officers.

General Saunders, Commandant of Cadets, said, "Gentlemen, as first classmen, you are starting out on your final summer of work. A year from now, you will have been graduated and assigned to tours of duty.

"But before that time comes, there are still areas of learning which we want you to experience.

"Tomorrow, you will leave for a one-and-one-half-week tour, to see the Armed Forces in action. You will visit the Army and Navy installations in the eastern part of our country.

"You have seen something of the basic principles of support and maintenance, as well as the operation aspects of the Air Force organizations. You have seen these during the past two summers, and each base you visited gave you a broader concept of what our branch of the service is trying to accomplish.

"This summer, you'll visit important installations belonging to the Army and Navy, and you'll see how they synchronize with our work."

Again, as during the summer before, the first classmen were taken to several military installations—only on this trip, the bases belonged to the Army and Navy. They spent some time at the Norfolk Navy Base in Virginia, where they met the midshipmen from Annapolis. One whole day was devoted to touring the carrier, U.S.S. *Ranger*. Here the Navy put on an air show with their navy planes.

Most of the cadets were very impressed with the skill and care the navy pilots exercised in taking off and landing on the huge carrier.

"Those pilots are really hot," Frank breathed after a particularly exciting landing.

"It's like landing on a pocket handkerchief." Pete's eyes were wide with admiration. "That's what I call real hairy."

And later, as the two roommates went back to their quarters, Pete moaned, "My poor dogs—I'll bet we walked 50,000 miles covering that ship today. Wow!"

The next stop was at the Marine Base, at Quantico, Virginia, where the corps showed the visitors a mock landing, with a whole invasion force coming in LST's.

"Look how those LST's drive right up on the land!" Pete exclaimed excitedly. "How will they get back into the water?"

Frank answered, "I read some place where the sailors anchor them out in the water. Then, when they want to return, the boats are pulled back out."

As each LST landed, the whole front opened and marines and tanks roared out.

The next stop was at Fort Benning, Georgia, an army installation. Here the men met some of the cadets from West Point and shared the experience with them. After the fire power demonstrations, the Air Force Academy cadets were allowed to fire many of the weapons that they had witnessed in action.

But the most exciting part was the introduction to parachute training which they received. Fort Benning is known as a "jump school," and the cadets learned something of the rigorous training necessary to ready paratroopers.

Later, Frank wrote to his dad,

I really have a lot of respect for paratroopers after our experience today. There's a thirty-four-foot tower with a kind of trolley wire that angles down to the ground. The idea is to give you the same experience you would get if you jumped from an airplane and your 'chute opened.

Well, I got up there and took hold of the straps of my 'chute. Then they let me go and I went streaming through the air and lit with a terrific thud. It was rugged.

When he and Pete were flying back to the Academy with their group, Frank said, "Well, it won't be long now until we're on our way to the Far East."

"Man, oh, man!" Pete answered. "I can hardly wait. Think of it! Alaska, Japan, Hong Kong, the Philippines and the Hawaiian Islands." Then he sat up straight suddenly and demanded, "Do you suppose we'll see the beach at Waikiki?" He started to hum, slightly off key and pretended he was strumming a ukelele.

19

"North to the Orient"

Dear Ann,

I'm going to write this for you in diary form, then will you please keep it for my scrapbook? I think that's the best way to record this wonderful trip we're taking.

We spent last night at McCord Air Force Base and now we're winging northward. It hardly seems possible that I'm going "north to the orient." I remember writing a book report in high school on Anne Morrow Lindberg's book with that title, but I certainly didn't dream then that I'd ever be doing the same thing.

Right now, we're flying at 17,000 feet. The jagged Canadian Rockies stretch endlessly below us, still snow-covered and quite forbidding-looking. The sky is a queer light blue, with a few clouds stretching out toward the horizon. An occasional lake looks gray and cold, not at all inviting. Not exactly the kind of country I'd want to sit down in and hack my way out.

Pete is complaining about the time element. Right now,

it is 0839 hours, and, although we've been flying for two hours, we didn't take off until 0845. He says he'd just gotten used to Eastern Daylight Saving time, which means that it's lunch-time back there, and we haven't had breakfast. You know Pete and his stomach!

1000, 22 June—Anchorage, Alaska

We were reminded last night of our trip to Europe last year. Then, too, we had this business of light most of the night. It was dark for about thirty minutes last night—the sun was still shining when we got in at midnight.

Anchorage looks exactly as I expected—like a raw frontier town. There are still tar-paper shacks (shiver!) and very little pavement. (Our nice shoeshines!!) One of the most interesting things we saw was at the local airport, where there are hundreds of light planes for bush flying—B-18's, B-23's and C-82's. Even a battered old B-24.

We're in our private MAT's C-121's now, flying to Fairbanks. Mt. McKinley is on our left. It looks a little like Pikes Peak does from Denver when it's covered with snow.

2000, 22 June—Fairbanks, Alaska

Here we stopped at Ladd Air Force Base, which, to our surprise, we found is larger than the town of Fairbanks. Now I feel as though I'm really in the Alaska that I've read stories about. You see signs saying: the Yukon, Point Barrow, the Arctic Circle, Fairbanks, the Ice Islands. Shades of Jack London!

2000, 23 June—Anchorage, Alaska

Yesterday we flew up to the Arctic Circle, then back here to Anchorage. That country is a little hard to describe. There are miles and miles of wasteland—tundra, it's called. There's plenty of ice, even though it's midsummer, and, you may be sure, very few signs of life. Not my favorite place to spend a long winter evening.

Today was a lucky day for me. I won a drawing to fly in a TF-102, the two-place trainer for the big delta wing interceptor. We flew a practice scramble, did a couple of intercepts and a few acrobatics. Pete is still green with envy.

This afternoon, we visited a living glacier. I still don't know for sure how they know the difference between a glacier and just plain ice. Anyway, this had a big lake at its base which was the beginning of a river, and there were huge chunks of ice floating around in the lake.

0800, 24 June—Shemya, Japan

We're enroute to Tokyo. We hadn't seen anything but water and more water since taking off until we landed on this little dot of an island. I don't know how the pilot ever found it. Anyway, there's nothing here to see or do—reminds me of what we call "wide spots in the road." You know, little towns where there is nothing and nothing ever happens—except something could happen here if you dared explore! The Japanese mined this island during World War II, and the north beach is still mined. I won't go near the north beach, I promise.

1800, 25 June—Tokyo, Japan

I'm not real sure about the date because we lost a day somewhere in the Pacific. However, I'm not going to change now—I'll pick it up on the way home!

This is the strangest city I've ever been in and the hardest to describe. It's like being flung into a huge kaleidoscope. East and West have finally met and they whirl around one another in a fantastic dance.

In spite of its mad activity, Tokyo looks very drab in the

daytime. Dun-colored buildings sprawl everywhere, and the people dress in sober colors. But you should see the place at night! Neon lights blaze blindingly everywhere, and many of the signs are bigger than the tiny places they advertise.

The Japanese—like the British—are all left-handed, so the traffic goes haywire for me. I'm forever looking in the wrong direction and just escaping with my life. It reminds me of those old Keystone comedy pictures you see on late, late TV. You know, where the automobiles, carts, horses, wagons, motorcycles, bicycles and people all race like mad and are forever just missing each other by a hair's breadth. I expect to see Buster Keaton or Laurel and Hardy come busting around a corner any minute.

1800, 26 June—Tokyo, Japan

Today we visited one of the U. S. military installations nearby. We spent a lot of time with the Fifth Air Force and were shown how they operate. They're the big dog in the Pacific.

Everything is very interesting and shows what we are doing to help the Japanese preserve their new democratic form of government. Red China perches like a menacing dragon over on the mainland, but the Japanese people are feverishly working to build up their country and maintain a good economy.

I admire these people very much. Most of them have so little in worldly goods and yet they seem to smile and make the best of everything. They are so grateful for the little they have.

I was talking with a young American officer and his wife who have been stationed here for two years. They love Japan and have made a real place for themselves among the people where they live. They rent the upstairs floor in a beautiful Japanese home and live Japanese style—no chairs, central heating, western stove or any of what we call the "comforts of life."

The Japanese family from whom they rent were very wealthy before the war. But the Communists took all their holdings in China, and they have only their home left. So they eke out a pitiful existence on the small rent which this American couple pays them. Our officer friend and his wife do everything possible to make life easier for their host and hostess.

We had another interesting experience—at least, we heard an interesting story. One of the Army chaplains told us about his experiences in Korea while he was stationed there. Everywhere our soldiers went, they saw orphans living in the streets, in alleys and ditches, on the banks of the rivers— anyplace where these poor kids could hole up and scrounge out some kind of bare existence.

Finally, this one group to which the chaplain was as- signed got together and found a half way decent shack, which they fixed up. Then they gathered up all the kids they could find and put them there together. They fed them from their rations. But best of all, the chaplain said when he got there, he was never so amazed as to see all those poor little boys and girls running around in strange-looking cos- tumes. They wore shirts and pants and skirts which the sol- diers had made from their own shirts and blankets. Now the payoff is this, those soldiers only had two shirts and two blankets issued to them, so every man had to give up one each in order to help these kids. It made a big lump come in my throat when the chaplain told us.

I was glad to hear these stories because we've heard some that weren't too good. I'm a little ashamed when I hear about how some of our armed service people—and the tourists—act. Why can't they realize that they are the showcase for our country—that people in other lands judge us by their actions? I hope I always act half way decent. (Please forgive the preaching!)

There was a reception last night and then most of us when downtown to see the sights. The thing that really floors us is the price of everything. We see something marked 1000 yen. Then when we think we can't afford it, some mathematical wizard like George Shelton reminds us that's only three dollars in good old U. S. money.

Pete was flabbergasted by the city. He kept exclaiming over and over, "Whata place, whata place! Wouldn't this make one heck of a bonfire if anybody ever lit a match to it?"

That's because there are thousands and thousands of tiny stores all lined up like pigeonholes. You wonder how *any-body* makes a living.

1800, 27 June—Yokohama, Japan

This was our day to visit the Navy. Captain Jenkins got real big-hearted and, after we had spent a morning touring maintenance, a destroyer and base supply, he said, "We've had it. I think these men would like to visit the Ship's Store."

Quite a few shekels were exchanged there for pearls, china, cameras and other things, but somehow it seemed queer to be buying Japanese articles in an American store.

Later, we spent some time at the Japanese Defense Academy, which is similar to ours in many ways. They gave us a bang-up exhibition of their ancient oriental sports—judo, karate and kendo. The best of all, though, was to see some of their men break a two-inch piece of pine with one blow or kick.

2130, 28 June—Tokyo, Japan

Today was a free day so Pete and I decided to go shopping. I'll try to describe our cab ride downtown, but what I really needed was a movie camera. Naturally, I can't put in all the dialogue, but you can imagine Pete.

We hailed a cab at the barracks. The cabbie took us at breakneck speed down the narrowest alley I've ever seen. Pete yelled, "Look out!" and the only reason we missed two people is because they faded into the wall.

We erupted out into a narrow street, where we played "chicken" with a ten-ton army truck, two cabs which seemed bent on squishing us between them, several motorcycles driven by maniacs, a trolley car which lumbered along as though we didn't exist, and pedestrians too numerous to mention who did various acrobatics to evade the assassin who was driving our cab.

"There's an open manhole!" Pete screamed at the driver, who paid no attention, but drove directly over it.

Heavy Saturday traffic became more congested in the center of town. This made no difference to our driver. He executed a U-turn in the middle of a block with a trolley in front of us, a trolley behind us and they were headed for each other! It was something like seeing a Sherman tank rolling down from either side when you're in a foxhole.

But our hero was equal to the occasion. Again he turned left in the middle of the block, drove up on the sidewalk, zoomed by two parked cars and angled down another alley. I saw arms and legs vanishing in every direction, but I never did see any bodies attached.

Pete kept moaning, "Let me out of here! Let me out of here! That guy is nuts!"

As we barreled out of that alley, there before us were two innocent pedestrians, caught between a parked trolley and a stalled truck. They didn't see us. We were getting close and they still didn't see us. The driver stepped on the gas and Pete yelled, "This Frankenstein monster is out to kill somebody!" He tried to climb out, but I grabbed his arm and hung on.

Still the poor pedestrians hadn't seen us and we were bearing down on them like the black plague. Finally, the driver honked his horn, but I couldn't stand any more. I closed my eyes. When I opened them, the two pedestrians had disappeared—where, I'll never know. The driver pulled up with a flourish before our stop and, grinning broadly, opened the door to let us out.

I climbed out first, praying that my knees would hold me. I glanced back at Pete, who looked like his own grandpa. He was as white as I've ever seen anybody—except when we were in that Cessna 170 that George Shelton clobbered that time. His eyes stuck out more than usual, and every freckle he ever had or ever will have stuck out on their stems.

If I hadn't been so shook, I'd have busted from laughing. As it was, I managed to pay that cousin of an idiot for the tumbrel ride. Pete staggered over and leaned against a wall, moaning, "I didn't think we'd live through that nightmare. Man, he almost gave us the kiss of death!" Then, for the first time since we'd left the barracks, I breathed. It took us fifteen minutes to get hold of ourselves.

As we walked into the nearest store, Pete said, "Now I know what those guys were talking about in the movie *The Bridge on the River Kwai*. This fellow must have escaped from that chain gang."

The Tokyo department stores are all very modern, and one of them was amazing. It had an open area in the center going up ten floors—something like the rotunda in the Brown Palace Hotel in Denver. And hanging down for nine stories was a mammoth mobile, turning slowly in the breeze. It was breathtaking!

One more thing before I sack out. I think Japan is a great place and I hope I'm stationed here some day. You'd love it here, Ann. The quaint houses, the beautiful trees and shrubbery, the kids who all look like dolls.

2330, 20 June—Okinawa

This is really a beautiful island, quite different from what I expected. I always thought of it in connection with World War II and imagined it would be a horrible place.

The American installations are something to behold! We got to see some F-100's in action. Man, those are sleek babies!

Surprise! Some of our former ATO's are here and we did some guff-guffing with them. I was really glad to see them.

2100, 30 June—Okinawa

The ATO's took us on a tour of the island today and we saw the largest native town, Naha. It was quite a surprise; it is so very modern. But in contrast, on the outskirts are many thatched huts—the way I'd pictured the island.

Pete and I had a break. We got to fly back to the base in a Marine chopper—that was great. This is the *blue* Pacific out here—the one you're always hearing about in songs and stories.

2330, 1 July—Taipei, Taiwan

This is the only part of free China left—a large island and several smaller ones nearby. It seemed almost like Chinatown in San Francisco—firecrackers, rickshaws, slit skirts.

The Chinese Nationalist Air Force treated us to a Chinese dinner—complete with chopsticks (you should have seen Pete) and then a Chinese Opera. Pete kept whispering in my ear, "What *are* they moaning about? Who is that queer creature who looks like a fugitive from *Grapes of Wrath?* Why does he keep moving things around all the time and then plunking himself down on the stage?"

One of the Chinese officers explained that he was the stage manager, but Pete couldn't quite dig that.

We inspected the Chinese Nationalists' installations. They are certainly persistent, and they're determined to hang on.

2300, 2 July—Hong Kong

Now I feel like I've been in a Charlie Chan movie. This is one of the last free ports in the world and a most unbelieveable sight. Most of the shops—and there are thousands of them—would fit on your back porch.

This is the only place I'm going to spend my money. Pete and I went out and were fitted for a couple of suits—this is the top spot for buying good suits of British material. And cheap! These will be the greatest for off-duty luxury and should wear for three or four years at least.

2315, 4 July—Hong Kong

What a strange place to spend the Fourth! No bands, no parades but plenty of firecrackers, only nobody would know why you were shooting them. This was our free day, so Pete and I had another fitting on our suits, then we took off to see the sights.

We rode a cable car to the top of what they call the "peak" in Hong Kong—it's 1500 feet high.

I never realized before how tropical Hong Kong is. The vegetation is lush; there are innumerable trickling streams, gorgeous colored butterflies—it's really like a technicolored dream. Away down on the deep blue ocean, Chinese junks and sampans drift across the water. It gives you the feeling of being unreal.

The humidity is so high, we are dripping most of the time, with the temperature staying in the high 90's. Oh, for a breath of cool Colorado air right now!

I spent the last of my hoard today. I bought two pairs of earrings—one pair for you and one for Mom. *I* think they're beautiful—yours are blue star sapphires, to match your ring. Mom's are gray star sapphires, a color she loves. I decided you'd both rather have something very nice, rather than a lot of tourist junk from every place. Captain Jenkins introduced us to the jeweler—the captain has been here before and knows the man is reliable.

We're airborne—even Pete, but this was the time we almost lost him. About an hour before we were to leave, he went down to pick up our suits and somehow or other got lost. He had a heck of a time getting back—I almost chewed my fingernails off. He still wasn't there at formation which worried me a little. But when the bus came to take us to the airport, I really got hot and bothered. Just as we left the hotel, I saw a wild figure racing down the street, two huge boxes bouncing and streaming out out behind him. He looked like Ichabod Crane. He dodged pedestrians—or they dodged him. I'm sure they thought he was a wild man.

As our bus driver paused for a stop sign, I asked him to open the door for a moment. Pete came hoofing it up alongside, I grabbed his arm and dragged him aboard before we were off once more. Whew! Close call.

2100, 5 July—Philippine Islands

It took us almost all day to get here. Now I know I'm in the tropics. Man is it hot!

We inspected the military installations and were briefed on the economic and political set up of the islands. I don't like the Philippine Islands as well as Japan, but they're interesting.

We toured a strange village, right here on the base, which belongs to the Negritos, tiny people something like pygmies.

"As you know, we're allowed to wear 'civvies' when we are off duty. Last night one of the officers came up to me at the club where they were entertaining us and said it was sure easy to see that I'd been to Hong Kong. When I asked why, he said, "Your suit. You can tell it's been especially tailored."

Pete almost split to keep from laughing when I said, "Indeed it was specially tailored by a Mr. J. C. Penney. He has a chain of stores in America."

0200, 8 July—Over the Pacific

Just before we took off today we had a rather hectic and unsatisfying ride through Manila. What really tickled Pete were the jeepies—World War II jeeps—decked out in chrome and bright red paint and used as taxis! They were fantastic.

Guam, next stop.

0000, 9 July—One hour out of Wake

It's the creepy hour of midnight. 9 July is beginning in Wake, but we passed the international date line a little while ago, which means that it was 7 July and now it's the 8 July all over again! Oh, what's the use? I can't figure it out tonight.

We had a two-hour orientation at Guam. This is a huge SAC base and the B-47's stand alert twenty-four hours a day.

The flight has been very dull. Everybody is either reading or sacking out.

1830, 8 July—Honolulu, T. H.

Everything here is exactly as you've seen it dozens of times in the movies and travel magazines. We were greeted by a bevy of beautiful girls with orchid leis for each of us.

(Don't get jealous, please. There weren't any as pretty as you.)

We spent the afternoon swimming at Waikiki Beach. Whatalife!

2330, 9 July—Honolulu, T. H.

One of the colonel's wives took Pete, Bob and a couple of other cadets and me on a tour of the island. It's the kind of place you dream about—lush, tropical, with miles and miles of white surf and Diamond Head like a painting against the horizon.

2340, 10 July—Honolulu, T. H.

We were briefed today and saw the defenses of the island. They look very formidable and rather incongruous against all the beautiful scenery.

On the way back to the base we spotted some coconuts up in a tree. Nothing must do but Pete had to shinny up that tree and get them. I wish you could have seen him. He looked like a red-haired monkey. One of them fell off and conked him on the head. He has a lump the size of a goose egg, but he said it was worth it.

We took the coconut that he managed to bring down back to our room and opened it with a machete that Bob had bought in the Negrito village in the P. I. But the coconut was too green to eat!

2200, 11 July—Honolulu, T. H.

We had a tour through Pearl Harbor this morning and an officer explained the whole attack which occurred on December 7, 1941. It really was dramatic, listening to him. I could almost see what had happened and shivers ran up and down my spine.

It's almost seventeen years since it all happened, but you

can still see the bullet holes on the buildings left by strafing aircraft. Just think—those marks were put there by a country that today is our biggest ally in the Orient!

We put a wreath on the wreckage of the *Arizona*. I found myself very much touched by this place. After all, there is that wonderful battleship lying in Pearl Harbor, only its mast showing above the water, a victim of Japanese torpedoes. And saddest of all was the thought of the 1102 bodies which are still aboard her.

It really makes you think, believe me. It makes me more determined than ever that we should keep peace in the world. This trip has convinced me that there are more people who want peace than there are people who want war. And I hope I can be one of those that will help keep the peace.

Right now, we're sitting in our aircraft, waiting for take-off. It's been a wonderful, unforgettable trip. And it will be wonderful to see you again.

Love,

Frank

20

Mission Accomplished

After their return to the Academy and a few weeks training in field operations there, Frank and Pete were assigned as part of the first classmen to supervise the week of bivouac which ended the fourth class summer training.

These fourth classmen had just completed eight weeks of extensive high-altitude physical and mental education as an introduction to their four years at the Air Force Academy.

Frank had been appointed a Squadron Commander of the New Cadet Detail, and Pete was one of his three Flight Commanders.

"I told you, if you kept working hard enough, you'd go forward in rank," Frank said when they were handed their assignments.

"Sure, sure, but I'm not exactly looking forward to this little detail. I'll bet we'll have our hands full with those doolies—some of them look plenty gross."

The last week was spent in fatigues and tents, windy showers, dodging rattlesnakes, eating from soapy mess gear and getting very little sleep.

"Wouldn't you know I'd draw the grossest doolies in the bunch?" Pete complained one evening after chow.

"The ones that call themselves the Zulus?" Frank laughed. "I wouldn't worry too much about that bunch of guys. Some of them have plenty of initiative. But they're getting caught in some of their monkey business. We'll wear them down to size before the year is over."

"I suppose so," Pete admitted, then he grinned. "Honestly, you have to hand it to them, just the same. Even though they get all the dirtiest jobs because they have to work off demerits, they have some real engineers among them."

"What do you mean?"

"Have you seen the garbage area lately?" Frank shook his head and Pete continued, "Well, you should. They've put up a fence with an archway and walks around it. Even planted flowers."

"That's what I mean," Frank said. "Men like that who will have that kind of initiative, even when they get all the dirtiest and toughest assignments, will come out all right."

Pete chuckled, "That Mr. G. C. Wilbur is one of the leaders. You know, I've had to tear up his resignation five times this week. Then he just gets mad and goes out and dreams up something else to do."

"Seems to me I can remember a certain Peter John Day who used to be a little gross when he was a lowly doolie."

Pete looked over his shoulder in mock anxiety and said, "For gosh sakes', dry up! I don't want these guys to know anything about my record."

Finally, then, the week was over and it was time to go back to the Academy. Only this time, instead of returning to Lowry Air Force Base, where the interim site had been, the buses would take the troops to the permanent site near Colorado Springs.

As soon as they loaded into the buses, most of the cadets

promptly went to sleep. Just before they drove up to the North Gate, Frank saw a large green and white sign stretched above the highway: THE UNITED STATES AIR FORCE ACADEMY.

His heart started to pound a little faster. This was the end of the third lap and the beginning of the last one—his final year at the Academy. As the cadets piled out of the buses at the North Gate and picked up their gear, Frank and other cadet officers shouted orders.

Just before he gave the command to march, Frank gazed toward the west and saw the Academy buildings sparkling in the bright Colorado sunshine. It was an exciting, imposing sight. Over to the left was Pikes Peak, dominating the scene—like a guardian spirit of some kind, Frank decided.

Then he shouted, "Forward, MARCH!" and his troops swung down the road and spread out in a tactical formation of columns of twos—one on either side of the road. They were wearing full field packs, fatigues and combat boots. Frank knew it would be a tough hike—there were still three and a half miles and a fifteen-hundred-foot climb to make up hill and down dale until they reached their new home.

They could see it across the valley, almost like a mirage, a whole new world of gleaming aluminum, glass and mosaic tile against a striking backdrop of the rugged Rockies.

Frank's heart beat faster in cadence with the marching feet of his hundred men. He thought back to his first summer and the ATO's who'd chewed his group out. Even Lieutenant Jenkins had been plenty hard on them at times, but the cadets always admired him. The thing was, Jenkins was always fair. He demanded—but he also produced in his leadership. Sometimes he had drilled the daylights out of Frank's squadron, but the result was good.

Frank tried again to analyze just what made the young officer's leadership dynamic. Then he became conscious of his heels clicking along in front of his men—hup, two, three, four; hup, two, three, four. Now he had it! Lieutenant Jenkins always *worked right along with his men*. And they knew he would make them measure up to what he expected of them.

Yes, Frank thought, as they swung left, certainly that was it! Anybody could be tough and rough and stop there. But to be fair and make men like it while you were being tough and rough was another thing. That was the real test.

He glanced back over his shoulder. His men were dirty; they were hot and tired; but they stood straight and marched with precision—hup, two, three, four, in good step, with faces straight ahead, and the old fifty-pound field pack on their tired shoulders.

Frank started joking with the men closest to him. He caught the flash of smiles and the sparkle in their eyes as the cadets felt his comradeship. He experienced a friendliness and relaxation, in spite of their keeping perfect step, correct stance, heads erect.

Suddenly, without thinking twice, Frank began singing a marching song which one of their doolies had written and set to music.

> Hey, 'A' Flight, as we march along,
> Let's everybody join in song.

The men next in line started humming, then singing. Down the column the tune was picked up:

> Hey, Mr. Goodenough, tell me, Mr. Veach,
> Why do you have two left feet?

> This Air Force life, it sure is fine,
> We see everything from double-time.

> Well, candy bars and ice cream,
> All week long that is our dream,

> But dust on desk and dirt on floor,
> These privileges we'll see no more.
>
> Saturday nights sure are a ball,
> You, men, halt! Now stand up tall!

Louder and louder, straight along the line of men, went the melody and words.

> Inspection in ranks sure is fun
> The AOC finds grasshoppers in my M-1.
>
> Camouflage, airplane, a rattlesnake,
> Boy, this bivouac's really great!
>
> Where's your name tag? Straighten that tie!
> Tell me, Mister, Why? Why? Why?
>
> All day long we sweat and strain,
> Oh, good Lord, let's pray for rain.
>
> The time for study's not enough,
> My poor flashlight's got it tough.

A wave of emotion swept through Frank as he recognized the sympathy and fellowship between him and his hundred men. Now he knew they'd be the best squadron of the twelve in the United States Air Force Academy!

From time to time, automobiles drove between the columns, heading toward the Academy. Frank didn't pay much attention, as he was intent on watching that his troops were in order. Suddenly, he was aware that Pete had marched up beside him. His roommate muttered, "How do you like that? Of all the dirty, low-down tricks!"

"What ARE you talking about?" Frank was puzzled.

"Those guys driving by—haven't you noticed all the convertibles and sports cars whizzing along?" When Frank shook his head, Pete continued, "Well, it just happens that some of our dear buddies are returning from leave. They're nice and clean—lucky dopes—and have girl friends or parents to *drive* them to the site."

"I was so busy I hadn't noticed. What can we do about it, anyway?"

"Nothing." Pete's voice was bitter. "But it really racks me to see them so smug and cheerful and look at us—dirty, bedraggled and ready to fold up, we're so tired."

"Buck up," Frank said sternly. "We're almost there."

And finally they were literally at the foot of the great Academic buildings. The band met them, and now the New Cadet Detail set foot on the long, long ramp for the first time. Marching in regular columns of threes, with normal intervals, they tried to look erect and military, in spite of their dirty fatigues, loaded backpacks and all the rest of the FASE.*

They marched into the marble, pebble and cement quadrangle known as the "Terrazzo," halted and, on order, threw down their packs.

"This is what I call 'organized chaos,'" Pete yelled at Frank. "Did you ever see anything like it?"

Frank shook his head and answered, "The thundering herd—now I know what the term means. And this is what I'd call a 'motley crew.' It really racks me."

An hour or so later, the two roommates picked up their own field packs and stumbled wearily toward their section of the dorm. Pete mumbled as they marched across the quadrangle, "Well, I suppose I may as well get used to this glittering spectacle. It won't be long until I'll be wearing my path in the Terrazzo." He groaned.

But Frank was too tired to answer. When they got to

---

* FASE—Forward Air Strip Encampment (Bivouac).

their room, where they had planned to shower and sack out until dinner time, they were confronted by a horrible sight.

Their trunks stood in the middle of the floor and gear was strewn about everywhere. The beds were unmade and leaning against the wall. Everything was in complete confusion. Pete sank down on the nearest chair, declaring, "This is the end. I'm finished. I simply *can't* start on this room now."

Frank walked over to the window and gazed out upon the magnificent mountain terrain spreading out for miles. He drew a deep breath, then said, "It won't be too bad, Pete. Anyone who is lucky enough to look out and see this sight every day ought to be able to put his room in order."

It took the pair the rest of the day, though, and part of the night, to get things squared away. The drudgery included unpacking, moving furniture, requisitioning supplies, organizing, finding lost articles, cleaning and orienting.

Early Monday morning, Frank and Pete joined the other cadet officers, in charge of the New Cadet Detail and they marched to the parade grounds. Here the first classman who was Commander presented them to the Wing Commander, who in turn officially accepted the new cadets into the Cadet Wing.

Now the doolies received those coveted titles: "Cadet Basics" or "Fourth classmen," as well as their shoulder boards. Frank looked at the young cadets with satisfaction. They had been a good group of men, and, although it had been a tough assignment, he'd enjoyed working with them.

Frank gave the order, and his squadron, along with the other three, passed in review for the entire Wing. Frank's heart began to pound and he found his back a little straighter and his head a little higher as they finally took their places alongside the rest of the Wing.

"Man, was I proud of them," he told Pete later. "They're

a good bunch of doolies and they have the makings of good cadets."

"Right you are," Pete agreed. "Even Mr. G. D. Wilbur."

After lunch that same day, Frank said, "Now I know academics have started."

"Why?" Pete asked.

"Because when we pick up our text books, classes begin."

It was a happy, though busy fall for Frank and Pete. Once more, they were back in the swing of studying, marching, drilling and parading, only now that they were first classmen, there seemed more purpose to everything.

Most Sundays they spent at the new glider area on the Academy grounds. Both Major Foster and Captain Jenkins were pleased with their progress in soaring and encouraged them to continue.

Now that Steve Clark was a second classman, Frank found it easier to be with him and to work with him whenever possible. There wasn't quite the same barrier as when Steve was a doolie and Frank an upper classman.

Steve usually was at the glider area, too, with his usual enthusiasm about flying. Soon after their return from summer activities, Frank asked him, "When you were at home on leave this summer, did you do any flying?"

"You bet I did!" Steve answered happily. "I saw a lot of my old pals in CAP, and we took some jaunts around the country. I told several of high-school kids, too, how much that CAP training had helped me here at the Academy. If they want to get into the flying game, that's a wonderful place to start."

"You really are their press agent!" Pete laughed. "That CAP outfit ought to pay you a salary."

"Well, Mister, I believe in them, and anything I believe in, I talk up. The same thing is true with the Academy. I really talked it up at home. I hope I lighted a fire under some top high-school material to try out for the Academy."

Frank was so pleased he found it hard not to beam. "Good for you, Steve! That's what I've been wanting to hear."

They were interrupted by Captain Jenkins, who told Frank and Pete that the gliders were ready for them to solo. They jumped to their feet and hurried toward the sailplanes. Frank heard Steve say, "Lucky dogs! Getting to solo. But don't worry, I'll be doing it myself one of these fine days!"

Frank found himself getting more and more involved in studies and his football activity. He still was on the team—not the first one, he had carefully explained to Ann soon after school started.

"This is my last year at the Academy," he said a little sadly, "and I know now I'll never be a first string man. But I'm on the third team, and I'll get to substitute whenever the coach feels he'll need me." Then his face clouded. "But I'm afraid I won't get a chance to win a letter."

"Why not?" Ann demanded. "You've been pretty loyal—sticking by them for three years. That's the least they could do—give you a letter."

Frank shook his head. "No—I have to earn it. I have to play in the required number of games and the required number of minutes. And by the looks of our schedule this year, I don't know if I'll get a look-in."

One of the highlights of the fall program, Frank and Pete decided, was a speech which their history professor, Colonel Farbee, arranged for the first classmen.

The colonel invited Colonel Gregory Starwell, USAF (ret.) to give a lecture to the cadets. Titled "Our Moment in History," the talk included something of what Colonel Starwell believed to be the American Way of Life. He said:

What is the American Way of Life? It was never clearly given us during the recent conflict. But in a land of free men, the individual citizen is under as much obligation as anyone to work out such matters for himself. One night in North Africa during the War, I made an attempt. The following ideas, I believe, we Americans have several times fought to protect, and would fight again to preserve:

A System of ordered justice . . . the writ of Habeas Corpus . . . the Bill of Rights . . . the separation of Church and State . . . the tradition of voluntary neighborhood benevolence and mutual aid as contrasted with the theory of the welfare state . . . Freedom of Speech, Assembly, Petition, Press and Worship . . . Government of laws instead of men . . . Personal independence, and self-reliance . . . Individual initiative and local responsibility . . . Responsibility for tested tradition, coupled with a healthy scepticism toward overconcentration of power and authority . . .

These ideas are the social and political expression of the Christian faith . . . brought across the Western Ocean by immigrants in frail sailing vessels, men and women who found the shoe fit too tightly economically, spiritually, politically, or socially, in the land of their birth, ideas soon domesticated in a new soil, tinctured by the wilderness, and flavored by frontier conditions.

Again and again, we violate each of these ideas, even as an individual fails in his personal code of honour, yet we come back to them as the center of our existence, for which we have fought, and for which we would enter the lists again.

To cherish, and, if need be, to defend these ideas whenever menaced is the test of our worthiness to survive. They constitute a basis of which no man need feel ashamed. . . .

Later, Frank said to Pete, "That speech Colonel Starwell gave certainly ties in with what we've been studying and working toward since we've been here at the Academy."

"Yes," Pete answered thoughtfully, "it's the kind of talk that makes you want to turn over a new leaf and work harder than ever."

Pete had two big assignments during this last fall of his school experience. In addition to being elected captain of the soccer team, he had been appointed managing editor of the *Talon*. During the past two years, he'd been so enthusiastic about his work on the school magazine that it came as no surprise to Frank to learn that he'd been selected for the responsible position.

Pete had also taken upon himself the job of keeping clippings about all the Academy's sports activities for himself and Frank.

One afternoon he came in with a newspaper and waved it around angrily. "Did you see this?" he shouted.

"Pipe down—I'm not deaf," Frank said. "See what?"

"The article in this paper. Those dopey sports writers say the Academy football team hasn't much chance this year. We're just the poor little underdogs and we'll be lucky if we come out alive! How do you like that?"

"Well, Pete, you'll have to admit we're up against the toughest competition we've had in our four years of existence—Oklahoma State, Iowa of the Big Ten and Colorado University, to remind you of a few."

"So what? We've got a good team this year. I *know* we'll show 'em."

"Well, one thing you may depend on, we will be in there trying. Right now, I had better post. I'm due at football practice. You know, I really like this new coach—I wish I could tell you in so many words how he inspires the team."

21

Football Triumph

The Academy Falcons sat in the dressing room, looking at their new coach—Barney Morrow—who had taken them over this fall. Frank liked his looks—his close-cropped black hair and honest blue eyes. There was a certain intensity about him that was catching. And he was very intense at this moment. Frank listened closely to what he had to tell the players.

"So we're not as experienced as some of the teams we're slated to play. So we're not as heavy. So we haven't the depth. Well, then, *let's make the most of what we have.* That's what one of our great presidents, Theodore Roosevelt, did.

"I was reading last night how a friend praised him for his hundreds of trophies of the hunt, for the shelves full of scholarly letters and writings he'd leave to posterity, for his unusual ability as a statesman. TR said, 'Don't praise me. I have very ordinary abilities. As a boy, I had wretched health, poor eyesight. I was the worst grammarian in my

236

class at school. When I first had to work with people, I was utterly fearful and lacking in confidence in my ability to handle human relations. But I have always had one humble talent. That's the talent for making the very most of very ordinary ability.'"

The coach paused and glanced briefly around at his players. "I think we, like TR, have one very ordinary talent—the determination to excel. All right, men. Let's go out there on that football field and use that talent!"

Frank found he had a little difficulty in swallowing. He busied himself with his football equipment, so nobody would notice how touched he was by the coach's faith in the team. He glanced about surreptitiously and detected an unusual quietness among the other players, as if they, too, had taken this talk to heart and were going to do something about it.

From then on, the football team was like a giant steamroller, or Sherman Tank, as Pete said. Nothing seemed to stop them. After each game he'd jump about with glee and talk it over, play by play.

Now, as the season's end approached, he told Frank he wanted to make a summary of the season for an article in the *Talon*. "You'll help me, won't you?" he begged. "Get out your newspaper clippings and we'll do some summarizing."

Pete pounded away at the typewriter while Frank leafed through the clippings. A few minutes later, Pete ripped the page out of the typewriter and his voice squeaked with excitement as he asked, "How's this for a beginning?"

The team had to win. They knew that out on the bleachers they were being supported by an almost fanatical Wing of Cadets.

They heard hundreds of voices sing:

Rev up and go, Falcons, to the fight
For our spirit is high.
Gear up and go, Falcons, surge ahead
On the field as on the sky.
For you will see silver and the blue
Reign supreme upon the field.
We will prove that we can't be beaten,
For the Falcons never yield.

"That's great, Pete! Now why not tuck in something like this?"

The two cadets read from a clipping:

The role of the underdog is not unfamiliar to the Falcons. It was a sudden plunge after three shakedown seasons against second-line opponents into big time. The fledgling Academy had no proven football scores, no football tradition to lean on, no stadium to call its own. In spite of this, the Air Force Falcons wrote the football success story of the year.

"O.K., O.K.," Pete said. "That's the kind of thing we want to get across. And I like this." He leaned over Frank's shoulder and read:

The team started out by ripping the University of Detroit and then fought mighty Iowa to a tie. In the Iowa game, the Fabulous Falcons pulled the upset of the year. It was the biggest dumper in the season. The twenty-eight-point underdogs tied the mighty Hawkeyes, the unbeatable, famed Iron Men, in a game considered so one-sided the gamblers didn't even put it on the cards. The Falcons put on a display of such unmitigated nerve that it ranks with the best in football history.

Frank laughed and said, "And don't forget about Mach One. That *must* go into your report. Here, you type and I'll dictate."

The once fledgling Academy soared into the blue yonder of big-time football altitude Saturday as they forced Iowa's tough and experienced Hawkeyes to fight for a 13-13 tie. The most startling mascot in U. S. football, a trained falcon called Mach One, that attends all U. S. Air Force Academy games, is no less spectacular than the team it represents. He'll get his letter this year at the Academy.

However, Mach One played a dirty trick at the Iowa game. He "chickened out." It was amid much fanfare that the big falcon took one look at the crowd of almost 50,000 persons and went AWOL.

Pete had to stop typing, he was laughing so hard. Frank sat down in a chair and held his sides. Finally he said between laughs, "That crazy bird! When I think that they finally found him perched on one of Iowa's sorority houses!"

Pete wiped his eyes and retorted, "He's not such a dumb bird. Like the cadets here, he knows where to find the best chicks."

"Let me jot down something about two or three other games, then I'll read and you can type it," Frank said.

A few minutes later he dictated:

Balance—that's the key to the Falcon's success. It was Elspy who pounced on a Stanford fumble early in the first quarter which brought the Falcons' first touchdown. In addition to his ball-hawking, Elspy has been murder on defense in every game.

Tom Henderson, a gritty and gambling quarterback, plucked the Air Academy off the brink of defeat as the Falcons came from behind in the final nine seconds to upend Oklahoma State, 33-39.

Frank paused, then exclaimed, "Gosh, those were wonderful games. I got to play five minutes in each game."

"What about New Mexico? What shall we say about that game?"

"I got to play in three periods in that game," Frank said with a sigh. "Those are things you never forget. Well, let's see—how shall we write it." He jotted down some lines on his paper and then read:

Airborne cheerleaders cut loose wildly as the Air Force Falcons scored against New Mexico by returning a 63-yard punt for a touchdown. No wonder fewer than 200 cadets attending the game outshouted a crowd of 15,000 people in Albuquerque.

"I have something to add to that." Pete pecked away at his typewriter. "How's this?"

Back home at the Academy the cadets who couldn't attend the game sent their own brand of enthusiasm. They got together to listen in an auditorium and had their cheers piped to the game by telephone line to encourage the team.

"Whoever had that idea was real hot!" Frank exclaimed. "The football team really appreciated those cheers."

Pete yanked the paper out of his typewriter, then rubbed his hands. "Whew, my aching knuckles! I don't know when I've typed so hard and so fast." He leafed through some more clippings, then picked up one and said, "How about this? I like this editorial from one of the Denver newspapers. Let's get permission to use it, too."

This has never happened before in football history. It probably will never happen again. And it happened only because these are young men who have been trained to believe that victory is the only answer to competition—whether it is on the football field or whether it is in war.

It was the team itself which, in its short life, under the wise direction of Coach Barney Morrow, has developed a personality like none I have ever seen before. This team really seemed to be one great football player acting as an individual. Its character was youth, resourcefulness, vitality, discipline; quickness to take advantage of breaks and un-flagging spirit. It is the will to win that surges through the Falcons' veins.

"That's true," Frank said softly. " '*The will to win!*' That's exactly what our coach instilled in us. I'll never forget his talks in the locker room. They were really something—I wish I had them written down. The one I remember best is the one he gave us the first time he met with us. It was about Teddy Roosevelt. I can't tell you, Pete, everything he said. But I do remember one important thing and I hope I never forget it. He said, '*Let's make the most of what we have.*' "

A couple of days later, Pete rushed into their room and sank into a chair, gasping for breath.

"What's the matter with you?" Frank couldn't help laughing at his roommate, who always seemed at loose ends when he got excited.

"You—you—won't laugh—when you—hear the news," Pete managed to gasp.

"All right, spill it. Am I elected Queen of the May?"

"We've had two Bowl bids!" Pete announced trium-phantly.

"What?" Frank yelled, jumping to his feet. He grabbed Pete by the shoulder and shook him. "You're kidding!"

"No, I'm not—I'm giving it to you straight. The rumor is out that *if* we win the Colorado University game, we'll get a bid to the Cotton Bowl, in Dallas, Texas, and to the Tangerine Bowl, at Tallahassee, Florida."

The news spread quickly through the dorms, and that night at dinner there was great excitement.

Next day, at football practice, though, Coach Morrow told the players that he wasn't concerned with the Bowl bids at this time. They had just one job before them—to beat Colorado.

The day of that game finally came—the Saturday after Thanksgiving. The bright Colorado sun took an edge off the crisp air. Folsom Stadium was filled to capacity and, down on the bench, Frank could feel the tension and excitement in the crowd.

He and Bob Elspy sat together and Bob said, "Well, Frank, this could very possibly be the last time we've suited up for the Air Force Academy. Have you ever regretted coming out for football?"

"Never!" Frank answered emphatically. "It's been a wonderful experience for me and I'll never forget it—thanks to you."

"Skip that part. The thing is, you've been a good sport, pal. I know it isn't always easy to stick by when you spend so much of the time warming the benches."

"Somebody has to keep them warm," Frank said with a laugh. "And I can't think of a better guy, can you?"

Bob clapped him on the shoulder and said, "I don't know how the game will end today, but I do know one thing for sure. No matter what the score, it's been the men like you and some of the others who have been out there faithfully every day, practicing. You'll deserve the praise just as much as any ball toter or lineman. Don't ever forget that, Mister."

As Bob ran away to take his place on the field, Frank felt his thoat tighten and his eyes grow misty. *Good old Bob!* he thought, he'd been a loyal friend through these four years.

Frank turned as Steve Clark sat down beside him. Steve had been making a pretty good place for himself on the team this year and Frank was glad for that. It gave the young cadet one more interest in his school.

Then Frank forgot everything except the game. It was a

rough and tumble one, with Colorado University gaining the most ground but never quite able to take full advantage of it. At the end of the half the score stood:

University of Colorado 6
Air Force Academy 6

Frank felt his heart beating faster as the blue-uniformed members of his team surged across the field to get into position for the start of the second half. The tension in the air almost crackled.

CU played courageously, but they paid heavily for fumbles and penalties. It took the Falcons less than five minutes to strike in the third period after another fumble, and the score stood:

University of Colorado 6
Air Force Academy 13

"Win! Win! Win!" yelled the Air Force Academy cadets. Their cheers and spirit helped their Falcons through unbelievable trap plays and power surges.

Frank felt rather than saw Steve jump up. The young cadet paused a moment, then said, "The coach wants me to go in."

Frank got up and slapped him on the back, "Good luck, Mister. Play the best game you've ever played."

He couldn't sit down again. The game was too exciting. A quick stab of emotion caught him as he realized that Steve, not he, was getting into this most important game. His throat tightened and he swallowed with difficulty. Then he said to himself sternly, "Cut it out, Barton. You want the best man in there to do the job."

The rest of the game went by almost in a daze for Frank. It was a series of diving, running and passing. The Falcons would jar the ball loose from the University, then pass and thwart the golden Buffs until the final moment of the game. Frank looked up at the scoreboard almost in disbelief:

University of Colorado   16
Air Force Academy   21

The cheering and yelling reached a tremendous din. He saw the blue-uniformed cadets spill over the stadium wall and spread out like a flood across the field. Some of them grabbed team members and put them on their shoulders. Others grabbed the coach. Others swarmed around the goal posts and ripped them from their foundations. It was a shrieking, frantic mob.

Frank finally fought his way back to the dressing room. He didn't know when he had felt so happy or elated. This was one of the most wonderful things that could have happened to his Academy. Now they were on the map! People all over the country would know there was an Air Force Academy!

After what seemed hours of pandemonium, the team was at last in their dressing room and someone managed to close the door and lock it. After the men had quieted down and were getting undressed for showers, the coach said, "You know, of course, that we've had some Bowl bids. I've talked it over with General Bridewell, our Superintendent. You have the permission of the Academy officers to accept, but we all feel that it is the team's privilege and right to make the final decision. Gentlemen, there are two bids: The Tangerine Bowl and the Cotton Bowl. First, let's have a show of hands for the Cotton Bowl."

Frank looked around and saw that every man on the team had his hand raised. Then there was a cheer as the coach announced, "Gentlemen—it's unanimous for the Cotton Bowl!"

22

Unhappy Landings

There was a tremendous pressure on the cadets the following week. The coach announced there would be only three football practices per week until after Christmas. Everybody at the Academy had to dig in for finals just before Christmas vacation. There was one high spot, though. Frank wrote home to his parents about it.

Dear Mom and Dad:

I haven't much time to write but I wanted to tell you the exciting news. Our football team decided that we should have an Air Force Academy Queen to represent us at the Cotton Bowl. She will reign along with the Cotton Bowl Queen at the game. And guess who was elected—Ann! You could have knocked me off the Christmas tree.

Bob Elspy put up Ann's name, and I was never so proud in my life as when the men elected her. I guess they thought she deserved it because of her winning essay.

I guess that kind of makes up for all the games I didn't get to play. Don't misunderstand—I'm glad I went out for

245

football, but it's hard to sit by and not get into the big games.

See you soon.

Love,

Frank

One evening Pete came into their room excitedly and told Frank, "You're not the only one who has nice things happen to him. Get a load of this. Captain Jenkins came over to the *Talon* office, where I was slaving away, trying to get out the next edition—"

"Get on with the important news and leave out the details," Frank broke in.

"Pipe down—this is my story. Anyway, Captain Jenkins said that several invitations have come from the Cotton Bowl officials. The Wing Commander, the head cheer leaders, the editor of the *Talon* and the captain of one other sport—soccer—are invited to be special guests."

"Congratulations! That's great!"

"But best of all—*their girl friends are invited, too.*" Pete jumped about in his excitement.

"Man, that's hot!" Frank exclaimed. "It means that Patty Peterson will come from Washington."

"Yep!" Pete's blue eyes gleamed. "Believe me, this is going to be a real ball."

There was one more important thing that had to be done before academics were over for the Christmas holidays. Frank, George Shelton, Pete and several cadets still had a navigation mission which they must fly to fulfill their first semester requirements.

It was scheduled for the next week end, and Lieutenant Porter, who was one of the navigating instructors, told the students they'd go down over the Gulf of Mexico, to get some experience in flying over water.

Next day, in class, Lieutenant Porter said, "I suppose

you've all read about the loss of one of our C-119's over in the Utah mountains last week. Five men froze to death. Well, we all know that no aircraft is perfect, and there will be accidents resulting from malfunctions from time to time. There is one thing, however, that I can't impress enough on you men.

"In addition to the normal emergency equipment aboard the aircraft, you should carry certain survival items with you. *Always* check your waterproof matches. As far as I'm concerned, they're about the most important item. If those men had had matches with them, the chances are that more of them would have survived through the sub-freezing weather encountered in the mountains after bailing out. A compass and a knife might come in handy."

Just before they were to report for their mission, Frank reminded Pete of what the officer had said. "I'm taking waterproof matches with me, I'll tell you that for sure."

The first half of the mission was uneventful, the cadets performing their various navigation assignments in routine fashion. At the prescribed check point, the pilot headed back toward Denver. They were well along on their return trip, cruising at about 17,000 feet, when Frank glanced out of the window and saw an alarming sight. It made his stomach tighten and his heart pound. He spoke into the intercom quickly, "Sir, the right engine's on fire."

There was instant activity on the T-29. Orders were snapped and the cadets got busy. This was something in preparation for which they'd had plenty of drill, but it was the first time they had had a real airborne emergency.

Frank could see the aircraft commander consult quickly with the flight engineer. Then his right hand reached up to the loudspeaker switch. His voice, calm—almost casual— came over the speaker, "The fire in Number 2 appears to be out of control. All cadets will bail out as briefed. Lieuten-

ant James, the flight engineer, and I will stay with the aircraft for another try at the fire. Lieutenant Porter is jump-
master. Take your assigned positions when I sound the
alarm bell and start abandoning the aircraft on Lieutenant
Porter's orders."

Frank's muscles tensed as the bail-out alarm sounded.
Then, almost without thinking, he went through the bail-out
procedure: harness tight, parachute snapped in place with
D ring on the right, everything out of the aisle.

There was still time, so he zipped up his jacket, put his
cap inside, pulled on his gloves and unsnapped a first aid
kit from the side of the fusilage. Somehow he remembered
to put a Hershey bar from his lunch in his jacket pocket.

Suddenly, with a *"swoosh,"* the air pressure changed and
Frank's ears hurt. The cabin filled up with a fine mist, for
the pilot had dumped the pressurization.

When the alarm bell rang again, the cadets moved quickly
to the door. There was no panic, even though Frank knew
everyone was scared. He looked at Pete, who grinned
weakly, his freckles standing out.

Lieutenant Porter jettisoned the emergency exit door and
Frank felt the quick rush of air. Noise filled the cabin. He
watched wide-eyed as each cadet stepped to the door, where
the young officer made a quick examination to see that the
harness of every one was tight and his 'chute was attached
properly.

He shouted to each to dive head first under the waist-high
strap which stretched across the doorway and to be sure
that he was clear of the aircraft before pulling the D ring.

When it was his turn, Frank closed his eyes for a second
and prayed silently, *Dear God, save us all.*

Then he looked at the earth, 17,000 feet below, and hesitated a moment. He realized he was holding up the others,
so he dived before they could yell at him to hurry.

As he tumbled over and over, Frank was reminded of diving from a very high board at the swimming pool. First there was earth, then sky. Using an old diving trick, he straightened his body and slowed the rotation. He caught a glimpse of the airplane far away against the blue sky and pulled the D ring.

With a sudden jerk, the 'chute opened, the rotating stopped, and there was a beautiful canopy of orange and white above him. He breathed a sigh of relief. The 'chute had opened and he was descending at a leisurely rate. As he looked at the D ring in his right hand, he felt good all over. He had kept his head and had made a satisfactory bail out. Now if he could just land safely!

The sensation of falling so slowly and smoothly was wonderful, but it didn't last long, for he soon felt cold. The ground looked far away and he began to wish he were touching down. He glanced about and saw two other cadets floating down, not too far away and a little below him. By twisting, he was able to spot still another. He thought he recognized Pete.

Frank realized it would soon be time to strike the ground. He recalled instructions the crews had given him when he first started to fly: feet together, knees bent slightly, face downwind, then tumble with the wind and grab the lower shroud lines, to dump the air out of the 'chute.

The ground coming up toward him looked bumpy and unfriendly—they should be over southeastern Colorado, if he recalled correctly their position when he'd seen the engine catch fire.

Then the ground seemed to rush at him. As his feet hit the earth, he remembered to pull in the shroud lines and spilled the air out of his 'chute. He stood for a moment, catching his breath, then glanced up. The T-29 was still circling, but the smoke no longer trailed behind. He decided the fire was out and the right engine was feathered.

Frank looked around. It was scrubby, deserted country, with no farms or towns nearby, he had noted as he floated down. He folded his 'chute as best he could, then started walking toward the place where he'd seen another 'chute dropping.

After he had gone several hundred feet, he rounded a small outcropping and their lay Lieutenant Porter, absolutely still. Frank hurried over to him, calling his name. The officer did not answer, and Frank knew something was wrong. He looked around anxiously, hoping that someone else would come soon to help out. Then he knelt and examined the officer. The lieutenant was unconscious, but alive. Frank breathed a sigh of relief.

He shouted a few times and, in a couple of minutes, George Shelton, Pete and Tom Henderson came running up.

"What happened to Lieutenant Porter?" Pete demanded.

"He must have cold-cocked himself on that rock," Frank answered. "He has a terrific bump on the back of his head."

George knelt and examined the officer, too.

After glancing around, Frank said in a strained voice, "I guess I'm the ranking cadet officer here, so I'll take charge. First thing, we'd better do is improvise a litter."

"There are some saplings we can use for handles. They're small enough to hack down with our knives," Pete said confidently.

"George, you and Tom rig up the stretcher from one of the 'chutes," Frank ordered. "Then we'll try to carry the lieutenant to the nearest road—or maybe we can find a farmhouse or something."

"This is mighty lonely country," Pete said as he started cutting down a scrubby little tree. "I don't remember seeing many signs of activity as we were flying over."

"I disagree," George said with something of his old assertiveness coming back. "I think somebody—I'd be glad to do it—should hike out and get help. I'm sure I saw a little town back there, just before we jumped."

"Well, I don't think we should split up," Frank said flatly. "We need four men—two at a time—to tote this litter and I want to try to get him out from here as quickly as possible. He may have a bad concussion."

"I saw the other two fellows' 'chutes disappear in that direction," Tom said. "When we get this litter fixed, why not go that way?"

"Yes," Frank said, "we'll have to. They may be in trouble or unable to travel, also. Now, hurry up, let's get going."

They finally managed to rig up a crude litter and they lifted Lieutenant Porter onto it very carefully. By now, the light was fading fast and Frank was anxious to get under way.

After they'd walked for some time, calling as they went, George asked, "Are you *sure* you saw 'chutes over here, Tom? Seems to me we should have found the other two men by now."

Finally, it was too dark to go any farther, so Frank ordered, "Think we'll stop here. We'll stretch out one of the 'chutes as a tent, for protection."

"What about food?" Pete asked.

Frank had to smile, in spite of his increasing concern. "Oh, you and your big stomach!" he said.

"I have some stuff in my pocket," Tom offered. "It was left from lunch."

Together, they managed to pool some candy bars, a bedraggled sandwich and some peanuts.

"At least we won't starve," Frank joked, "and we can have a fire to keep warm."

"Yeah, if anybody has any matches," said George. "I didn't bring any."

"Well, I did," Frank said. "I remember what Lieutenant Porter said about that crew in Utah that froze to death because they didn't have any matches. Now scrounge around and pick up some wood."

The cadets scattered out and finally brought back some dry sticks and they managed to get a small fire going. As the night grew darker, it also got colder, and they all shivered.

Lieutenant Porter moaned and squirmed, but he didn't regain consciousness and Frank was worried. Maybe he'd made the wrong decision. Maybe he should have let George and one of the others strike out for help. Off in the far distance, a coyote howled. Gosh, it sounded lonesome, Frank thought.

They took turns dozing and listening, in case any airplane came looking for them during the night.

By morning, all of them were stiff and tired, and George was particularly grumpy. "I'm hungry," he said. "If you had let me go on yesterday, I would have had help back here by now," he complained. "I've a good notion to strike out this minute. It's light enough."

Frank walked over to the big blond cadet and looked him in the eye. "No, you won't, Mister. You'll stay right here with us. I hate to remind you, but I'm in command here, and," his jaw tightened, "what I say, goes."

"He's right," Pete's voice shrilled. "You could go up for court martial for disobeying a senior officer," he reminded the rebellious cadet.

George didn't answer for a moment. Finally, he said grudgingly, "All right, you win. But just remember, as ranking officer, you'll have to assume all of the responsibility for your decision."

Frank cleared his throat to steady his voice. "I'll take that responsibility, Mister."

"Well, I was just trying to help," George said crossly.

Frank paused before answering. He was thinking of what their officers had told them many times about keeping the confidence and morale of their men. "I'm sure you were, George, and I appreciate it. Now let's post. We'll start walking toward the east, the way this small stream runs. Sooner or later, we should run into a fence or road or something."

After a few miles of stumbling over the rocky ground, Frank saw a wisp of smoke ahead of them. He pointed this out to his companions, adding, "It could be more of our men—or it might be a cowboy."

"I don't know which I'd rather see," Pete said. "If it's our two men, we'd know they were all right. If it's a cowboy, maybe he'd have some food. My stomach's beginning to think my throat's been cut!"

Frank didn't answer. He was in no mood for joking. He was getting more and more worried about Lieutenant Porter. The officer had spent a restless night, and now he was beginning to mumble and toss about on the litter. Frank felt the injured man's forehead apprehensively. He hoped he wasn't getting a fever.

"George, you and Tom go find out what that smoke means," he ordered. "Pete and I will stay with the lieutenant."

A few minutes later, Tom returned to say that it was the other two cadets, and one of them had broken a leg. George was staying with them until Frank sent other orders.

Frank felt again the terrific sense of responsibility that the ranking officer must assume. These were his men, and he must try to make the right decisions. Finally, he said, "We'll carry Lieutenant Porter over to where the other wounded man is. Then we'll decide what to do."

As they walked toward the other camp, Frank made up his mind. He would leave Tom with the two injured men. Then he, George, Pete and Chuckovitch, the other unhurt cadet, would each take a direction and walk until they found help.

Frank told the others of his decision. They settled the two men as comfortably as possible for what might prove a long wait, then mapped out their courses. Frank had decided that he would travel east because somehow he felt that he might find help fastest in that direction.

After he'd walked for about a half hour, he heard a humming sound and, looking up, saw something in the distance that made his heart jump. He narrowed his eyes and shaded them with his hands. Yes, it was a chopper—a helicopter, probably out looking for them. The Air Force takes care of its own, he thought.

He started running forward, waving his hat and shouting. Soon the 'copter swerved over toward him, then lowered. When it was hovering just above him, the door opened, and an officer yelled at him, "Are you alone?"

"No, sir. I have several men back there," he pointed. "and two of them are injured."

A rope ladder was lowered and the officer said, "Climb on and show us where to go."

Frank asked, "What about the T-29?"

"They made it in O.K."

A few minutes later, the helicopter landed near the injured men and their relieved guardians. Frank hurried over to Lieutenant Porter, who had regained consciousness. "How are you, sir? Are you better?" he asked anxiously.

A worried frown wrinkled the officer's forehead, then he said, "I hit something—now I remember. The two cadets

left with me told me you've been in charge, Mr. Barton."
He smiled weakly and his gray eyes seemed to light up.
"Well, Mister, you've helped me out before. Remember that
time I conked out in the plane when you were a third classman?" Frank nodded. The officer closed his eyes for a
moment, then continued, "And that darned cat—"

Frank said hastily, "Better not try to talk, sir."

"And now—you're all right, Mr. Barton. You're a good
cadet. I've always thought so." He closed his eyes again.

Frank replied warmly, "Thank you, Lieutenant Porter.
And you—you're a good officer, sir." He saluted smartly
as two of the cadets came up to help lift the officer into
the 'copter.

Just before they closed the door, the lieutenant opened
his eyes, raised his head a little and looked at Frank. "Don't
worry, Mister," he said, "I'll still get to the Bowl game."

Frank gulped. There'd been so much excitement, he'd
forgotten all about the Cotton Bowl game. Then he yelled,
"Of course, you will, sir. We couldn't have it without you."

The officer in charge of the helicopter said, "I've radioed
your position. If you'll walk about two miles northeast,
you'll find a road. An Air Force truck will pick you up
there. Good luck!"

As the 'copter lifted upward, then flew northeast, Pete
asked, "Why didn't they bring us some breakfast? They
might know we're starved."

"That's what I say," George agreed. "I could eat that
coyote we heard howling last night."

Frank said, "Come on and quit griping. Just think, if
we're lucky, we'll be back in class tomorrow!"

23

The Falcon Flies High

And now it was the day after Christmas and Frank was en route to Dallas, to join his teammates and practice for the Cotton Bowl game. As he got on the airplane at Kansas City, the first person he saw was George Shelton.

Darn, he thought, why couldn't it have been Pete? Then he felt ashamed of himself. He and George had been making a pretty good go of things for the past year and this was a chance to become better acquainted. After all, at the Academy the cadets had very little time to get to know each other personally.

After exchanging greetings and finding seats together, the two settled down to discuss the prospects of the game. George had brought several newspapers and they scanned the sports' pages.

"Look at this," he said and read aloud, " 'The Air Force has a versatile, beautifully coached football team. But I think they'll meet their match when they play Texas Christian University in the Cotton Bowl.'"

256

"How about this?" Frank answered and read, " 'There's probably not a citizen in the heart of this big land called Texas who doesn't think the Horned Frogs will give the Falcons a thrashing.' "

George leaned back and exclaimed, "Man, oh, man, this is one game when we're going to play for keeps!"

Frank agreed. "We'll have to give it everything we've got—and then some. But we will—I know the other men feel the way I do."

George continued, "These sports writers really pour it on. 'The Horned Frogs, expected to power and pass their way through and over the Falcons . . .' "

"Yes, and listen to this: 'The Frogs are supposed to grind the lighter Falcons to bits on the ground . . . supposed to wear down the Falcons in the late stages.' And here's another, 'The Falcons will have met two of the nation's toughest conference champs—Iowa of the Big Ten and, on New Year's Day, Texas Christian of the Southwest.' Well, we're keeping big company, aren't we? *But so are they.* If I haven't learned anything else in these past four years at the Academy, I've learned to have a little more self-confidence."

George folded his paper. "Yep! We're sure on the defensive all the way. But, here's hoping. You know, Frank, I really should have been a great football player because I've been on the defensive, too, all my life."

Frank glanced at his companion in surprise. This certainly didn't sound like George Shelton—Shelton, who always knew all the answers.

"I think I've learned a few things at the Academy, too." George seemed to be talking to himself as much as to Frank. "*You* didn't have enough confidence. Well, *I* had too much. At least, I always made myself act that way. And getting the chance to play on this team—though never as a first string man—has been a real eye-opener."

"I know what you mean," Frank responded quietly. He was almost afraid to speak because he sensed that the other cadet wanted to put some of his pent-up feelings into words.

George continued, talking softly and not at all in his usual cocky manner, "I needed to have my ears beaten down—clear to my chin—but I hope it doesn't show too much. As I look back now, I can see that my life has always been something of a football game. There was always some goal up there ahead, and I felt I had to win, regardless. So I elbowed, bullied, boasted and bluffed my way toward that goal. Not only that, but *I* had to be the great quarterback—the one who called the signals, the one who usually carried the ball."

Frank squirmed and said protestingly, "Oh, it hasn't been that bad, George. We've all had to learn things."

"You're darned right we have. But I can never thank the Academy enough for cutting me down to size." He paused, then continued, "I'm going to tell you something I've never told anybody before. You know, Frank, we haven't always seen eye to eye, but, deep down underneath, I've always liked and admired you."

"Thanks, Mister. I—I learned to like you, too." Frank knew he could say this honestly. He'd found a steadily growing awareness and more and more to like about the big blond cadet during the recent weeks.

"Now," George continued, "I'm going to talk about something that's hard to put into words. But I'll say it—and then I'll forget it and start from scratch. I've always been ashamed of my father." George spoke so low that Frank had to lean forward and strain to hear him.

"Oh, he's a good guy and has always given me everything I wanted, but he's different. It took me the past four years at the Academy to figure out why. He didn't have much education and that was one thing he admired more than anything in the world, so he pushed me hard to make top grades and get the best schooling in the country. He, in turn, made himself a financial wizard. But his poor schooling put him on the defensive and made him too ambitious for me.

"My mother—well, I never knew her. She seemed to have other plans—they didn't include my dad and me. Those two things—my mother's desertion and my father's lack of education—really drove him. He saw that the success bug bit me early. And it almost fouled me up in the best place I've ever been in life." George looked out the window.

Frank cleared his throat before replying, "We've all learned plenty at the Academy, George. And we've all had our problems. I just hope I remember a few of the important lessons I've had pounded into me."

George reached over and gripped Frank's hand, then he changed the subject abruptly and began talking about the Cotton Bowl prospects.

The next week was spent in practicing until the day before the big game. In the meantime, Ann had arrived. Frank could only talk with her on the phone because of his heavy schedule.

Pete, who constantly bubbled with news, bounced in and out of their quarters. "Patty is coming!" he exclaimed excitedly. "Her dad—you remember the general in Washington, the one I spilled punch on—he's bringing the family down in a commercial plane, so Patty and I will really see the sights."

Although Frank couldn't see Ann because of being on the team, he did manage to get a ringside seat for himself for the parade. It was a thrilling sight to see the blue and silver float moving along the street, bearing Ann in her royal red velvet gown and matching cape. She looked every inch a queen, he decided proudly.

When she saw him, she waved gaily, then touched something over her heart and he knew that's where she wore the silver wings he'd given her.

Then it was New Year's Day, dawning bright but cold. Everything seemed at a fever pitch and Frank felt the tension in the dressing room. His hands trembled as he tied his shoestrings, and he fumbled with his headgear.

Soon, they were out in the stadium and Frank watched as the Falcons spread over the field and the stands broke into cheers. He glanced back and saw the Cadet Wing—a solid blue phalanx behind him. Wave after wave of yells swept down.

He took his place on the bench, where George joined him a moment later. A wave of friendliness toward the other cadet swept over him. Maybe they were bench warmers, but, by golly, they'd be the best ones in the country, he vowed.

The sparks really flew, Frank thought, when the two teams came together.

"This is going to be the toughest game we ever fought," George said. "They outweigh us twenty pounds to a man, but we've *got* to hold that line."

"He fumbled!" the crowd groaned and Frank jumped to his feet.

Tom Henderson had lost the ball on the AFA's 23-yard line, and it was TCU's first break of the game, early in the first quarter. But the Falcons pushed the Frogs back to the 27-yard line, and in three plays they forced the Frogs to try a place kick, which was no good.

It was give and take over most of the field for the first two quarters, until, finally, the Falcons punched out short yardage in four straight first downs to the TCU's eight-yard line. Now they were in position to score.

Frank felt as though he couldn't breathe. He stood with

his hands clasped together, the nails biting into his palms.

"Pass the ball—pass the ball!" the Cadet Wing yelled.

Two running plays gained merely a yard, then Ray Gilbert overthrew a pass to Art Grigsby. The only thing left was to try for a field goal, just twelve yards back from the goal posts.

"This is a wonderful chance," Frank said to George. "Bob has kicked several of these goals and pulled us out of worse holes than this."

But Bob missed and a great groan went up from the Cadet Wing. At the end of the half, the score stood:

AFA 0
TCU 0

In the dressing room between the halves, Bob said to Frank, "If we get another crack at a field goal, I'm asking the coach to send you in to hold for me."

"I'll be glad to, Bob," Frank answered, but his voice shook slightly as he thought of what a tough spot it would be. Then he squared his shoulders. This was what he had wanted for the past three years—to get a crack at the ball in a big game. Maybe it would happen!

As the Air Force team ran out in the stadium Frank was amazed to see the Cadet Wing come streaming out of the stands and make a corridor for their players to run between. A great thrill surged through him at the realization that their buddies were giving them every ounce of backing they could. This spontaneous outburst of confidence seemed to make the feet of the team fly.

As he sat down, Frank glanced across at the royal stands, where the Cotton Bowl Queen and the Air Force Academy Queen were presiding. He quickly spotted Ann in her pretty blue suit—Air Force blue, like the skies. He wished he were closer, to wave at her, but he imagined that she was looking toward him and his heart beat faster.

Once again, the two great teams spread out over the field and Chuckovitch kicked off to his own 41-yard line. A few minutes later, the Falcons got the ball on a fumble and started a drive that Frank felt sure would pay off in a score.

The AFA alternated runs and passes until they had peeled off three straight first downs and were on the 20-yard line. On the first down, Henderson threw a pass to Bob in the end zone, but the TCU quarterback knocked it down. Then Ray Gilbert ripped off eight yards on the next play. Henderson went through the line for a first down, but the penalty marker was down.

"What happened?" Frank groaned.

"Our back field was illegally in motion," George answered. "There's so much noise from the stands, they can't hear the signals."

"That means Bob will probably try for another field goal," Frank said. He looked expectantly toward the coach, who motioned for him to go out on the field. Frank's heart started pounding loudly, and his mouth felt dry as ashes as he jogged across the field. He kept flexing his fingers, hoping his hands wouldn't shake.

"You can do it," he said to Bob as they took their places on the 23-yard line.

But the kick was wide to the right, and the score remained,

AFA   0
TCU   0

Frank stayed in for two more plays, then the regular man was sent back in and Frank returned to the bench.

When the fourth period opened, George said, "We're in

the best place we've been all day. That ball is on TCU's own six-yard line."

"Oh, for a good fumble from them now!" Frank moaned.

But TCU was in there to win, too, and they unleashed their best attack of the day. They used their devastating fullback traps and off tackle plays, culminating with a spectacular pass play—a 38-yard pitch off a double reverse to the fullback, who caught the ball, then fumbled. They recovered and went on down to the AFA's eight-yard line.

Frank found his breathing very difficult. He beat one fist on the other. This was the toughest spot they'd been in today, and it could mean a score for the Frogs. TCU went into the air with a wild pass, and Bob intercepted for the AFA.

Again the Cadet Wing went wild. Frank's ears rang and he took great gulping breaths of air to fill his starved lungs.

Bob punted his team out of danger, then the Frogs banged back to the AFA 15-yard line. But the Falcons' line held like a stone wall.

Now Frank realized that TCU was in scoring position. "They'll try a field goal," he told George. "They're in the same place they were last quarter!"

"Block that kick! Block that kick!" yelled the Cadet Wing.

Frank hugged his arms to himself and watched in fascination. This could be the deciding point in the game, he knew.

"Block it! Block it! Block it!" George shouted in his ear.

The Falcons didn't block it, but the ball missed the goal. Frank watched it with relief, then turned to George and yelled above the screaming mob behind them, "It's the wind —I knew it when I was out there. There's a tricky crosswind cutting around the base of the stadium. Bob should never have missed that goal—and neither should TCU!"

A few minutes later, the final whistle blew and the score-board still read:

AFA   0

TCU   0

The AFA team was surrounded by a howling mob of cadets, who yelled and slapped them on the shoulders.

As they hurried toward the dressing room, Frank said to George, "Well, they can stop calling us the 'Cinderella' team now. We've played the best lineups and we're still undefeated."

"Yes," George answered, "and even if it was a tie game, that's better than losing."

Back in the dressing room, Frank was reluctant to undress. It suddenly swept over him that this really was the last time he'd ever suit up for the AFA Falcons, and it made him a little sad.

Then he noticed Bob over in the corner. By the sag of his friend's shoulders, he knew something was wrong. He walked over to him and asked, "What's the matter, Bob?" Suddenly he realized the big half-back was actually sobbing.

With tears streaming down his cheeks, Bob answered, "Those field goals I missed. If I had kicked them, we'd have won."

Frank was speechless. He'd never thought Bob would take it so personally. He put his arm across his friend's shoulders and said, "It wasn't your fault, Bob. Your kicks were true. I held that ball for you and I know. It was that tricky crosswind swishing around the base of the stadium. *Nobody* could have made them."

But Bob wasn't to be consoled. He shook his head and turned away. Frank tried again, "TCU missed in almost the same place. I know what I'm talking about—*it was the wind.*"

Bob rubbed his arm across his eyes and smiled weakly at his friend. "Thanks, Frank. I appreciate what you've just said. And I suppose you're right. Only just now it's hard for me to accept it." He turned away to get dressed.

Then the coach stood up and everyone was silent as he spoke. "Men—there's one thing I want you to know. You were the better team out on the field today."

Frank noticed that, for the first time that day, disappointment had crept into his voice.

A commotion at the door drew everyone's attention. Pete charged through, clasping a football tightly. "I got it! I got it!" His voice rose higher and higher. "One of the TCU players tried to take it, but I got it away from him."

He jumped up and down with excitement, then said, "Here, Coach, this ball is for our trophy case. Now we have the windup ball for every game we've won this year under your coaching."

The coach smiled broadly as he accepted the ball and the team whistled and clapped.

Then Pete turned to Frank, explaining, "Man, oh, man! Patty's prettier than ever. She is one slick chick." He grinned and added, "You know, I think her dad—the general—is a little absent-minded. He doesn't seem to remember the punch cup deal." He changed the subject abruptly. "Do you know what happened to Mach One during the half?"

Frank shook his head, and his roommate continued, "Well, he took off and flew to the roof of the Texas Hall of State, on the Fair Grounds. So the handler had to use Mach Two. Of course, *he* made a big hit with those 75,000 people out there. You know how the crowds love to see the falcon perform. But I think, when we get back to the Academy, you're going to have to go down to the falconry and give that Mach One a pep talk. It's the second time this year he's gone AWOL. . . . Well, I'll be seeing you." He bounded away, chuckling.

Frank got dressed quickly, then went out into the stadium. He gazed over to the canopied section, where Ann had reigned as queen that afternoon. The crowd was thinning out now. He saw her blue dress. She turned—and waved to him.

He hurried across the field, his thumb rubbing hard over the now familiar ring on his third finger. He felt the crest, which he knew by heart—a four-pointed star, the eagle and the clusters of laurel. Laurel was for peace, he always reminded himself. The bolts of lightning—yes, he'd fly in storms many times. The engraved numeral ONE—because his was the first class to graduate. The falcon—well, he and Mach One had plenty to be proud of together.

He heard some excited voices and looked up in time to see Mach One swoop down to the field. Then he saw the handlers out there with the lure and realized that the falcon had come back from its high perch to the cadets to whom it belonged.

The thunder of a jet ripped the sky above Frank and reminded him that before long he'd be flying one of those quick-silver speed merchants himself. He took the steps two at a time to join Ann.

That evening, Frank proudly escorted the Air Force Academy Queen to the dinner at which the football awards were given out. He was glad to see Bob stand up confidently as captain of their team and accept the Cotton Bowl trophy to put in their award case at the Academy. TCU graciously allowed the Falcons to take this one, agreeing to wait for a duplicate.

"How does it seem to be co-champion of two conferences?" Pete asked Frank between speeches.

"What do you mean?"

"Well, we're co-champion with Iowa of the Big Ten, and now with TCU of the Southwest Conference."

Frank laughed happily.

Next, each player on the team was given an award blanket, an engraved wrist watch and a ten-gallon hat as souvenirs of the game.

The dance later was all that it should have been, all that Frank had hoped it would be. It was the perfect ending to a perfect day and a perfect year.

Ann looked pretty special in her white chiffon and Frank noticed with pride that there were plenty of admiring glances turned in her direction.

And then it was the next day and the football team was winging its way back to the Academy, in the chartered commercial plane. This time, Ann and Pete were in the airplane, too, along with several Air Force Academy officers and their wives, who were chaperons.

Pete seemed dejected at first and when Frank asked him what was the matter, he replied, "I wish Patty could have come back with us, but her school starts in a couple of days."

His good humor soon returned, however, and he was the first one to spot Pikes Peak. He rattled excitedly, "'Pikes Peak or Bust'—that's what the old-timers used to say. Well, it's Pikes Peak for us—but we're not about to bust!"

Frank chuckled as he turned to Ann, who was seated beside him. "That Pete—he's incorrigible!" Then he surreptitiously took her hand and held it down between them. He decided that they couldn't exactly call it PDA here on this plane. Anyway, he thought, as he glanced around, nobody was paying any attention to them.

Ann was pointing now with her other hand, and he leaned over toward the window to look down. There was the Academy, spread below them—all steel, aluminum, glass and colored tile. How it sparkled in the sun! And there were the gliders in which he'd made his first solo flight.

He remembered back to the time he'd flown over the site, almost four years ago, when these buildings were just a dream. He'd had a dream then, too, of graduating from the Academy. Now part of the dream had come true. And, just as the buildings were a reality, so his dream of graduating from the United States Air Force Academy was coming true. Only six more months and he'd have his second lieutenant's bars, his navigator's wings and a commission in the United States Air Force.

"Isn't the Academy magnificent, Frank?" Ann asked, breaking in on his reverie. Then she looked at him searchingly. "Are you going to be sorry to leave it?"

Now the stunning white mass of Cathedral Rock swept into view. How strong and sturdy it was, Frank thought. It was really a symbol of strength—for him, for his class, for the men who would follow them. Those men would continue to make tradition and add to the stature of the Academy, he knew.

A wave of humbleness and thankfulness swept through him as he answered Ann. "Yes, I'll be sorry, but I'll be glad, too. I have a certain reluctance to leave. It has been a wonderful life—one I'll never forget. Of course, I'm eager to graduate and get out into pilot training and the business of flying. I hope I can measure up to that challenge, too."

Ann put her hand on his arm and said, "Of course you'll measure up, Frank. That's what all your training has led toward."

Frank straightened his shoulders and answered, "I'll measure up. I know it's part of my job to go out and fly with those wings that I have earned here—wings for peace."

MARIAN TALMADGE AND IRIS GILMORE

After finishing *Wings of Tomorrow,* the writing team of Talmadge-Gilmore became so interested in the experience of the cadets of the Air Force Academy, so captivated by the intelligence, imagination, knowledge and discipline of these young men, that they continued to keep in close touch with their activities.

Work with youth is natural for these authors. For twenty years the team directed a Children's Theater, taught private drama, worked in radio, directed a marionette troupe and were professors at the University of Denver.

Throughout these years, they wrote plays, stories, articles and radio scripts. In 1956, they won the *Boys' Life-Dodd, Mead Prize Competition* with their teen-age book, *Pony Express Boy.*

Mrs. Gilmore's summers are spent conducting the teen-age program at Geneva Glen Camp, Indian Hills, Colorado, which her husband directs. Mr. Gilmore and their married daughter are also interested in writing, and the family's other hobby is music.

Mrs. Talmadge and her accountant husband are amateur gardeners and travel extensively. On their many trips they manage to include two of Mrs. Talmadge's hobbies—collecting antiques and western historical material to add to her voluminous files of Americana.